SPIDER-MAN®

THE VENOM FACTOR

Diane Duane

Illustrations by Ron Lim & Keith Aiken

**BYRON PREISS MULTIMEDIA
COMPANY, INC.
NEW YORK**

BERKLEY BOULEVARD BOOKS, NEW YORK

Special thanks to Lou Aronica, Lucia Raatma, Eric Fein, Danny Fingeroth, and Julia Molino.

SPIDER-MAN: THE VENOM FACTOR

A Berkley Boulevard Book
A Byron Preiss Multimedia Company, Inc. Book

PRINTING HISTORY
Puttnam hardcover edition / October 1994
Berkley Boulevard paperback edition / November 1995

For all our friends at Baycon '94 and
Ad Astra '94, Toronto
. . . who watched it happen

Thanks to Keith, who suffered,
well, *we* know what

PROLOGUE

t was very cold three hundred feet down, very dark; but not very quiet. Outside the skin of the sub, the noise of near-shore seas rumbled and clattered and moaned against the hull—a muted chainsaw rattle of engine noise from ships passing overhead, the clunk and burp of bells or horns from nearby and distant buoys, even the occasional soft singing moan of a whale going about its lawful occasions. The man in the center seat of the submarine's bridge looked thoughtfully at his charts. He sighed at the thought of his upcoming leave and of the relative peace and quiet of being surrounded by air instead of water.

The spot where he sat was not really the center seat, of course. Not yet: his boat was still three years off its refit. Eventually all U.S. subs' bridges would come to resemble the original one of a famous television starship, the circular design having eventually been appreciated by the powers-that-be as the best and most efficient presently available. But right now, the bridge of SSN-45, the *USS Minneapolis*, was still a tangle of panels and conduits arranged around the obstructive central column of the periscope. The captain's chair was no plush over-seeing throne, but a folding chair stuck under the lighted chart table: not very aesthetic, not very comfortable. It was not meant to be. Captains spent most of their time on their feet.

Right now, though, Captain Anthony LoBuono was sitting and didn't care who saw him. He could not wait to get this boat into dock and out again. Eight days from now, after final unloading at Greenland, he would get his butt off her, and the back cargo section emptied out once and for all. *Never again*, he thought. *Never again.*

Realistically, though, he might be commanded to carry such a cargo again, and he would take his orders and do as he was told. In fact (and the thought made him twitch) it occurred to Captain LoBuono that, since he had managed this mission well enough, he might easily be given the same task again at some later date.

He swore gently under his breath. He would not soon relish another week and a half like the last one. His crew were on edge, which was no surprise, for *he* was on edge: and such things communicated themselves, no matter how hard you tried to keep them under wraps. *You should be grateful*, he thought to himself. *It's one of the things that makes your crew as good at their jobs as they are. They hear you thinking, anticipate you, jump faster when they have to.*

All the same, he would have preferred to pass on this last week's case of nerves.

His Ex appeared at his shoulder. LoBuono looked up. Bass Lorritson—no one called him Basil, no one who didn't want a drink later spilled on them "accidentally"—favored his captain with a calm look that fooled LoBuono not at all. "Coming shallow as scheduled at the north end of Hudson Canyon, sir," he said. "Do orders mandate a specific course, or are they letting you play this one by ear?"

LoBuono smiled grimly. "We're inside the limit," he said, "and safely under the birds by now. No mandate, except to avoid the Hudson Canyon/Barnegat lanes—too much routine traffic there. Plot us in toward the Coast

4

Guard beacon at Democrat Point, and then take your preferred route to the Navy Yards."

Bass raised his eyebrows, thought a moment. "Jones Inlet," he said, "East Rockaway Inlet, Rockaway Point, Ambrose Light, Norton Point, Verrazano Narrows Bridge, and up."

LoBuono nodded. "Don't stop to pay the toll this time. How's the tide at Ambrose?"

"About three knots, the CG says."

The captain nodded. "Coast-creeping. I guess it suits the situation. Call Harbor Control and give them our ETA. Then call New York Yards Control and tell them I want that stuff waiting at the dock and loaded no more than fifteen minutes after open hatches."

"Yes, sir."

"I'm not fooling around, Bass. I don't want to linger."

"I'll tell them so, Captain."

"Go."

Bass went. Captain LoBuono got up and stepped over to the periscope. "Depth," he said.

"Two hundred, Captain," said Macilwain on the number-two radar. "Periscope depth in half a minute."

LoBuono waited, staring at the shiny scarred deck-plates. It seemed about a hundred years, now, since he had reported aboard the *Minneapolis* at Holy Loch after returning from his last leave and had been handed the sealed envelope. That aspect of his life he was used to: usually a whole looseleaf binder full of mission info stamped "SECRET," which in the present scheme of things normally meant "not very." But this envelope had not been the usual color, but an eye-rattling air-rescue orange, and it had had the new barcoded utter-security seals in it. Two sets of seals: one for the envelope itself, and one for a package which had been waiting on a lowloader by the dock. The package had been about eight feet square, a metal case with a very large cordon of armed and jumpy MPs around it—an escort which, in a lighter mood, would have suggested to Captain LoBuono that possibly the President himself was inside. As it was, he went down belowdecks, swiped the barcode through the reader in his quarters, opened the envelope, swiped the barcode on the inside envelope, opened that, sat down, and read.

And swore. But then, as now, there was nothing he could do about it, any of it—not the envelope, the box, or either of their contents. The box was loaded on, and he had told his crew not to ask questions about it because he had no answers for them. Then *Minneapolis* had headed out.

The door of the secure-cargo compartment way in the back, where the uneasy MPs had deposited the box, was now sealed with the second set of barcode seals, and a sign which one of the MPs had slapped on the door at eye-height: "DANGER—RADIATION," with the familiar three triangles, red on yellow. At the bottom of this sign, over the past few days, some wit had scrawled in ballpoint, "SO WHAT ELSE IS NEW?" Whoever had done it had a point: *Minneapolis* was an attack sub and carried nuclear-tipped torpedoes—what her crew did not know about radioactives would fit in a very short book indeed.

"FULL ALERT," his orders had said, "HOLY LOCH

TO GREENLAND: TRIPLE WATCHES: RADIO SI-
LENCE UNTIL COASTAL WATERS NY." And so it
had been done. LoBuono had known what effect this
would have on his crew. They were an intelligent and
stable bunch—no news there: neither the stupid nor the
unstable were allowed on nuclear-armed submarines.
But it made them uneasy to be carrying out secret orders.
It made them feel as if their superiors didn't trust them,
and they didn't know which superiors to be annoyed
with—the brass higher up or their captain.

For his own part, Captain LoBuono knew how they
felt. His annoyance was more focused. Without knowing
what he carried, it was hard for him to take all possible
and prudent precautions, thus jeopardizing the mission
itself.

"Periscope depth, sir," said the number-two radar
man.

"Thank you, Mr. Macilwain," LoBuono said. "Up
periscope."

It slid up before him, and he draped himself over its
handles and peered into the hood. Someone had left the
starlight augmenter on, so that everything in view glared
green. He *hmphed* to himself, toggled it off, and looked
again.

Dead ahead of them he could see Ambrose Lightship,
some six miles away, rocking slightly in the offshore
swells despite its anchoring. He looked north toward
Norton Point, got a brief glimpse of Coney Island,
walked around the 'scope housing a little, gazing to
northeastward, and saw the brick tower in the middle of
Jones Island, with its pointed bronze-green top. He

7

smiled slightly. It was a long time since he had pestered his folks on summer weekends to take him down to Zachs Bay near that tower, where he could sail his toy boats in the quiet water near the Playhouse—

". . . don't know," he heard someone whisper off to one side, partly behind him.

"You think he does?" the whisper came back from down the Bridge.

Silence: probably the sound of a head being shaken. "I think that's what's steaming him these last couple days—"

This was the other thing Captain LoBuono hated about sealed-orders runs: the rumor mill that started running when the engines did and didn't stop until some time during the crew's next leave, if then.

"I heard different." Another voice, whispering too.

"What?"

"Some kind of *thing* they're studying. Something they found."

"Thing? What kind of *thing*?"

Captain LoBuono swung gently around so that his back was broadside-on to the conversation. He looked idly south toward empty water, then swung slowly around to gaze westward, spotting the familiar landmarks: the Coast Guard observation towers on Sandy Hook, and the Sandy Hook Light, oldest in continuous use in the country; the low rise of the Highlands of Navesink, marking the southern boundary of New York Harbor.

"I don't know. Something—not from *here*."

A little further around LoBuono swung, toward the conversation. It stopped.

"Verrazano Narrows," his Ex said.

"So I see," said Captain LoBuono, looking through the periscope at the graceful upstrokes of steel and curves of cable. "Got five bucks, Bass?"

There were smiles around the bridge. Three trips ago, they had come this way, and Bass had been easing *Minneapolis* out of harbor in storm weather while LoBuono attended to paperwork business in his quarters. A nasty unsuspected riptide had pushed *Minneapolis* into one of the stanchions of the Narrows Bridge. She had taken no damage worse than a good scrape on the hull, but Bass had been mortified, and the crew had teased him good-naturedly and offered to pay the toll for him if he wanted to get onto the Bridge that much.

"Fresh out of small bills, Captain," Bass said.

"Good man. Sound surface. Steady as she goes, then twenty degrees starboard."

"Sounding surface." The usual clangor began. "Twenty degrees aye. Yard Control says our packages are loaded and waiting for us, Captain."

"Very well, Mr. Lorritson. Surface. Anything from Harbor?"

"Routine traffic west of Gowanus Bay," Macilwain said. "We pass eastward, starboard of the separation zone. Course to Buttermilk Channel and north to the Yards is clear."

"Proceed," Captain LoBuono said.

They sailed on up out of the Lower Bay and into New York Harbor proper, taking their time. LoBuono turned a bit again to admire the view of the skyscrapers towering up over lower Manhattan, or to seem to. He heard no more talk behind him, though, except the normal coming-to-berth chatter. "Tide's at two," said Loritz, the second navigator, one of the crewmen who had been whispering before.

"Mind the Spider," Bass said. LoBuono's mouth quirked. The treacherous crosscurrents of that name, which ran to the starboard of Governor's Island, were what had caused Bass his old trouble with the bridge. But this time of day, with high water still two hours off, they were at their least dangerous.

Without more incident they sailed on up through the East River and under the Brooklyn Bridge. Traffic on the bridge slowed down as motorists, seeing the *Minneapolis*'s sail, braked to stare and point. Captain LoBuono smiled slightly with pride, but the pride did nothing to ease his tension. *The sooner we're loaded and out of here*, he thought, *the better I'm going to like it.*

A few minutes later they passed under the Williamsburg Bridge, where the same slowing occurred, and then turned slightly out of the main East River "deepwater" channel.

"Wallabout Bay," the second navigator said.

The Navy Yards at last. "Down scope. Pop the top," Captain LoBuono said. "Mooring crew to the aft hatch. Down to one knot, Bass."

"One knot aye. Mooring crew reports ready."

"What's our berth?"

"Sixteen."

"Take us in."

They crept slowly through the outer Shipyard harbor mole. Not much business came this way anymore, what with defense cutbacks and other curtailments on spending: the Brooklyn Navy Yards, once the talk of the world, full of half-laid keels and the rattle of rivets and air-hammers, were now mostly home for mothballed ships and massive lifting cranes whose hooks swung empty in the wind off the Harbor. Still, the Navy used the Yards for occasional nontechnical repairs and provisioning work.

"Twenty-five degrees right rudder," Bass said. "Half a knot."

"Five hundred yards, sir."

"Very good. Rudder back."

A crewman was working the wheel that popped the forward hatch. Captain LoBuono waited for him to get out of the way, then went up the ladder to get a look at the day and the mooring.

There was a brisk wind blowing: it had already mostly dried the sail and the superstructure. LoBuono leaned on the sail's "balcony rail" and gazed down at the dock to the starboard of slip sixteen as *Minneapolis* sidled gently into it. The dock was stacked with plastic-wrapped crates and packages on dollies, ready to be hauled up onto the superstructure and passed down the hatches. Very slowly, very gently, the boat nudged sideways into the dock.

Bump.

And then, abrupt and terrifying, came the screaming hoot of collision alarms. The whole ship shook, abruptly, and shook again. "What the—" LoBuono started to mutter, and didn't bother finishing, as he dove down the ladder again.

By the time he reached the bridge, Lorritson was already running out of the back of it, toward the source of the alarms. "Hull breach!" someone yelled at the Captain as he raced past them.

"Bass!" LoBuono yelled at the back of his Ex, running in front of him.

"Not me, Captain!" Bass yelled back. They kept running.

Ahead of them they could hear the most dreaded sound of boat men, the thundering rush of uncontrolled water. They could also hear a slightly more reassuring sound, that of watertight compartments with automatic doors, dogging themselves closed. First Bass, then Captain LoBuono came to the final door, the one down at the far end of the weapons room, and found it closed as well. Behind it, they knew, lay the door with the "DANGER—RADIATION" sign. They looked at each other as they stood there.

LoBuono grabbed a mike that hung nearby and thumbed its "on" button. "Bridge! Everybody accounted for?"

"All accounted for, sir," said the Crew Chief's voice. "No one's back there."

"Get someone out in the water and have them see what the damage is!"

"I've got a man out there now, Captain," the Crew Chief said. "One moment—" There was an unintelligible squawking of secondhand radio conversation. Then the Crew Chief said, "We've got a breach about a foot and a half by two and a half, from the looks of it. Deck crew are getting a temp-patch on it. We can pump out the aft compartment in a few minutes."

"Go," LoBuono said.

He looked at his Ex. Lorritson opened his mouth, and the Captain said, "Sorry, Bass. The currents in the Narrows are one thing, but I know you'd never make a goof like that in dock." He made a slightly sour smile. "Put it down to nerves."

Lorritson nodded. "It's been—difficult," he said.

"All around—"

"Patch is in place," the Crew Chief said. "Pump's started."

They heard the throb from the in-hull pump motors starting. For a few minutes more they hummed unobtrusively. Then LoBuono heard the coughing noise that meant they were running out of anything to pump.

"Right," he said, and turned to Lorritson. "Got your dosimeter?"

Bass patted his pocket, where the little radiation-sensitive patch hung.

"If it turns any interesting colors, get your butt out of here," the Captain said. He turned the wheel to undog the door.

Clunk! went the latch. LoBuono pulled; the door swung slightly open. He peered around its edge.

His dosimeter, one of the new ones with a sound chip in it which essentially made it a small geiger counter, ticked gently to itself—a slow watch-tick, serious enough but hardly fatal. "Let's keep it short," the Captain said, stepping through and looking around cautiously.

There was nothing to be seen but wet floor, wet walls, wet ceiling, and the silvery-gray metal crate in the middle of it all, as wet as everything else. Slowly LoBuono walked around it. The front was fine. The sides were fine.

The rear of it, though, had an oblong hole about a foot and a half wide and two and a half feet long punched through it. The bent rags and tags of metal around the hole in the crate were all curved outward. LoBuono's dosimeter began to tick more enthusiastically, as did Lorritson's when he came up beside the captain and peered through the hole in the crate. There was nothing inside.

They looked at the hole in the hull, now sealed with pink plastic fast-patch. It very closely matched the one in the crate, both in size and in the direction of impact—from inside, punching toward the outside. Whatever had been in the crate, it had waited until the most opportune moment and then had left under its own power . . .

Lorritson looked at the hole in the hull, reached out to touch it, thought better, and let the hand drop. "I guess we'd better call the lost and found."

Captain LoBuono shook his head. "The lost part we seem to have handled," he said sourly. "We'll be in enough trouble for that very shortly, I would imagine. As for the found part—are you sure you would *want* to?"

Lorritson shook his head like a man unsure of the right answer. "Come on," LoBuono said, "let's get on the horn to the brass. We might as well start the trouble ourselves as wait for it to come to us."

But as they walked to the Bridge, LoBuono found himself wondering again, against his own orders, just what *might* have been in that box . . . and he shuddered.

H e had been in many strange and terrible places, in his time. He had been off Earth, on other planets, to other galaxies, even. He had faced threats terrible enough to make all Earth shudder, and had come away from them alive. All in all, he didn't have a bad record so far.

But right now, Peter Parker stood outside the doors of the 48th Street midtown branch of the First Manhattan Bank and cursed at the way his palms were sweating.

Behind him, the city made its accustomed roar. People on the sidewalk rushed past, going about their business, no one noticing the young man standing there paralyzed by his own unease—he refused to call it "fear." *I'm a super hero*, he thought. *Why am I standing here twitching?*

No answers came. Peter scuffed one sneaker on the sidewalk, staring at the chrome and plate glass of the bank. He had never been entirely comfortable with the term "super hero," at least not as applied to himself. Some of the other people he consorted with in his line of business—mutants or other humans unusually gifted with extraordinary powers—seemed to him really to merit description with the word "hero": many of them exhibited a level of courage or nobility which inspired him and sometimes shamed him. In his own case, "super" couldn't be argued with. But the way he often felt while out on his rounds—frustrated, enraged, sometimes terrified—struck him as less than heroic. *This kind of thing . . . this is different. Harder, in a way. This is just life.*

The people on the sidewalk just kept streaming past

him. It was lunchtime, and they had more important things to pay attention to than a reluctant super hero, had they even recognized one in his street clothes. Peter let out a long sigh, squared his shoulders, and walked into the bank.

He made his way through the soulless cheerfulness of the front of the bank, filled with gaudy posters shouting about mortgages and favorable interest rates, and went to the customer service counter. For all the attention anyone paid him for the first five minutes, he might as well have stayed outside. The young woman who finally came over to him did so with the air of someone engaged in much more crucial matters than serving a customer. "Yes?" she said, and popped her bubble gum.

"Mr. Woolmington, please?" Peter said.

"He's out to lunch."

This chimed well with some of Peter's private opinions about the man, but he was hardly going to say as much in public. "Can you tell me when he'll be back?"

"Dunno," said the young woman behind the counter. "This afternoon sometime." She turned away.

"Can you take a message for him, please?"

Popping her gum in a manner which suggested she had been a machine gun in an earlier life, the young woman said, "Yeah?"

"Please tell him—" Peter had a powerful urge to say, *Please tell him that Spider-Man was here to see whether his debt-consolidation loan's been approved yet, or whether he has to get one of the Avengers to cosign for it.* He restrained himself. "Please tell him Peter Parker stopped in to see if there was any news on his loan approval."

"Uh huh," said the young woman, and she turned away again.

Peter watched her go, then walked back out to the street again, feeling—actually, a little grateful. He was so sure the answer was going to be "no" when it came, that not finding the guy there to give him the bad news was a blessing, in a way.

He walked on down 48th Street toward Fifth Avenue, hands in his pockets, staring at the sidewalk—as much from self-defense as anything else. No matter how much you fined people for not cleaning up after their dogs, it never seemed to help much.

Banks.... Peter thought. This had been just one more of many situations in his life lately which had made him wonder whether being able to invoke the inherent cachet of superherodom openly would be any use. Or, would it just make matters worse? There were some heroes who functioned without secret identities, and when you saw them socially—if you did—they seemed to be managing okay. All the same, Peter suspected their answering machines were always full when they got home from heroing, or even from doing the shopping, and the thought of how much junk mail they must get made him twitch. Even without anyone knowing his own secret identity, Peter got enough to make his trips to the recycling bins a trial for anyone, super hero or not. And when you added MJ's endless catalogs to the pile....

He smiled slightly as he crossed Madison and headed on along toward Fifth. Mary Jane Watson-Parker was quite a celebrity in her own right—or had been, until she had left the soap opera *Secret Hospital*. Even before that, she had been well enough known for her modeling work. As a result, every mail-order house in the country, it seemed, sent her notifications of its new product lines . . . and she went through every one lovingly, pointing and oohing at the goodies.

But, of late, not buying from them. Things had gotten—well, not desperate, but tight. It was easy to forget how lavish money from TV work was until you lost it. Until then, MJ had spent some months persuading Peter to lighten up a little, to go ahead and spend a little money, buy himself that jacket, eat out more often. Peter had resisted at first. Finally, because it made her happy, he had given in—gotten used to enjoying himself, gotten used to having more funds to work with, gotten out of the habit of dreading the time the credit card bills came in.

And then, just as he had gotten used to it, it had all changed.

Now the mailbox was once again a source of uneasiness. The rent on the apartment, easy enough to handle on the combined incomes of a minor TV star and a freelance photographer, had now become a serious problem. Breaking the lease before it expired so that they could move somewhere smaller and cheaper was proving near impossible. So was keeping up the rent on just a freelancer's salary. They had some savings: not a huge sum, but it would last a while. MJ was out there getting every interview and audition she could scrape up. She was getting depressed, too, at not having been hired for something else right away. But Peter, just as nervous about it all as she was, had been purposely staying cheerful, trying to keep her spirits up and prevent her from getting discouraged. At the same time, he desperately wished there was someone to keep *him* from getting discouraged.

Being a super hero is all very well, he thought. *I just wish it paid better.*

I wish it paid, period!

He stopped at the corner, waiting for the light, while around him people hurried across anyway, daring the oncoming traffic. Whether heroing paid or not, he had to do it. Just as he had to take pictures, because he loved to, whether he got paid for them or not. Just as he had to study science, whether there seemed to be a job in it for him later or not. The old habit, the old love, went back too far, was too much a part of him now to let go.

He just had to make everything work together, somehow.

The light changed. Peter crossed, heading up Fifth to West 49th, then over to the shop where he usually got his photographic supplies. He had a couple of hours' work in the darkroom before him. Usually he tried to wind that up before MJ got home from her day out and complained about the smell of the developing solution (as well she might). It wasn't always easy. Darkroom business had become a lot more complicated, and more expensive, since the *Daily Bugle*'s front page had gone color. Now a photographer who aspired to lead-story work had to be able to manage quality color processing at home—a one-hour place wouldn't cut it. And color chemicals were four times the cost of black-and-white.

Nothing he could do about it, though. Peter swung into the store, waited a few moments: Joel, the owner, was busy trying to sell a guy in a leather jacket a large and complicated camera case. After a few minutes the guy shook his head and went off.

"Hey, Petey," Joel said, "you need a camera case?"

Peter snorted. "That thing? With the plastic hardware on it? It wouldn't last a week."

They both laughed. It was an old game: Joel would push something useless at Peter; Peter would push it back. Then they would gossip a while. Peter had learned not to cut the gossip short—Joel sometimes knew about potential news stories in the area, and once or twice Peter had been able to bring in hot pictures to the *Bugle* as a result, before anyone knew anything about the news story in question.

"Hey," Joel said, bending down to rummage under the counter for a moment. "Got that gadget you were asking me for."

"Which one?"

"Wait a sec." Joel vanished below the counter, and things began to appear on it: rolls of film, brushes, lens caps, lens hoods, and lots more small pieces of equipment. After a moment he came up with a little black box with a clear plastic lens on the front.

"Strobe slave," Joel said.

"Got one already," Peter said. It was a useful accessory for a photographer, a second flash cabled to his camera and "slaved" to the first, so that they went off together. That way you could add light to a dark scene, or fill in unwanted shadows from the side.

"Not like this, you haven't," Joel said. He picked up the little box and turned it to show Peter a tiny secondary lens on the side. "Wireless. It goes off when your flash does by sensing sudden changes in the ambient light."

Peter picked it up and looked at it thoughtfully. He had been thinking about some improvements to his present rig. "Any way you could hook a motion sensor to this, you think?"

Joel nodded, pointing to a jack socket on the back of the slave flash. "One of my other customers did something like that. Nature photographer. He picked up one of those passive infrared things, you know the kind—the doohickey that turns on your outside lights when someone gets close to the door. Saved him having to watch the birdie so much." Joel chuckled. "The bird moves, the camera takes its picture before it flies the coop."

Peter smiled. "I can use this. How much?"

"Forty."

He sighed, did some hurried addition in his head and pulled out his credit card. "Okay. And give me another package of three-by-five stock and a bottle of three-fifty, would you?"

"No problem." Joel went back to the shelves, came back with the gallon bottle of developer solution and the photo paper. For a moment he worked at the cash register. "Your lady find work yet?" he said.

Peter shook his head. "Still hunting."

"Hmm. You know, I have a guy comes in from the network place around the corner, the studios for the daytime stuff. Yesterday he told me they're hiring actors all of a sudden. Some kind of high-class soap, he said." Joel chuckled. "*Is* there such a thing?"

"You've got me. But I'll tell MJ to check it out."

The cash register dinged. "Sixty-two thirteen," Joel said.

Peter winced and handed his credit card over. "Did the price of the three-fifty go up again?"

"Yup. Another four bucks. Sorry, Petey."

"Not much we can do, I guess," Peter said, as Joel swiped the card through the reader.

"Don't I know it. The distributor says he can't do anything since the manufacturer's raised *his* prices . . ." Joel sighed. The reader beeped twice: Joel looked down at it, then raised his eyebrows. "Uh oh. They declined it."

Peter swallowed. "Didn't get the payment yet, I guess."

"Wouldn't be surprised. Did I tell you I sent my sister-in-law in Brooklyn a birthday card two weeks early, and it didn't get to her until two weeks *afterwards*? I ask you. You'd think we were in Europe or something. Come to think of it, I get letters from my cousin there *faster* than I do from Cecile."

Peter dug out his wallet and produced the necessary cash, noting sadly that this process left him with the munificent sum of one dollar and sixty cents. "Yeah," he said. "Here you go."

"Right." Joel handed him his change. "Hey, Petey—"

Peter turned, already halfway to the door. Joel waggled his eyebrows at him. "Don't let it get you down. It can only get better."

Almost against his will, Peter smiled. "Yeah. See you, Joel."

"See you."

All the same, as he walked on down the street, it was hard for Peter to see any way that things would get better any time soon. *There's only one thing*, he thought, *that's going to make it seem worthwhile.*

Tonight. . . .

The apartment was empty when he got there. It was big and roomy, with a nice enough view of the skyline, and a slightly less impressive view of the next-building-over's roof, about ten stories below their own and in this weather well covered with people in bathing suits trying to get a tan through the smog. The apartment's big windows let in plenty of light on white walls and a polished oak floor. There, as in some of MJ's show-business friends' apartments, it might have stopped, finding not much else to shine on. But unlike them, MJ had no patience with the presently fashionable minimalist school of decorating which considered one couch and one throw rug "enough furniture" and left the place looking barren as a Japanese raked-sand garden. Mary Jane Watson had been something of a packrat—though in the best possible taste—and Mary Jane Watson-Parker remained so. Her tastes ran more toward Laura Ashley than Danish Modern: big comfy sofas and chairs to curl up in, cushions scattered around, lots of bookshelves with lots of things on them—vases, bric-a-brac old and new (mostly old), and lots of books. It made for a comfortable and welcoming environment, though it was a pain to keep properly dusted.

Dusting, though, was not on Peter's mind at the moment. The new strobe slave was. Peter made his way back to the darkroom, unloaded the developing chemicals and the paper, and went back out to the front of the apartment to see what the answering machine had for him. Two invitations to subscribe to the *New York Times* (which they already did), one offer to clean their carpets (there weren't any), two anonymous please-call-this-number messages (probably bill collectors: sighing, Peter took the numbers and wished the machine had thrown one of its occasional fits and lost the messages). No offers of work, no parties, no sudden legacies, no good news.

Oh well. Tonight. . . .

Peter got up and went back to the table where he had dropped the new strobe slave. It was often difficult to take decent pictures when you weren't behind the camera, but in front of it as Spider-Man. It was tough to pay much attention to *f*-stops and exposure times when you were duking it out with some bad guy. It was the devil to keep the camera pointed at the action when you were swinging by your webline from one rooftop or another. Also, criminals, both the elite supervillain types and your ordinary garden-variety crooks, were generally not very amenable to staying in the camera frame while you were having it out with them. Peter had been trying to find a solution to both of those problems for some while.

Now, though, I might have one. On the table, left over from where he had been fixing MJ's sunglasses the other night, was a set of ultra-tiny screwdrivers which he also used for jobs like maintenance on his web-shooters and getting the faceplate off the microwave when its LEDs failed. Now he picked up the third-largest of the group, undid the screws on the bottom and sides of the strobe, and carefully pried the backplate off, taking a long look at the insides. It was a fairly straightforward array, though some of the soldering on the chip at its heart was slapdash. A transistor, some assorted diodes, all labeled for a change; an LED to tell you when the gadget was armed; the light sensor; and a bypass circuit to take it out of commission when you had some other triggering mechanism jacked into the input.

Fair enough. Peter had one other piece of hardware which would communicate with this readily enough, with some programming. Miniaturization had worked enough wonders of late, but there was one that not a lot of people but researchers in the sciences knew about. To take up less room on the lab benches, some bright guy in the Far East had taken a whole PC computer mother-board and worked out how to fit it on a board the size of two cigarette packs laid end to end. That, with enough RAM chips, was enough machine-smarts to run a fairly sensitive motion-control apparatus—and that was what Peter had been working on for a while now. The Engineering Department at Empire State University had assumed that one of the doctoral candidates was doing a little good-natured slumming when he came down to pick their brains about the fine points of motion control programming. Privately they thought that the guys up in Nuclear Physics were getting twitchy about handling the radioactives themselves, and were trying to teach the computers how to do it for them. They could hardly have suspected the real purpose of Peter's visits. Pretty soon, though, he would have something of considerable use to a photographer who was also a crimefighter. Bit by bit, he was building a camera which, with the right motion sensor attached, would turn by itself to follow the action taking place around it, and which could be remotely triggered, and which (if the aforesaid crimefighter got too busy) would follow his movements and fire at preset default intervals. Once this creature was built, his bosses at the *Bugle* would have fewer complaints about the poor composition of Peter's shots compared to other photographers'.

And his credit card company would be *much* happier with him.

For half an hour or so he fiddled with the slave strobe. The actual movement-controlling hardware, the guts of an old portable telescope's cannibalized and much-altered clock drive, had been ready for a while. All Peter had needed was a suitable actuator. This new slave would do fine until something more sophisticated came along. The afternoon shadows moved across the apartment, and finally the windows lost the sun. Peter barely noticed, finishing his adjustments to the slave itself and then going to fetch the system's moving parts and the camera itself. It was his best one, a Minax 5600si, with an extremely advanced automatic exposure- and shutter-control system—which it would need, when its owner was hanging by synthesized spiderweb from the top of some building, swinging after a crook, tens or even hundreds of yards away. The camera screwed into a little platform with a ball-and-socket joint able to yaw, roll, and pitch. That, in turn, screwed into the top of a small collapsible tripod which had the motion-control motors and the teeny PC motherboard, each bolted to one of the tripod's legs in a small shockproof case. The whole business, when collapsed, would fit comfortably into a backpack or one of the several elastic pouches that Peter had built into his costume over time.

Finally, there it all stood, ungainly looking but theoretically functional. He took the camera off its stand, popped off its back, rooted around in a nearby desk drawer for some of the time-expired film he used for tests, loaded the camera, and seated it on the stand again.

The instant the camera was turned on, it whirled on the stand. The camera's inboard flash went off as it took his picture, and another one, and another, and another. . . .

"Oh jeez," he muttered, "cut it out." He stepped away, trying to come around the setup sideways to turn off the slave. Unfailingly the camera followed, taking pictures as fast as it could wind itself, about one per second. The flash was beginning to dazzle Peter. He jumped over the table and took a few steps further around it. The camera tried to follow, fouled itself on its own motion-control cables, and got stuck, still taking picture after picture, its motor making a pitiful and persistent little *hnh, hnh, hnh* noise as it tried to follow him right around the table. Peter reached out and caught the tripod just as it was about to fall over.

It *hnh, hnh*ed in his hands for a few more seconds before he managed to pull the motion control system's jack. *Well, it works*, Peter thought, turning back toward the table. *Even if it is a little light on the trigger. I'll take it out tonight and see how it does.*

A key turned in the apartment door, which then obligingly opened. The camera in Peter's hands flashed. MJ stood in the doorway, caught open-mouthed with a couple of heavy bags of groceries, and looked at Peter curiously.

"It's not my birthday," she said. "And I don't remember calling the media. What's the occasion?"

"Your glorious homecoming," Peter said, putting the camera down. "C'mere. I want a hug."

MJ offloaded the bags onto a table near the door, and Peter collected the hug, and a couple of serious kisses, while behind them the camera flashed and flashed and flashed. After a few seconds, MJ detached herself by a few inches, took his face between her hands, and said, "Gonna run the batteries down that way."

"What, mine?"

She laughed. "Not yours, lover. Eveready, that's you. Just keeps going, and going, and . . ." Peter poked her genially in the kidneys, and MJ squealed slightly and squirmed in his arms. "What, what, why are you complaining? It's a *compliment*. Lemme go, the frozen stuff's going to defrost. It's like an oven in here. Didn't you turn the air-conditioning on?"

"I didn't notice," Peter said, letting her go. He picked up one of the bags while MJ got the other, and they headed into the kitchen.

"It may be just as well," MJ said as she started unpacking one of the bags: salad things, a couple of bottles of wine, ice cream, sherbert. "I turned the air conditioner on this morning and it didn't go. Made a sort of gurgly noise for a while, but no cold air. I shut it off—thought it might recover if I left it alone."

Peter sighed. "That's what it did the last time it broke. The compressor, wasn't it?"

"Yeah. The guy said it might not last much longer. . . ."

She reached down into the bag for a couple of cheeses, then picked the bag up and started to fold it. Peter opened his mouth to say something about how they really couldn't afford to have the air conditioner break just now, there were too many other bills . . . and then he stopped. MJ looked so tired and woeful. Perspiration and the heat of the day had caked the makeup on her, her hair was all over the place, and she had a run in her stocking. He knew she hated looking like that, and she was so worn down and miserable that she didn't even care.

He went to her and hugged her. Somewhat surprised, MJ hugged back, and then she put her head down on his shoulder and just moaned softly, a little sound that hurt him as badly as any supervillain tapdancing on his spleen.

"Nothing today, huh?" he said.

"Nothing," MJ replied, and was silent for a little while. "I can't stand this much longer. I *hate* this. I'm a good actress. At least, they all used to say so. Were they just saying that because they wanted to stay on my good side? And if they weren't just saying it, *why can't I find another job?*"

Peter didn't have any answers for her. He just held her.

"I've been all over this town," MJ muttered. "I'm either too tall, or too short, or too fat, or too thin, or my hair's the wrong color, or my voice is wrong somehow. I wouldn't mind if I thought the producers *knew* what they wanted. But they *don't* know. They don't know anything except that I'm *not* what they want. Whatever that is." She breathed out, hard. "And my feet hurt, and my clothes stick to me, and I want to kick every one of their sagging, misshapen butts."

"Oh, come on," Peter said, holding her away a little now, since her voice told him it was all right to. "Their butts can't *all* have been misshapen."

"Oh yes they can," MJ said, straightening up again and reaching for the second paper bag, while Peter still held her. "You should have seen this one guy. He had this—"

"Who's all this food for?" Peter said suddenly, looking at the counter, which was becoming increasingly covered with stuff. Chicken breasts, more wine—dessert wine this time—fresh spinach, cream, fresh strawberries. "Is someone coming over for dinner, and I forgot about it? Ohmigosh, you said we were inviting Aunt May—"

"It's for *us*," MJ said. "Why do we only have to have nice dinners when people are coming over? Besides, May is *next* week. You have a brain like a sieve." She folded up the other bag, picked up its partner, and shoved them into the bag drawer.

"No question about that whatsoever," Peter said, abruptly glad of an excuse not to have to tell her immediately about the bank, or the credit card, or the answering machine. "Sieves R Us. What's for dinner, sexy?"

"I'm not telling you till you set the table. And tell your little droid friend out there that he doesn't get a high chair. He can sit in the living room and I'll give him a can of WD-40 or something." She hmphed, an amused sound, as she pulled a drawer open and started taking out pots and pans. "Flashers. I have enough problems with them in the street without finding them at home."

Peter chuckled, picked up the camera tripod and its associated apparatus and carried it into the living room, where he left the camera with its face turned to the wall. Then, humming, he went to get the tablecloth.

Tonight, he thought. *Tonight we'll see.*

Much later, well after dinner, the lights in the front of the Parker apartment went out.

The lights in the back were still on. MJ was in bed, propped up in a nest of pillows, reading. If someone heard about this tendency and asked her about it, Peter knew, MJ would tell them one version of the truth: that she was just one of those people who found it constitutionally impossible to get to sleep without first reading something, *anything*. The other truth, which she only told to Peter, and no more often than necessary, was that she needed to do something to take her mind off his "night job," as opposed to his day job. His night job's hours were far more irregular, the company he kept was generally far less desirable, and sometimes he didn't come back from it until late or, rather, early. Peter knew

MJ restrained herself from saying, much more often, how much she feared that one night he would go out to the night job, and *never* come back from it. He had learned to judge her level of nervousness by how big a book she took to bed with her. Tonight it was *The Story of the Stone*, a normal-sized paperback. So Peter went out in a good enough humor, as relaxed as he could be these days, when he was no longer quite a free agent.

It was perhaps more strictly accurate to say that Peter Parker opened the window, and turned off the lights. Then, a few minutes later, someone else came to the window and stood for a moment, the webbed red and solid blue of the costume invisible in the darkness to any putative watcher. It was always a slightly magical moment for him, this hesitation on the border between his two worlds: the mundane standing on the threshold of the extraordinary, safe for the moment . . . but not for long.

Tonight he hesitated a shorter time than usual. The camera and its rig were collapsed down as small as they would go, slipped into the back-pouch where they would stay out of his way. If anyone caught sight of him on his rounds tonight, they would probably find themselves wondering if they were seeing some new costumed figure who had decided to emulate the Hunchback of Notre Dame. He chuckled under his breath at the thought. *Would one more costumed figure attract any attention in this city anymore?* he wondered. Lately the place had been coming down with them. Meanwhile, there would be the usual stir if one of the natives spotted him, one of the more familiar, if not universally loved, of the super heroes in town.

Under the tight-fitting mask, he smiled. Then Spider-Man slipped out the window, clung briefly to the wall, and closed the window behind him, all but a crack.

Carefully, as usual, he wall-crawled around the corner of the building—theirs was a corner apartment—and around to the back wall, where MJ's bedroom window was. The window was open, in the hope of any cool breeze. He put his head just above windowsill level, knocked softly on the sash. Inside, on the bed against the far wall, the reading light shone. MJ looked up, saw him, smiled slightly, made a small finger-waggle wave at him: then went back to her book. She was already nearly halfway through it. *I still wish she could teach me to read that fast*, he thought, and swarmed up the back corner of the building, making for the roof.

He peered cautiously over the edge of the roof balcony. There was no one up there this time of night: it was too hot and humid, and their neighbors with air conditioners seemed to have stayed inside to take advantage of it.

Can't blame them, he thought. It was a heck of a night to be out in a close-fitting costume. All the same, he had work to do.

About a third of a block away stood a tall office building. Spider-Man shot a line of web to a spot just south of the roofline near the building's corner. *And we're off,* he thought, and swung.

He had five different standard exit routes from the apartment, which he staggered both for security—no use taking the chance someone might see him exiting repeatedly and figure something out—and for interest's sake. Security was more important, though: he didn't want to take the chance that someone would find out where he was living by the simple expedient of following him home.

By now the business of swinging through the city had become second nature, a matter of ease. Tarzan could not have done it more easily, but then, Tarzan had his vines hanging ready for him. Spider-Man made his swinging equipment to order as he went. He shot out another long line, swung wide across Lexington and around the corner of the Chrysler Building, shot another line way up to one of the big aluminum eagle's heads, and swarmed up the line to stand atop the head and have a look around.

This was a favorite perch: good for its view of midtown, and it had other attractions. This was the particular eagle-head on which Margaret Bourke-White had knelt while doing her famous plate photos of the New York skyline in the late forties. Spidey stood there a moment, enjoying the breeze—it was better, this high up—and scanned his city.

It moved, as always it moved: restless, alive, its breath that old soft roar of which he never tired, the pulse visible rather than audible. Red tail-light blood moving below him in golden-lined sodium-lit arteries, white light contesting the pathways with the red; the faint sound of honking, the occasional shout, but very faint and far-off-seeming, as heard from up here; the roar of late jets winding up, getting ready to leap skyward from

LaGuardia; lights in a million windows, people working late, home from work, resting, eating meals with friends, getting ready to turn in. Those people, the ones who lived here, worked here, loved the place, couldn't leave—those were the ones he did this for.

Or had *come* to do it for. It hadn't started that way, but his mission had grown to include them, as he had grown.

Spider-Man breathed out. While Spidey had never established a formal communication with the various lowlifes, informants, and stoolies that populated the city, he still heard things. Over the last couple of days, he'd heard some rumblings about "weird stuff" going on on the west side. Nothing more specific than that, just "weird."

Spidey slung a long line of web at the Grand Hyatt, caught it at one corner and swung on past and around, halfway over Grand Central, then shot another line at the old Pan Am building, swung around that, and headed westward first, using the taller buildings in the upper Forties to get him over to Seventh Avenue, where he started working his way downtown. That was something he had learned fairly early on: when traveling by web, a straight line was often not the best way to go. It wasn't even always possible. Buildings tall enough to be useful are not necessarily strung for a webslinger's convenience in a straight line between him and his destination. Over time Spidey had learned where the tall buildings clustered and where they petered out. He learned to exploit those clusters for efficiency, discovering that an experienced slinger of webs could gain as much speed slingshotting around corners as he lost from not being able to go straight as the crow flew.

Shortly he was down in the mid-Twenties, and he slowed down to take in the landscape. This time of night, things were more than just quiet, they were desolate. There were few restaurants in this area, not even many bars, and almost no one lived here, except the occasional tiny colony of homeless squatting in some unused or derelict structure. Not even much traffic passed by. Here the street lighting was iffy at best, the lamp bulbs missing or sometimes blown out by people who liked the dark to work in. The presence of that kind of person was one of the reasons he patrolled here on a more or less regular basis. Left to themselves, the children of the night might get the idea that they owned this neighborhood, and it was good for them to know that someone else had other ideas.

He paused on the roof of one building, looked up and down its cross-street, and listened carefully.

Nothing. He shot out another line of web, swung across another street, and waited. It was not only sound for which he listened.

Nothing.

So it went for some good while. Not that he minded. Every now and then, he lucked into a quiet night, one which left him more time to appreciate the city and required less of his time worrying about it. The problem was that the worry came a lot more easily than it used to. The city was not as nice as he remembered it being when he was a child—and he chuckled softly to himself, remembering what a dirty, crime-ridden place it had seemed to him when his aunt and uncle first brought him from Queens into Manhattan. By comparison, that New York of years ago—and not that many years, really— was a halcyon memory, a pleasant and happy place, where it seemed the sun had always been shining.

Not anymore.

He paused on another rooftop on West 10th, looking around. Nothing but the muted city roar. Locally, no traffic—but he could hear the grind and whine of a diesel truck, one with a serious transmission problem to judge by the sound of it, heading north on 10th Avenue. *We've got a dull one*, he thought. *No "weird stuff" in sight. Normally I'd be grateful.*

Then it hit him.

Several times over the course of their relationship, he had tried to explain to MJ how it felt, the bizarre experience he had long ago started to call his "spider-sense." It was, first of all, very simple: there was nothing of thought or analysis about it. It wasn't a feeling of fear, but rather of straightforward alarm, untinged by any other emotion, good or bad. It was the internal equivalent of hearing a siren coming up behind you when you knew you hadn't done anything wrong. It had seemed to him that, if as simple a creature as a spider experienced alarm, it would feel like this.

It also made him feel as if he was tingling all over. He was tingling now.

He stood very still, then slowly turned. The sense could be vaguely directional, if he didn't push it. Nothing specific northward, nothing to the east. Westward—

He shot out some web and swung that way, over several decrepit-looking rooftops. Unlike the buildings closer to midtown, these were in rather poor repair. There were gaping holes in some of the roofs, places where the tar and shingles and gravel had fallen in—or been cut through. *Looks like there's precious little to steal in most of these, though.*

The spider-sense twinged hard, as abrupt and impossible to ignore as the nerve in a cracked tooth, as he came to one particular building. He had almost passed it, an ancient broad-roofed single-story building with big skylights which looked mostly structurally intact, though most of the glass in them was broken. Well, all right . . .

He shot out another length of web, cut loose the last one from which he had been swinging, and let it lengthen as he dropped toward the old warehouse's roof. After a second or so he impacted, but so lightly he doubted anyone inside would have heard him.

Softly he stepped over to the skylight with the most broken glass, dropped beside it to show the minimum possible silhouette, and peered inside.

A very old place indeed. Down on the main shop floor, if that was what it was, lay toppled or discarded timbers, piles of trash, and puddles of water from other spots in the roof that leaked. His gaze took in old oil-drums lying on their sides, some of them split and leaking, and old newspapers plastered to the floor and faded by the passage of time.

Spider-Man shuddered. It was in a place very like this one that he had found the man who killed his uncle.

At other times, it all seemed a long time ago. His life had become so busy since. But here, it all seemed very close. The memory was reduced, now, to quick flashes. That afternoon in the science department at college, the experiment with what was mildly referred to as "radioactive rays." He could almost laugh at that, now. It had taken him years of study, nearly to the master's level, to really understand what had been going on in that experiment—and he now knew that the professor conducting it hadn't fully understood what was happening, either. There was more going on than the generation of plain old gamma rays: the radiation source had been contaminated by unusual elements and impurities, producing utterly unexpected results.

A spider had dropped gently downwards between the generating pods and become irradiated. Its DNA so quickly uncoiled and recoiled into a bizarre new configuration that it was actually able to survive for a few moments and bite Peter before the changes in its body chemistry killed it. The memory was frozen in Peter's mind like a slide from a slideshow: the tiny glowing thing falling onto his hand, the sudden rush of pain and heat as their respective body proteins met in what started as an allergic reaction, but turned into something much more involved and potentially deadly. Only the tininess of the spider and the minuscule amount of venom from its bite had saved his life. As it was, the radiation-altered proteins in its body fluids complexed with his own, the change a catalytic one, sweeping through Peter's body faster than mere circulation could have propelled it. Ten seconds later, he almost literally had not been the same person.

Another slide-image: the building he jumped halfway

up, frightened by a car horn behind him, his hands adhering to the brick as if glued to it, but effortlessly. A standpipe that he accidentally crushed with what seemed a perfectly normal grip. Soon he had realized what had happened to him and, after the initial shock wore off, decided to market it.

He made a costume, not wanting his quiet home life with his Aunt May and Uncle Ben to be affected, and started making public appearances. The media ate it up. Sudden fame, to a guy who had always been regarded by his peers as a useless bookworm, was heady stuff. So it was, one night after a television appearance, that a man brushed past him and dove into an elevator. The cop in pursuit had shouted at Peter (still in costume at that point) to catch the running man. Peter had let the guy go, not particularly caring about him. He had other business to think about, appearances to plan, money to be made. What was one thief, more or less, to him?

Until a burglar, surprised in the act, shot and killed his Uncle Ben.

Weeping, raging, Peter had struggled into his costume, going to join the pursuit. There was an old warehouse not too far away where the burglar had gone to ground. By ways the police couldn't manage, he had gone in, cornered the burglar, disarmed him, battered him into submission—and then had found himself looking, horrified, into the face of the man he hadn't bothered to stop.

That face hung before him again, now. Other memories might mercifully fade. Not *this* one. Since that awful night Spider-Man had learned the lesson that with great power comes great responsibility. The weight on his conscience of his uncle's lost life had perhaps lightened a little over the intervening years, but he doubted he would ever be completely free of it—and maybe he didn't want to be.

Now he looked down into the warehouse, alert, and saw nothing but what was actually here. *As good a chance to test this as any,* he thought, and silently unshipped the camera apparatus, set it up near the edge of the skylight, checked its view and made sure that the pan-and-tilt head worked freely and without fouling itself. He wasn't using a flash tonight; instead he had loaded the camera with a roll of the new superfast ASA 6000 film, which would let the camera work by available light and keep it from betraying its presence to unfriendly eyes.

Right, he thought. *Now let's see what the story is in here.*

Softly he walked around to another of the skylights and peered inside. There was more glass in this one, and the view through it was somewhat obscured: he rubbed at one pane with a gloved hand and looked through. *Nothing.*

Spider-Man went along to the third skylight. This one, as the first, was missing most of its glass. Now, though, he heard something: voices muttering, the clunk of something heavy being moved, metal scraping laboriously over metal. He peered down. There was a shape on the floor. He squinted.

A security guard in uniform lay askew, crumpled and motionless. *Unconscious? Dead?*

He went through the biggest pane of glass with a crash, uncaring, taking only time enough to leave a strand of web behind him to ride down as it lengthened and break his fall to the floor. Landing, he took in the surroundings in tableau, as if frozen—four men, thuggish-looking, caught in the act of loading big oil-drum-like metal canisters onto a truck backed into the warehouse's loading ramp. Wide eyes, mouths hanging open, certainly unprepared for his arrival.

Not that *unprepared*, Spider-Man thought, as one of them pulled a gun. But the man was moving at merely human speed, and his opponent had a spider's swiftness of reaction. Spider-Man flung out one arm, shot a thick, sticky line of web at the gunman. It stuck to the gun, and Spidey yanked it out of the man's hand and threw it across the warehouse into the piles of trash in the shadows. The man yelped—apparently his finger had gotten stuck in the trigger guard, and now he stood shaking the hand and cursing.

"Serves you right," Spidey said as the others came for him, one of them pulling his own weapon. "But come on, now, didn't you see what just happened?" He threw himself sideways as the second man fired, then came up out of the roll, shot another line of web and took the second gun away, flinging it after the first one.

"Anybody else?" The first of the four came at Spidey in an attempt to get up-close and personal. "Oh well, if you insist," he said, resigned but amused. Spidey side-stepped the man's headlong rush, shot a line of webbing around his ankles, and got out of the way to let him sprawl face-first to best effect. The second one, now deprived of his gun, swung a board at Spider-Man and missed in his excitement. Spidey cocked one fist back, beginning to enjoy himself, and did *not* miss. That sound of a perfect punch landing, so bizarrely like the sound of a good clean home run coming off a bat, echoed through the warehouse. The man went down like a sack of potatoes and didn't move again.

"Glass jaw. Guess the gun is understandable," Spidey said, as the third of the four came at him. This one didn't just dive headlong, but stopped a few feet away, turned, and threw at Spider-Man what under normal circumstances would have been a fairly respectable rear thrust-kick. Unfortunately, these circumstances were *not* normal, as Spidey had been having two-bit crooks throwing such kicks at him since the craze for kung-fu movies had started some years before. While the kick looked good, the man throwing it had obviously never heard about the defenses against it, and Spidey simply stepped back a pace, then grabbed the foot hanging so invitingly in the air in front of him, and pulled hard. The man fell right down off his inadequately balanced stance on the other foot, and straight onto his tailbone with a crunch and a shriek of pain.

"I'd get that X-rayed if I were you," Spidey said, throwing a couple of loops of restraining web around the man before he could struggle to his feet. "Now then—"

His spider-sense buzzed sharply, then, harder than it had on initially seeing the warehouse. Spidey threw himself instantly as hard and as far to the right as he could. It was just as well, for just to his left there was a deafening *BANG!* and an explosion of light, and dirt and trash from the warehouse floor were flung in all directions through a thick roil of smoke.

The light and the noise were horribly familiar: Spider-Man had run into them entirely too often before. *Pumpkin bomb*, he thought. He came up into a crouch, aching slightly from the concussion but otherwise unhurt, and stared through the smoke at its inevitable source. Tearing through the smoke, standing on the jetglider which was one of his trademarks and his favorite way of getting around, was the orange-and-blue-garbed figure of the Hobgoblin.

Spidey jumped again as another bomb hit near him and went off, then leapt one more time to get out of range. "Hobby," he shouted, "why can't you stick to playing with cherry bombs, like other kids your age? This kind of antisocial behavior's likely to go on your permanent record."

A nasty snicker went by Spidey overhead: he rolled and leapt again, to be very nearly missed by an energy blast from one of Hobgoblin's gauntlets. "Spider-Man," Hobgoblin said in that cheerful, snide voice of his, the crimson eyes glinting evilly from under the shadow of the orange cowl, "you really shouldn't involve yourself with matters that don't concern you. Or with anything else but your funeral arrangements."

A couple more energy blasts stitched the concrete in front of Spider-Man as Hobgoblin soared by low overhead. Spidey bounced away from the blasts, hurriedly throwing a glance toward the four thugs. They were already showing signs of recovery, and the webbed ones were struggling to get loose. *Not good.* Spider-Man looked at the truck. *This may not go exactly as planned. I need a moment to plant a spider-tracer on that—* Another pumpkin bomb hurled near him and, warned again by his spider-sense, he jumped one more time, but almost not far enough. He felt the concussion all over the back of his body as it detonated. "Hobby," he shouted, "I expected better of you. How many of these things have you thrown at me, all this while, and not gotten a result?"

"One keeps trying," Hobgoblin said from above, over the whine of the jetglider. "But since you insist—"

Immediately it began to more or less rain small knife-edged electronic "bats" which buzzed dangerously near. It was too dark to see their edges glint, but Spidey had had occasion before to examine them closely, and they were wicked little devices—light graphite and monacrylic "wings" with individual miniaturized guidance systems and razor-sharp front and back edges. *Me and my big mouth*, Spidey thought, resisting the urge to swat at them as they buzzed around him—they could take off a finger, or even a hand, in no time flat. He ducked and rolled out of the way as fast as he could, slipping behind a couple of standing canisters in an attempt to confuse the razor-bats.

"Is this better?" Hobgoblin said sweetly.

Spider-Man didn't answer, intent as he was on dodging the bats. He spared a glance upward. *Came in through the skylight. I wonder*, Spidey thought, *did the camera get him? Well, we'll see. Meanwhile, I want him out of here—he's got too much of the advantage of mobility, and inside here I'm a sitting duck for these things.*

Also, I've got a better chance of snagging him out in the open.

Spider-Man shot a line of webbing at the edge of the skylight where the camera was positioned and climbed at top speed. "Coward! Come back!" he heard Hobgoblin screech.

Outside, he looked up and around. Several buildings in this block and the next were ten stories high or better. He shot a webline at the nearest of them and went up it in a hurry. Behind him, to his great satisfaction, he heard the camera click, reposition itself, click again. *Good baby. You just keep that up.*

Hobgoblin, standing on the jetglider, soared up out of the skylight without noticing the camera. *Whatever else happens*, Spidey thought with slightly unnerved satisfaction, *these pictures are going to be dynamite.*

The bright, noisy detonation near him in midair reminded Spider-Man that he had more immediate explosives to worry about. *Now if I can just keep clear of those*, he thought, *long enough to snag that sled.*

For that, though, he needed to get himself anchored to best advantage, ideally in a situation that Hobgoblin would fly into without adequate forethought. Little time to manage such a situation. *All the same*, Spidey thought, *there's a chance. Those two buildings there are pretty close.* He swung around the corner of the building to which his webbing was presently attached, but instead of shooting out more webbing to the next anchorage and continuing around, he pulled himself in close to the side of the building and lay flat against it. Hobby shot on past and kept going, apparently assuming that Spidey had done so as well. *Good. He always tends to overreact a little.*

Now Spider-Man swarmed around the side of the building, back the way he had come, shot several strands of web across to the next building, felt them anchor; moved down and shot a couple of more, anchoring them in turn. In the dark, they were almost invisible. *Now all I need to do is swing across there with Hobby behind me, and one or another of those lines is going to catch him amidships and take him right off that glider.*

He wall-crawled as fast as he could up to the top of the building, peered around, saw nothing. *Good.* He anchored another strand of web, waited—

—and suddenly heard the buzzing all around him. The razor-bats had followed him up out of the warehouse.

Without hesitation he jumped off the building and web-slung for all he was worth, working to shake the things by swinging perilously close to the wall of the next building over. Several of the razor-bats hit the wall, disintegrating in a hail of graphite splinters. But the rest followed, and one of them got in close and nailed him in the leg. He managed to kick it into the building in passing, but his leg had a two-inch-long razor cut in it now, shallow but bleeding enthusiastically. *Next best tactic*, he thought, and shot out another line of webbing, heading upward toward where Hobby was gliding by, watching the fun and laughing hysterically.

"Yeah, this whole thing is just a bundle of laughs, isn't it? Let's see if it stays this funny," Spidey shouted, and made straight for him, energy blasts and pumpkin bombs or not. Even Hobgoblin had cause to be a little twitchy about being caught in a rapidly approaching cloud of his own flying razors. Sure enough, Hobby backed off slightly, tossing spare pumpkin bombs and firing off energy blasts as best he could. Spidey smiled grimly under the mask, noticing that his enemy was swooping toward the space between the two buildings where he had stretched his trap of weblines—

Then, without any warning, Hobgoblin turned, his great cloak flaring out behind him, and threw a pumpkin bomb right at Spidey. Caught up in Hobby's barrage, he was unable to dodge it, and it went off, seemingly right in his face.

He fell. Only an uprush of spiderly self-preservation saved him, the jet of webbing streaking out to catch the edge of the nearest building and break his fall to the roof of the old warehouse. It was not enough to cushion that fall, though. He came down hard and lay there with the world black and spinning around him.

Dead, he thought, *I'm dead. Or about to be.*

He could just hear the whine of the jetglider pausing in midair above and beside him, could just feel the sting of the roof gravel its jets kicked up. He knew Hobgoblin was bending over him.

"It doesn't matter," Hobby said, and laughed, not quite as hysterically. There was purpose in the laughter, nasty purpose, and the sound of genuine enjoyment. "Right now you wish you'd never heard of me, for all your smart talk. And shortly the whole city will wish it had never heard of me." More laughter. "Wait and see."

The laughter trailed away, as did the sound of the jet-glider. Spider-Man could just barely hear Hobgoblin scolding his henchmen down in the warehouse, yelling at them to hurry, get themselves cleaned up, get the truck loaded, and get it out of here! He must have passed out briefly: the next sound he heard was the truck being driven away, fading into the greater roar of the city.

It was some while before he could get up. *Click, whirr, click, whirr,* he heard something say. The camera, its lens following his motion, the motion of a very dazed and aching Spider-Man staggering toward it, holding his head and moaning. *Click, whirrrrr,* said the camera. Then it said nothing further. It had run out of film.

He sat down next to it, hard, picked up the camera after a moment, and pushed the little button to rewind the film. *This worked, at least,* he thought. *But whatever else was going on down there, there's no way to tell now. I didn't even have time to put a tracer on that truck. Oh well—I bet we'll find out shortly. Whatever it is, it's big—Hobby wouldn't be involved otherwise.*

Meantime, I'd better get home.

TWO

"**A**nd the WGN news time is one forty-five. It's eighty-four degrees and breezy in New York. Looks like we're in for worse tomorrow—our accu-weather forecast is for hazy, hot, and humid weather, highs tomorrow in the mid-nineties with expected humidity at ninety-two percent."

"I wish to God," said a weary voice off to one side, "that you'd turn that bloody thing off."

Harry sighed and reached out to turn it down, at least. "Can't get to sleep without my news," he said, turning over in the thin, much-flattened sleeping bag.

From his companion, half inside a cardboard box, wrapped in discarded Salvation Army blankets and numerous alternating layers of newspapers and clothes, there came a snort. "I can't sleep with it. Why don't you at least use the earphones, since you've got them? Jeez." There was a slight rustle of the other turning over restlessly in his box.

Harry grumbled acquiescence and started going through his things in the dark, looking for the small bag that contained the earplugs for the transistor radio. The sound echoed through the empty old warehouse: nothing else was to be heard. That didn't stop Harry from wrapping himself in several layers, despite the heat. You never knew what would be crawling around—or who. Best to keep protected, and keep what few possessions you had as close as possible.

He and Mike had been here for about six days now, having wormed their way in through a back-alley service entrance—the door to one of those ground-level elevators which, when they were working, came clanging up through the sidewalk to deliver crates and cartons to the storage area below a building. In the case of this particular freight elevator, it had been many years since it had worked. Some careful prying with the crowbar that Mike carried for self-defense got them in. They squirmed and wriggled their way through and found their way into a subcellar, then up a couple of flights of crumbling steps to the warehouse floor.

It wasn't as old as some of the buildings around here; it looked to have been built in the late forties and fifties, when there was still something of an industrial boom going on in this part of town. To judge from the general look of the place, Harry thought, it had been let go to seed for the past ten years or so. Now it looked like no one had been in to clean or maintain it for at least that long. There were chips and fragments of old paint and downfallen plaster all over the floor, and much of the light-blocking stuff they used on the glass windows had also peeled off. In other places, sun on the other side of the building had burnt the glass to translucent iridescence. There were some big old dusty canisters stacked up against one wall, forgotten, no doubt, by the previous owner, or the present one, whoever they were.

There were no signs of other habitation, which was unusual in this neighborhood. Squatters and dossers were all over this part of town, looking for a place to spend a night, or five, or ten. This building's quiet was a treasure, a secret that Harry and Mike kept very close to themselves and never spoke of when they were out on the street during the day, going through the trash and cadging the cash they needed for food.

"Money you spend on batteries for that thing," Mike muttered, "you could get food for."

Harry sniffed. His friend was single-minded in pursuit of something to eat: whatever else you could say about Mike, he wasn't starving. But his conversation wasn't the best. Harry, for his own part, might be homeless, but he liked to keep up with what was happening around him. He would not be this poor forever—at least, he tried to keep telling himself so.

At the same time, it was hard to predict how he was ever going to climb out of this hole he had fallen into two years ago. Job cuts at Bering Aerospace out on the Island left him an aircraft mechanic out on the street, unable to get a job even at McDonald's, because they said he was too old, and overqualified.

At least he had no family to support, never having married. So, when Harry's savings ran out, and he lost his apartment, there was no one else to feel grief or shame for. He had enough of that for himself. He kept what pride he could. He availed himself of a bath at least once a week at the Salvation Army; he only resorted to the various charities which fed homeless people when he absolutely had no choice. Most of all, he did his best not to despair. He kept himself as well fed as he could, and not on junk food, either. When he had the money, he bought fresh fruit and vegetables to eat. Whereas others might paw through garbage cans strictly for half-finished Big Macs, Harry as often as not would be distracted from his growling stomach by something in print that looked interesting, a foreign newspaper or a magazine. And there were, as Mike complained, nights when Harry went without anything to eat so that he could afford batteries for the transistor. That little radio had been with him a long, long time, a gift from his father many years ago, one of the first truly transistorized radios. It was on its last legs, but Harry refused to throw it away before it gave up the ghost on its own. It was, in a way, his last tie with his old life, and it kept him in touch with the rest of the world as well.

He pushed the earplug jack into the transistor and listened.

"A Hong Kong investment group is close to a deal with Stark Industries to finance a $3 billion housing development on the Hudson River site where real estate developers had once planned to build Television City. The plan for a vast media center on the Riverside between 59th and 72nd Streets foundered nearly a decade ago when attacked by city planners and neighborhood activists as a leviathan that would tax the area's infrastructure and environmental resources. It is believed that Stark's plan to introduce low-income housing for the area will meet with far greater approval—"

"I can still hear that thing," Mike said loudly. "Can't you turn it down?"

Harry was strongly tempted to tell his companion to wrap a pillow around his head and shut up. Since they started dossing here some six nights ago, Mike's constant complaining had been getting on Harry's nerves. There wasn't much he could do about it, though. He was aware that his companion was a bit of a sneak and a bully, and if Harry did anything to push him out of this warehouse, Mike would tell others about it. Shortly thereafter, the place would be full of other people, who would crowd in and steal from each other and get falling-down drunk on cheap booze, or blitzed on drugs, and would generally make the experience even more unpleasant than it already was. So Harry turned the transistor down just as far as he could, and lay there listening.

"District Attorney Tower has announced that he will be running for another term this year, citing his excellent conviction record and his toughness on paranormal criminals. He is expected to run unopposed—"

Harry waited to see what Mike would say. For the moment, at least, he lay quiet. At the end of that story, the radio said, *" . . . and if you have a news story, call 212–555-1212. The best news story of the week wins fifty dollars."*

Harry yawned. He knew the number by heart, but the odds of him seeing anything newsworthy enough to win such a fabulous amount were less than nil.

"I can't stand it," Mike said. "I can still hear it!"

Harry opened his mouth to say, "You're nuts!" and then shut it again. He knew that he had just recently been discharged from the Payne Whitney Clinic across town. Or more accurately, he had signed himself out, after having been brought in half-crazed from drinking what seemed to have been bad booze—or maybe it had been Sterno. In any case, Mike had taken advantage of seventy-two hours' worth of good food and a cleanup before signing himself out. "Had to get out," Mike had said to him when they met again on the street. "They talk to you all the time—they never stop. I woulda gone nuts for sure. And there were rats in the walls."

Privately, Harry believed otherwise. He was no expert, but he thought that Mike sometimes heard and saw a lot of things that weren't there. The complaining about the radio was probably more of the same.

"I can't turn it down any further," he said.

"Well, you're a bastard, that's all," Mike said mildly, "just a bastard." He crawled out of his box and shed the first two or three layers of his wrappings.

Harry watched warily, wondering whether Mike was going to try to start a fight with him again, as he had a couple of nights ago, when he claimed Harry had been whispering all night. It had been more of an abortive struggle than a fight, but it had wound up with Mike ostentatiously hauling his bedding over to the other side of the warehouse—his mien indicating that this was meant as a penalty for Harry's bad behavior.

"I can't stand the noise," Mike said. "I'm going to sleep over here." And once more he proceeded to drag his box and his various bags full of belongings, one at a time, with a great show of effort and trouble, over by the canisters stacked up against the wall. This left at least fifty feet between Harry and Mike, and Harry was just as glad: it was that much further for the lice to walk.

Mike started the arduous business of rewrapping and reinserting himself into the bedding. Harry, with only a touch of irony, waited until Mike was finished with all this, then shouted, "Can you hear anything now?"

"Nothing but your big mouth," the answer came back after a moment.

Harry raised his eyebrows in resignation and went back to listening to the radio.

"An amino acid has been found for the first time in large galactic clouds, proving that one of the molecules important to the formation of life can exist in deep space, researchers say. Yanti Miao and Yi-Jehng Knan of the University of Illinois at Urbana reported Tuesday—"

"Hey," Mike's voice came from the other side of the warehouse floor, "I hear something!"

Oh, God, Harry thought. *I was almost asleep.* "What?"

"I dunno. I heard something outside the wall— bangin'."

Harry rolled his eyes. This, too, was a story he had heard before. Things banging on the wall, rats, things walking on the roof—"For God's sake, Mike, just wrap a pillow around your head, or something. It'll go away!"

"No it won't," Mike said with almost pleased certainty. "It didn't in the hospital."

Harry sighed. "Look, just lie down and go to sleep!"

"It's still there," Mike said. "Bangin'."

Unutterably weary, Harry took the earplugs out of his ears and listened.

Bang.

Very faint, but definitely there. "You got one this time, Mike," he said softly.

Bang. And definitely harder, so that he felt it through the floor. Bang.

"Now what the hell could that be at this time of night?" he wondered.

The two of them lay there, across the floor from one

another, staring into the near-darkness and listening. Only a faint golden light came in through the high windows from outside—the reflected streetlights from the next street over. It gleamed faintly in their eyes as they turned to look at each other.

Then, silence—no more bangings.

"Aah, it's probably someone unloading something," Harry said after a while. "Maybe that Seven-Eleven over in the next block getting a late delivery."

Mike groaned. And groaned again, then, and Harry realized abruptly that it was not Mike at all, but a sound that was coming from the wall itself. A long, slow, straining sound of—metal, perhaps? He stared at the source.

In the darkness, your eyes fool you, so at first he simply didn't believe what he saw. The wall near the canisters was bowing inward toward them, almost stretching as if it were flexible, and being pushed from behind. Then a sudden sagging, the whole shape of the wall changing as it went to powder, and almost liquidly slumped away from itself, bowed further inward—

And then with a dreadful clanging crash, several of the big canisters were tipped away from the wall by what was coming through it, pushing them—the lowest ones fell over sideways and rolled. One of them stacked higher, slightly over to one side, teetered, leaned away from its stack, then crashed to the floor and burst open.

It fell right on the cardboard box where Mike had been sleeping. At the first dreadful noise the wall made, he had scrambled out and was now standing safe from the canister's fall, but not safe from its contents, with which it sprayed him liberally as it burst. A sort of metallic chemical smell filled the air.

Mike shook himself all over and started jumping around and waving his arms, cursing a blue streak. "What the hell, what is this sh—"

The last of the canisters fell down, missing and rolling away, drowning the sound of his cursing. And then something jumped through the hole in the wall.

Harry looked at it, and swallowed—and had to swallow again, because in that second his mouth had gone so dry, there was nothing left to swallow with. In the shadows of the warehouse, the thing that stood there was blacker still. Whatever light there was in there fell on it and vanished, as if into a hole. It was man-shaped, big, and powerful-looking, with huge pale eyes—

Mike, still waving his arms around, jumping and swearing, took a long moment to see it. Harry concentrated on staying very still and very quiet, and not moving in his bag. He might not have a television himself at this point in his career, but he certainly looked at them when he passed the TV stores on the Avenue. And he knew that dreadful shape—it had been in the news often enough lately. A terrible creature, half man, half God knew what. And Mike, infuriated, spotted it, and went at it waving his arms.

For the moment it seemed not to have noticed. It was crouching like some kind of strange animal. From a huge fanged mouth it emitted an awful long tongue, broad and prehensile and slobbering, and it began to lap at the stuff which had burst from the containers. Mike lurched toward it, windmilling his arms inanely as if he were trying to scare off a stray dog.

For a few breaths' worth of time, it ignored him. Harry lay there, completely still, while the sweat broke out all over him, and the blood pounded in his ears. The black creature seemed to grin with that huge mouthful of fangs as it lapped and lapped with the huge snakelike tongue.

But Mike was far gone in annoyance or paranoia, and he went right up to the creature, yelling, and kicked it.

It noticed him *then*.

It noticed his leg first, the tongue wrapping around it and sliding up and down it as if it were thirsty for the stuff which had drenched Mike. Mike hopped and roared with loathing and annoyance, and he batted at the dark shape.

Then he roared on a higher note, much higher, as it pounced on Mike.

It was not long about exercising its teeth on him. Harry lay there transfixed by horror, now, not by fear for himself. Eventually the screaming stopped, as the dark shape ferreted out the last few delicacies it was interested in, and finally dropped the hideous form that had been Mike.

Then it went back to its drinking, decorous and unselfconscious as some beast by a pool out on the veldt. It cleaned up every last drop of the spilled stuff on the floor . . . not despising or declining the blood.

And then it stood up and looked around thoughtfully, like a man, with those great pale glaring eyes.

Its eyes rested on Harry.

He lay there frozen, on his side, watching, a trickle of drool running unnoticed out of his shocked-open mouth.

The creature turned away, whipped a few more of the nastily dextrous tendrils around several of the canisters, and effortlessly leapt out the hole in the wall with them, silent in the silence.

Gone.

It was a long, long time before Harry could move. When he did, it took him a while to stand up, and he stood still in the one spot, shaking like an old palsied bum, for many minutes.

Then, carefully, avoiding the still-wet spots, and the gobbets and tatters of Mike that lay around on the floor, he made his way out through the hole the creature had left . . . feeling in his pocket for a quarter to call the radio station, and collect his fifty dollars.

It took Spider-Man a long time to get up after the fight. First he saw to the camera, unloading the film and tucking it away in his costume, and then he found that he didn't feel very well. He sat down, breathed deeply, and tried hard not to throw up. It was as usual: the reaction hit him later, sometimes worse than other times.

Finally he decided he really had to get himself moving. He started web-swinging his way home, taking his time and not overexerting himself. His whole body felt like one big bruise, and several times he had to stop and blink when his vision wobbled or swam. He found himself wondering whether the pumpkin bomb had possibly left him with a borderline concussion along with everything else. *Hope not*, he thought. *At least I wasn't uncon-*

scious at all. It was a relief. Going to the emergency room as a walk-in patient held certain complications for superheroes with secret identities—especially as regarded sorting out the medical insurance. . . .

The digital clock on the bank near home said 4:02, with two bulbs missing, and 81 degrees. *Lord, the heat.* . . . There was this blessing, at least: the city seemed mercifully quiet as he made his way back.

Very wearily he climbed up the wall toward their apartment, avoiding the windows belonging to the two nurses on four who were working night shift this spring and summer, and the third-floor windows of the garbage guy who was always up and out around four-thirty.

He found the bedroom window open just that crack, pushed it open, and found the lights all out inside as he stepped carefully over the sill and closed the window behind him. He looked at the bed. There was a curled-up shape there, hunched under the covers. He looked at it lovingly and was about to head for the bathroom when the shape said, "Out late tonight. . . ."

"Later than planned," he said, pulling his mask off wearily, "that's for sure."

MJ sat up in bed and turned the light on. She didn't look like she'd slept at all. "Sorry," he said, knowing she hadn't.

She yawned and leaned forward, smiling a small smile. "At least you came back," she said.

The issue of his "night job," and his need to risk himself webslinging for the public good, had been a source of concern. Peter had felt for a long time before they got serious that a costumed crimefighter had no business having a permanent relationship with someone who, by that relationship, would be put permanently at risk. It hadn't stopped him from dating, with various levels of seriousness, both superheroes and mere mortals—something that MJ was always quick to point out when the subject came up. She also pointed out that there were other costumed crimefighters and superheroes who were happily married and carried on more or less normal family lives, even without their alternate identities being known. That much he himself had shared with her. There was no reason they couldn't make it work as well. "All you have to do," she kept saying at such times, "is give up the *angst*."

Anyway, *now* she said nothing about those other discussions, though the memory of them clearly lurked behind her eyes. "You made the news," MJ said.

"I did?" He blinked as he pulled the costume top over his head. "That was quick. Didn't see any news people turn up before I left—"

"Yup. You made WNN."

"What??" That confused him. "Must have been a pretty slow news night," Peter muttered. "I still don't see how they managed to find out about that—"

MJ laughed at him softly, but there was a worried edge to the sound. She swung out of the bed. "Boy, you must be getting blasé. After what's been going on around this town the past few years, it is *not* going to be considered a slow news night when Venom turns up again—"

"What?!"

The laugh definitely had more of the nervous edge to

it. She turned and felt around in the semidarkness for the nightgown left over the bedside chair. "Venom," she said, and then looked at him. Her mouth fell open. "I assumed—" She shut the mouth again. "You *weren't* out fighting Venom?"

"Hobgoblin, actually." But now his head was spinning.

She stared at him again. "It was on the news, like I said. Something about him having been seen at a warehouse downtown. There was a murder—and then he made off with some—radioactive waste, I think they said."

"Who was murdered?"

MJ shook her head. "Some homeless guy."

Peter was perplexed. "Doesn't sound like Venom," he said. "Radioactive waste? What would Venom want *that* for? As for murdering a homeless person—" He shook his head too. "That sounds even *less* like him."

He handed MJ his costume top. "I thought," she said, "when you were out late. . . ." Then she looked down at her hands and wrinkled her nose. "This can wait," MJ said. "I think I'd better wash this thing." She held the top away from her, with a most dubious expression. "And I think you'd better change your deodorant. Phooey!"

"You didn't have the night that I had," Peter said, "for which you should be grateful."

"Every minute of the day," MJ said, with her mouth going wry. "Have you given any thought to making a summerweight one? This can't be comfortable in this weather."

"In all my vast amounts of spare time," Peter said,

"yes, the thought has crossed my mind, but picking the right tailor is a problem." MJ winced, then grinned and turned away.

"I'll just wash it," she said. "Did you buy more Woolite yesterday?"

"Oh, cripes, I forgot."

"Oh well. Dishwashing liquid'll have to do. *Don't* forget the Woolite this time."

"Yes, master."

"Have you got everything off of the belt? All your little Spidey-gadgets?"

"Uh huh."

She looked at his abstracted expression and, smiling, handed him back the costume. "You'd better go through it yourself—I can never find all those compartments. The thing's worse than your photojournalist's vest."

Peter took it, obediently enough, and removed from the top a couple of spider-tracers and some spare change. Then he shucked out of the bottom and gave it to her.

"You go get in the tub, tiger," MJ said, turning away again. "You can use a soak to relax."

"And to make me fit for human company?" he shouted down the hall after her.

A slightly strangled laugh came back. "After you're done," she said, "we can look at WNN. It'll be back on again."

Peter sighed, went to the hall closet for a towel, then ambled to the bathroom.

It was just like life to pull something like this on him

now. Venom. But he's supposed to be in San Francisco—

Then again, this sudden appearance was not necessarily a surprise. Every time in the past he had thought Eddie Brock, the man who had become Venom, was out of his life, back he would come.

And thinking this, not watching particularly where he was going, Peter tripped on the bathroom threshold and fell flat on the tile floor. Only a quick twist sideways kept him from bashing his forehead on the sink.

"You okay?" came the worried call from down the hall, in the kitchen, where MJ was filling the big sink to wash the costume.

"If 'okay' means lying under the toilet with the brushes and the Lysol, then, yeah. . . ."

He heard MJ's footsteps in the hallway as he started to lever himself up. "You fell down?" she said, sounding confused. "That's not your style, either."

"No," Peter said, getting up and rubbing one of his elbows where he had cracked it against the sink on the way down. "No, it isn't. Ever since—"

And then he stopped. The spider's bite had conferred a spider's proportional strength on him, along with its inhuman agility, and the spider-sense always helped that agility along, warning him of accidents about to happen, non-routine dangers, and even routine ones like trips and falls and people blundering into him. Now it was just gone. Then he remembered that he had also gotten no warning whatsoever when Hobby tossed that last pumpkin bomb at him. He should have received *some* sort of warning. He rubbed his ribs absently, feeling the ache.

He said to MJ, "Some time ago when Hobby and I first tangled—Ned, not the current version—he had managed to come up with a chemical agent that killed my spider-sense for a day or so at a time. He used to deliver the agent as a gas out of the pumpkin bombs. However—" He bent over to finger the shallow cut on his leg.

"You're going to need stitches for that," MJ said, concerned.

"No, I won't. It looks worse than it is. But it was deep enough for one of the razor-bats he threw at me to give me a good dose of the anti-spider-sense agent, whatever it is."

MJ looked at him. "How long is it going to last?"

Peter shrugged. "Well, Jason Macendale isn't quite the scientific whiz that Ned Leeds was. If *Ned* were still the Hobgoblin, I'd have reason to expect much worse—an improved brew every year, at least. But I think this'll just last a day or so."

"Well, be careful," MJ said. "Just get yourself into the tub and try not to drown, OK?"

"Yes, Mom," he said with some irony.

He turned on the tub's faucets, put in the drain-plug, and sat and watched the water rise. Hobgoblin was enough of a problem, but the addition of Venom to the equation—if the news story was accurate—made the situation even less palatable.

In a city filled with super heroes with complex life-histories and agendas, and villains with a zoo full of traumas, histories, and agendas almost always more involved than the heroes', and inevitably more twisted, Hobgoblin stood out. Originally "he" had been another villain entirely, one called the Green Goblin, who had taken a particular dislike to Spider-Man early in their careers. He had spent a long time repeatedly hunting Spidey down and making his life a misery. Norman Osborn had been the man's name: a seriously crazy person, but nonetheless a certifiable genius with a tremendous talent in the material and chemical sciences. Like many other supervillains, he picked a theme and stuck to it with fanatical and rather unimaginative singlemindedness, establishing himself as a sort of spirit of Halloween gone maliciously nuts—wearing a troll-like costume with a horrific mask and firing exploding miniature "pumpkin bombs" in all directions around him from the jetglider on which he stood. He took whatever he liked from the city he terrorized, and he frightened and tormented its citizens as he pleased.

Spider-Man, naturally, had been forced to take exception to this behavior: and the Green Goblin had taken exception to *him*. Their private little war had gone on for a long time, until finally Osborn died, killed by one of his own devices—but not before he had caused the death of Gwen Stacy, an early love of Peter's.

Peter paused, looking for something aromatic and soothing to put in the bath water. There didn't seem to be anything but a large box of Victoria's Secret scented bath foam. *I can't imagine why she buys this stuff*, he thought. He started going through the bathroom cupboards and finally came up with a bottle of pine bath essence.

Green, he thought. *It would have to be green. . . .* He

shrugged and squirted some in, then sat down again, watching the bubbles pile up.

No sooner had the Green Goblin died—and Peter, after a while, had come to some kind of terms with his grief—than history began to repeat itself. Some petty crook stumbled onto one of the Goblin's many secret hideouts, sold the information of its whereabouts to another, better-heeled criminal, who found the Green Goblin's costumes, bombs, energy gauntlets and jet gliders intact and in storage. He had done some minor work on the spare costumes—alterations and changes in color— and had emerged as a more or less off-the-rack super-villain, the Hobgoblin.

Hobby had been a reporter named Ned Leeds—ironically, both a colleague of Peter Parker's at the *Daily Bugle* and the husband to another of Peter's early loves, Betty Brant. This man too, in his new identity, began bedeviling Spider-Man in an attempt to keep him busy while Leeds tried to mine the secrets of Norman Osborn's rediscovered diaries—which Spidey feared also might include information on his own secret identity, which Osborn had learned. Leeds also synthesized the odd chemical formula which had given the Green Goblin his terrible speed and strength, but he ignored the warnings in Osborn's journals that the formula might also cause insanity in the person who used it for maximum physical effect.

It did, of course. It made Leeds as crazy as Osborn had ever been, and he too died, killed by a rival criminal. And then the weaponry, the costume, the persona, and the ruthlessly opportunistic and money-hungry personality surfaced again, this time in another man called Jason Macendale. Macendale had eagerly made himself over as Hobgoblin Number Two, or perhaps Two-A. Hobby Two-A thought, in concert with his predecessors, that it would be an excellent idea to get rid of Spider-Man, one of the most active local crimefighters and the one most likely to cause him trouble on a day-to-day basis.

Peter turned the faucets off, tested the water. It was at that perfect heat where, if you stepped in carefully and lay perfectly still, it would boil the aches out of you, but once in, if you moved, you'd be scalded. He climbed in, sank down to bubble level, and submerged himself nearly to his nose. *Hobgoblin*, he thought and sighed. *Him I could deal with. But Venom, too. . . .*

He closed his eyes and let the hot water do its work on his body, but his mind refused to stay still.

Venom was entirely another class of problem.

The trouble had begun innocently enough, when he was off-planet—Peter chuckled at how matter-of-fact it all sounded, put that way. He had been swept up into a war of superheroes against unearthly forces at the edge of the known universe and conveyed by a being known as the Beyonder to a world out there somewhere. While there, his trusty costume had been torn to shreds and, not being the kind of crimefighter who felt he was at his best working naked, he looked around for another one. A machine on that planet, obligingly enough, provided him with one. It was quite a handsome piece of work, really—that was his thought when he first put it on, and when he wore it during the Secret War, and afterwards, on his return to Earth. It was every superhero's dream of a costume. Dead-black, with a stylized white spider on the chest—graphically, he thought, a more striking design than his present red-and-blue one. Possibly the machine had read the design from some corner of his mind which thought it knew what he really wanted to look like.

The costume was more than just sleek-looking. It responded instantly to its owner's desires. You didn't have to take it off: you could think it off. It would slide itself away from your mouth so you could eat or talk; it would camouflage itself, with no more than a thought, to look like your street clothes; at the end of a hard day, it would slide off and lie in a little puddle at your feet, and you could pick it up and hang it on a chair, where the next morning it would be perfectly fresh and clean and ready to go.

It was *so* accommodating, in fact, that Peter began to find it a little unnerving. He began to have odd dreams about that costume and his old one, engaged in a struggle for possession of him, threatening to tear him apart. Finally he took the costume to Reed Richards, the most scientifically inclined of the Fantastic Four, and asked to have it analyzed.

He was more than slightly surprised to discover that what he had been wearing was not a costume, not a made thing—or *made* it possibly was: but it was not just cloth. It was *alive*. It was an alien creature, a symbiote, made to match his physiology, even his mind. And its intention was to bond with him, irrevocably. They would be one.

Peter shivered in the hot water and then winced

slightly as it scalded him. He slowed his breathing down slightly, trying to deal with the heat and the discomfort of the memory.

It had taken a fair amount of work to get the costume off him. He had not been prepared for a relationship of that permanence, intensity, or intimacy—not for anything like it at *all*. It took all Reed Richards' ingenuity to get the symbiote-costume off Peter's body and confine it for further study. Sonics were one of its weak points; against loud noises, and specifically, focused sound, it had no defense. But even when it was finally off him, that did not solve Peter's problem.

The costume desired him, and a great rage was growing in its simple personality. If it ever escaped its durance, it would find him. It would bond with him. It would punish him for his rejection. And in the act, it would probably squeeze the life out of him. The irony, of course, would be that in so doing, in killing the host for which it had been created, it would probably then die itself. But from Peter's point of view, the irony ran out with the prospect of his own death.

The symbiote had eventually escaped, of course— these things have a way of not ending tidily—and it did indeed hunt Peter down. The only way he had been able to get rid of it was to flee into the bell tower of a nearby church, and let the brain-shattering ringing of the bells drive it off him. Most of the symbiote, he had thought, perished. But a drop or two, it seemed, remained. With unearthly persistence it replicated itself—and found another host.

That new host was named Eddie Brock: once a journalist who worked for the *Daily Globe*, the *Bugle*'s primary competitor, but who had been fired over a misunderstanding, a misjudgment of a news story he had been reporting. Spider-Man had been involved in a less visible aspect of the same story, which involved a masked killer called the Sin-Eater. Spidey had revealed the genuine identity of the killer to the media, when Brock had thought it was another person entirely, and had written and published his story based on insufficient data.

Once fired, Brock had decided that Spider-Man was the cause of all his troubles and needed to be killed. And one night, in that same church, something dark oozed out of the shadows and found Eddie Brock. He was joined. He welcomed the hating unity that the symbiote offered him—he became one with it, part of it; and it, part of him.

Hatred can be even more potent than love as a joining force. So it proved for Brock. The costume, though not saying as much in words, gave him to understand its hatred for Spider-Man, for whom it had been made, and who, in its view, had heartlessly rejected it. And in Eddie Brock's opinion, anything that hated Spider-Man was only showing the best possible taste.

They were one. Eddie Brock became one of those people who could say "we" and did not need to be royal to make it stick. Since then, he, or they, as Venom, had successfully hunted Spidey down in apartment after apartment in New York—not beneath frightening MJ in their attempts to get at Spider-Man. That dark shadow—black costume, white spider, and the formidably fanged mouth and horrific prehensile tongue that the symbiote liked to grow—that shadow came and went in Peter's life, never bringing less than dread, often terror, sometimes pain and injury nearly to the point of death. They had slugged it out, how many times now? Up and down the city, and each time only skill and wits and sometimes luck had saved Spider-Man's life.

After many encounters, though, something strange had happened. In one final battle on a lonely Caribbean island, Spider-Man (already nearly beaten to a pulp) arranged for Venom to believe he had died in a gas explosion—leaving charred human bones and the remnants of his costume as evidence. He himself swam like mad into the nearby shipping lanes, looking for a ship to take him home, and found one.

And Venom, Eddie, convinced that his old enemy was dead at last, found a sudden odd peace descending on him. For a while he stayed on that island—maybe, Peter wondered, recovering some of his sanity there? At any rate, some time later Eddie turned up in San Francisco. He stayed there only long enough to discover that Spider-Man was still alive, and began hitching his way eastward to come to grips with him one last time.

But on the way, a gang of thugs attacked the kind family which had offered him a ride cross-country. It was here that Eddie began to find a sense of purpose, as Venom stood up and utterly destroyed the thugs attacking this family and the other people in the truckstop. He decided there might be something else for him to do in this life. He would protect the innocent, as (he thought) Spider-Man had betrayed him.

Or, at least, those he thought were innocent. One had

to remember that Venom was not remotely sane. Still, he was no longer a figure of pure malice, either. There was an ambivalent quality to his danger now. He would probably always be a threat to Spider-Man, on some level or another. But the poor and helpless had nothing to fear from him—at least as far as Peter understood. That was why this news about some homeless person's murder rang so false.

"How you doing in there?" came the call from down the hallway.

Peter bubbled.

MJ put her head around the corner of the door. "Need anything? Should I scrub your back?"

"Maybe later," Peter said. "Has the news come around yet?"

"No. You just make sure you dry off before you come out, and don't drip all over the floor like last time." She turned away. "Things are wet enough in here as it is."

"From what?"

"Your costume. Keeps trying to climb out of the sink."

"Don't even joke about it," Peter said, and submerged to his nose again.

It was bad news all around. He sighed, bubbling. His spider-sense was gone for at least a day, or so he thought. Even if it had been in working order, his spider-sense didn't react to the symbiote Venom now wore. It had, after all, been designed by that alien machine not to interfere with his own powers.

Bad, he thought. *If I were Hobgoblin, I would be gunning as hard as I could for Spider-Man over the next day. I'm just going to have to be super careful tomorrow. I've got no choice about going out, either.* He looked out at dawn's early light beginning through the bathroom window. *As soon as I get myself out of the tub and dried, I've got to start getting those pictures developed . . . so I can do something about that credit card bill. Assuming they* want *the pictures.*

He frowned for a moment. The job market had been tightening of late; there were a lot more freelancers competing for the same number of photo slots in any given day's paper. *The competition is fierce now, but it's hard to pay attention to composition,* he thought ruefully, *when someone's lobbing pumpkin bombs at your head.* Peter had a lively respect for the acuity and quality of results that war correspondents got in their photographs. He knew how they felt, and how it felt to be on the firing line . . . and often he would have given a great deal to be shot at just with bullets, instead of energy blasts or weird gases.

"Yo, tiger! I think it comes on after this bit. C'mon."

Peter got out of the tub, ouching again as the water scalded him, toweled himself passably dry, wrapped the towel around his waist and padded down the hall to the living room. The TV was showing another of those horrifically frequent commercials for something called Flex-O-Thigh, in which people who plainly had no need of physical exercise whatsoever smilingly worked various springy pieces of machinery in an attempt to convince you that the exercise was effortless, and the machinery results beyond your dreams. Toll-free numbers flashed, and a friendly voice urged all and sundry to Call Now!

Then the news came back on again. "Super-villain Venom has been implicated in a burglary and murder tonight in New York," said the voice. "Venom, whose last known appearance was in San Francisco, according to California law enforcement officials, allegedly murdered one man in an incident in a warehouse, then stole several containers of what City authorities have confirmed is nuclear waste—"

The camera showed the warehouse: a big jagged hole, but odd in its jaggedness, almost as if the edges had been pulverized—or melted? Peter looked at the picture curiously, but it changed to a view of a sheeted form, surprisingly small, being carried out of the warehouse on an ambulance's gurney and loaded into a paramedic wagon. The announcer said, "An eyewitness was treated for shock at St. Luke's Hospital and later released."

Peter and MJ found themselves looking at a stubbled, shaggy-haired man who was saying, "Yeah, he just came in through the wall—knocked some of the canisters over—and then—" He stammered. "He killed Mike there. He just ripped him up like a paper bag. Little bits came off the Venom guy—you know, like the pictures in the paper from the last time—little bits, they just shredded—" He turned away from the camera, making short chopping motions with one hand. "I'm sorry. I'm sorry, I just wanna go—" He stumbled away.

Peter and MJ looked at each other. " 'Shredded'?" she said softly.

"He could if he wanted to," Peter muttered. "But it's just—it's just not like him."

"Maybe he had a bad day," MJ said doubtfully.

"New York City authorities have begun a search for Venom, but reliable sources within the NYPD have told WNN that they doubt the police will have much luck in finding him. Venom's *modus operandi*, they say, has been to lie quiet until some set of circumstances aggravates his old hatred against Spider-Man—at which time Venom makes his presence known abundantly. The people of New York can only hope that Spider-Man maintains a low profile for the immediate future. Lloyd Penney, for WNN News, New York."

"And to think that meanwhile," MJ said, "you've been out aggravating someone else entirely."

"Hush, woman." He chuckled, though it wasn't really all that funny; and briefly he told MJ about the evening's confrontation with Hobgoblin, while WNN went on briefly about the new Madonna movie and details of a press conference the Avengers had recently called. "And there was nothing in there," he said at last, "but some big canisters . . . ." His voice trailed off.

"Like those you just saw on the news?" MJ said, raising her eyebrows.

"Like those. . . . I can't go to sleep," he said, getting up with a groan. "I've got to get those pictures developed and get them in to the *Bugle*, and I've got to get a look in the morgue—"

"The morgue," MJ said dryly, "is exactly where you're going to wind up if you go out in this condition."

There was no point in arguing with her in this mood,

Peter knew. He sat there quietly, thinking about which stock to use for developing the pictures, and drank what MJ gave him. But the decaf coffee was mostly milk, and Peter sat back, just for a few moments. . . .

MJ stood up, smiled, looked at him and shook her head. "It's the hot milk," she said with satisfaction. "That tryptophan does it every time." She went away to get a quilt to cover Peter, turned off the TV, and then slipped into the kitchen to see about her own pot of coffee.

THREE

Peter blinked at the sunshine suddenly filling the living room. He blinked harder. *Oh, God, I overslept.* "MJ, why didn't you get me up?!" he said.

No answer, nor would there be one, he realized. The apartment had that particular empty sound. As Peter sat up on the couch, the quilt fell to the floor along with a note. Moaning a little—the bruises from last night had now had time to stiffen up—Peter bent over to pick it up. "Gone out for Daily Variety and H'wd Reporter," it said. "Had hot tip this morning, might mean work. See you later. Love love love love," followed by a little tangle of X's and O's.

Peter dropped the note onto the coffee table, yawned, stretched, moaned again, stretched some more regardless. The smell of coffee was drifting through the apartment. *Just like MJ to have made a pot and left it for me. . . .* He staggered to his feet, wandered into the kitchen, poured himself a cup, added a couple of sugars, stirred and drank. When the caffeine buzz started to hit, he headed down the hall to the bathroom, this time to hunt down the extra-strength aspirin.

Peter took a couple of aspirin and a long drink of cold water, then turned the shower on and climbed in, letting the hot water pummel him into some kind of flexibility again. When he could move without whimpering, he turned the water to cold and let the change in temperature blast him awake. Another fifteen minutes saw him dressed, combed, downing another cup of coffee, and heading for his darkroom.

He turned on the red light and closed the door behind

him. He glanced at his workbench, where someone had placed his camera and a plastic-wrapped sandwich on a plate, with a note on top. The note said, "NOW YOU EAT THIS, DUMMY! XOXOXO," and had a lipstick kiss imprint on the bottom of the page. Smiling, Peter unwrapped the plastic and sniffed. Tuna salad: good enough for breakfast.

He spent a few moments hauling down the jugs of developing chemicals and mixing them, getting them ready in the various pans. Then he pulled the string for the exhaust fan to get rid of the stink, and began to break the camera down, pulling out the rewound film. He stripped it carefully out of the canister, dropped the long coil into the first developer pan, and started the timer.

He chomped down the first half of the sandwich while squinting to see how the negatives were doing. In this light, as usual, it was impossible to tell. For him, this was always the worst part of photography: waiting in hope. A picture that seemed useful at first might have inequities of grain, or color, or contrast, which would turn it into so much mud on the printed page. There was no way to tell until you did the contact prints, and in some cases not even then—sometimes you had to do trial blowups of a print in which you were interested to see whether it would really work—and there was that much paper and chemical gone as a result, money down the drain if the picture was no good. One of the risks of the art. . . .

The timer went off. He reached into the bath with a pair of tongs, swished the film around a little, then hoisted it out and dropped it into the fixer. The first

glimpse looked good. A lot of the pictures had strong di-
agonals, he could see that much even now. Whether the
fine detail would be good enough, though, remained to
be seen. He started the timer again, and waited.

While watching the timer tick its dial around backwards, Peter started on the second half of the sandwich.
Venom, he thought. *Now there would have been someone
to have pictures of.* The only problem, for him at least,
was that when Venom was in the neighborhood, he was
usually too busy trying to keep his skin in one piece to
worry about photo opportunities of any kind. *If Venom
really is in town, though, I'm going to have to deal with
him quickly.*

Probably soon, too. When Venom suddenly reap-
peared, it didn't usually take long for him to hunt Spider-Man down—or worse, to do the same to Peter
Parker. That had been one of the worst problems of all.
Venom knew his secret identity, knew where to find him,
and knew where to find MJ. Venom's big, broad-shouldered silhouette was not one he ever wanted to see on
his living-room wall again.

The timer went off. He pulled the film out of the fixer,
held it up to the red light, and took his first good look at
the negatives. "Awright," he breathed. There were some
good jumping shots of him, good shots of the Hobgoblin, and nice ones of the two of them. The motion sensor
was doing its work. He wondered if he could slightly im-
prove its effectiveness by adding to the motion-control
system some routines from the software which managed
his spider-tracers. *Plant one on the super-villain*, he
thought, *so that the computer keeps him in frame all the*

time. He was not so egotistical as to care whether he was in those shots, particularly. The city knew pretty well what Spider-Man looked like; it was the super-villains who fascinated them, and in any shot containing both a hero and a villain, it was best to have the villain better centered.

And then he saw something else he had hoped for—one of the first shots in the roll, and as a result one of the last ones he came to—a shot of the robbery actually in progress. "Not bad," he said softly. "This'll get their attention, if nothing else does."

He looked thoughtfully at the big canisters in the photo. One thing the camera was not good at, unfortunately, was zooming. He couldn't really make out much beyond the big "warning—radiation" trefoil on the side. No use trying for an enlargement, really.

Now then—prints. He pulled a pad close and began scribbling notes. *Two, six, seven, eight, nine . . . fourteen, sixteen . . . eighteen. . . .* He marked which of them he would print, checked the ones he wanted as eight-by-tens rather than three-by-fives, then shrugged a bit. *A contact sheet, six eight-by-tens, then this one, this one . . . that one. . . . Done.*

After that, things moved quickly. Picking the exposures was always the worst part of the work for him. You had to anticipate your editor. Sometimes it was hard to tell what they would prefer: did they want the more carefully composed picture, or the one with more fine detail? The best you could do was pick the best of each, bring a sampling of the others, and a contact sheet. That sheet—which showed a thumbnail of every picture on the roll—

had saved his bacon more than once when his editors had chosen a picture that Peter hadn't bothered to make into a print for one reason or another.

He got to work, pulling out his printing stock, setting up the enlarger, cutting the negatives down to more manageable strips of five. The developing took him about another three-quarters of an hour.

The clock was running, now. Two o'clock was the cutoff for the five-o'clock evening edition, and no one would thank a photographer who came in on the stroke of two, just as the big web presses were being prepped. One o'clock would be good, noon better still—but noon was pretty much impossible now. He twitched slightly at the thought of which photographers might have beaten him down to the office with other pictures. Some of the editors at the *Bugle* in particular felt that a picture in the hand was worth any two in the bush, regardless of quality, but there was no telling which editor was going to make the call on your photos, either. If Kate Cushing was in today, Peter knew she liked to have pictures in early, rather than good—though she wanted them good as well.

Shortly the pictures were hanging up on the little "clothesline" of string. Peter snapped the white light on and looked at them, while fanning them dry with his hand. They were a fairly good-looking bunch. It had been a good first test of the camera's motion control. The camera had gotten one particularly good chance shot, a full-face view of Hobby running straight at the camera without his having been aware it was there. Peter looked at the grinning face, slightly strained out of shape by the speed of the turn Hobgoblin had just made, and thought, *That's the one. If she doesn't want that one, I can't imagine what her problem is.* Assuming the editor in question was Kate. She could sometimes be a dreadful stickler for quality—not necessarily a bad thing, when you were in competition with all the other newspapers in town, but annoying to the photographer with credit card bills to pay.

Peter smiled as he took down that head-on shot, and two others: one of Spider-Man leaping directly at Hobby, the webline reaching up and out of frame at a most dramatic angle, another of the warehouse floor, Hobgoblin streaking up and out past the camera's point of view, a very lucky shot both in that Hobby could as easily have come up out of any other of the skylights, and that he might also easily have tipped the camera over as he zipped past. *Gotta find a way to lower the center of gravity on that tripod*, he thought as he took down the last of the prints and flicked its edge with one finger to see if it was still tacky. It wasn't. Peter slipped it and its companions into a compartmented paper portfolio, put that in turn into his leather photo envelope, packed in the negatives as well, and finished the last of the tuna fish sandwich. *Payday today*, he thought, in as hopeful a mood as he could manage, and headed out to the *Bugle*.

Half an hour later he was standing in the air-conditioning just inside Kate's office door, while one by one she peeled the photos out of the paper portfolio and dropped them on the desk. "Not too bad," she said, dropping the one with the canisters, and "That's OK, a little dark." Then, with an intake of breath and a smile, "What an ugly sonofabitch he is."

Peter heard the faraway sound of cash registers. He knew that smile, slight as it was. "He won't win any beauty contests," he said.

Kate held up the full-face picture of Hobgoblin. "How did you get that one?" she asked, cocking an eye at Peter.

He shrugged. "Long lens," he said.

The look she threw at him was amicably suspicious. "Since when can you afford lenses that give you that kind of detail without grain? Then again, this is that new ASA 8000 film, isn't it?"

"Six," he said. "I got a price break on it."

"You must have," Kate said. "Buy much of that stuff at the regular prices and you just about have to go into escrow. Well—" She held up the Hobgoblin shot. "This one with the canisters—this is the actual robbery itself, isn't it?"

Peter nodded.

Kate looked sidewise at him. "Enthusiasm is a good thing," she said, "but you want to watch you don't get reckless. What you were doing up on that rooftop, that time of night?"

Peter opened his mouth, thought better of it and shut it again. Kate just smiled. "Long lens," she said. "I remember." Then she added: "Came in with this a little late today, didn't you?"

"As soon as I could."

"Yes, well, I sent someone down to the crime scene

already," she said. Peter's heart sank. "And he's back, and the pictures are developed, and already in the system for pasteup. Now I'm going to have to get into the system again and pull them out. You could have saved me some trouble by being a little earlier. I hate that damn new software."

Peter smiled. This was a common complaint all over the *Bugle*. They had just gone over to a new computer-based pasteup system, and everyone was moaning about the endless inservices needed to learn how to use it, especially since they were used to the old system, no matter that this one was supposed to be so much more flexible and usable. "Anyway," Kate said, "anybody who's out with this 'long lens' in the middle of the night and gets pictures like this, deserves a little over his rate."

She scribbled for a moment on a pad, looked at the numbers, made a change. "Here," she said, "this should help you get some sleep tonight." She reached for another pad, the sight of which made Peter's heart rise again: it was the voucher pad, and you took the filled-out form on it to the cashier downstairs. Whatever she was writing, Peter could see that it was in three figures.

She tore off the sheet and handed it to him, and Peter could see which three figures. He suppressed the gasp. This figure was half the Visa bill, on the spot. "Thanks, Kate," he said.

She waved a hand at him negligently. "You do the work, you get the pay," she said. "The composition on these is a little better than what you've been showing me lately."

Peter said nothing, but was silently glad that the motion sensor was performing as advertised.

"Initiative, I don't mind. Enthusiasm is fine. Just you be careful," Kate said.

"Yes, ma'am," Peter said, and walked out.

He wandered down the hall clutching the voucher, looking at it once or twice to make sure it wasn't actually a typo or a mistake. But she had written the amount both in numbers and words. As Peter went down the hall, he could hear two familiar voices. Had they been anyone else's, he would have called what he was hearing an argument. As it was, when one of the voices belonged to J. Jonah Jameson, the noise going on was merely a discussion. "What the hell am I paying you for?" J. Jonah was shouting out his open door. This, too, was an indication of the casual level of the discussion; for a real argument, JJJ would have been right out into the hall.

"How could you possibly be so obtuse? Here we have the biggest super-villain ever to hit this city, and one of the worst, and you know why he's here."

"I don't, actually," said Robbie Robertson's calm voice. "He seems to have forgotten to fax me his itinerary again."

"Don't get cute with me, Robbie." JJJ emerged into the hall, gesticulating. "All the other papers are going to be all over this like a cheap suit. You know perfectly well that any time Venom turns up, Spider-Man turns up as well, and they begin bashing each other all over this city, trashing buildings, driving the city's garbage-removal budget through the ceiling, and doing all the other

97

kinds of things that make news." He stalked back into the office again, apparently waving disgustedly at the computer. "And we're stuck with two-bit break-ins, and secondhand reporting about flying hooligans zooming around, flinging exploding squash in all directions. We should be coming down a lot harder on this Venom story. It's just not the same as—"

"As the newsworthiness of having the flesh flayed off your bones? No, I suppose not," the answer came back. "But the police are saying that the forensics are looking a little funny. We don't have enough—"

"Funny? Now how can they *not* look funny when the thing that committed the murder is half psychopathic human and half some kind of mind-reading man-eating amoeba with a bad body image? Yet another little present to our fair city from Spider-Man, let me remind you. I tell you, there is not a garbage can in this town that you won't find the damn webslinger at the bottom of it—"

"There is not enough data to lean really hard on the Venom story," Robbie said calmly, "and I would sooner be late than be wrong. Extremely wrong."

"C'mon, Robbie," JJJ grumbled. "Right is doing it first. And I know it's right. I know it's Venom. I can feel it in my bones. This is some kind of plot between Venom and Spider-Man. I've seen it before. One turns up, and the other turns up, and the city gets trashed. And I refuse to miss the chance to cover it in my paper!"

"With all due respect—" Robbie said quietly.

"Yes, yes, with all due respect, you're not going to do what I say, because I'm not editor-in-chief anymore, and you are."

"Something like that," Robbie said, "yes. You can say what you like about it in your publisher's editorials. But while I'm editing, I edit. When I don't think there's enough data to set a story on, I let it build up until there is."

"I don't know what this business is becoming these days," JJJ bellowed, coming out into the hall again, with Robbie ambling along behind him, sucking resignedly on his empty pipe.

Peter was standing nearby, leaning as respectfully as he could on the wall nearby—being careful to put his pay voucher out of sight lest JJJ should get a glimpse of it and start going on about his freelancers being seriously overpaid. He couldn't resist putting in his two cents. "But, Jonah," he said. "Spider-Man—"

JJJ whirled on him. "And what would you know about it?"

"That Spider-Man wasn't anywhere around there," Peter said. "He was off fighting Hobgoblin when Venom showed up."

"Oh? Who says?

"I saw him," Peter said. "I got pictures of it."

"Did you, now?" Robbie said, his eyebrows going up.

"Hmm," Jonah said. "Think, Parker, use your brains! Don't you know what it means?"

Peter looked at Robbie, who just gave an infinitesimal shake of his head. "No, sir," Peter said.

"It means Spider-Man, Venom, and Hobgoblin are all in it together! Hobgoblin strikes in one spot, then Spider-Man turns up to pretend to fight him, and while they're drawing attention away, Venom is off murdering people on the other side of the city, or committing some other kind of weird crime! Drinking toxic waste, it looks like, for pity's sake. As if that monster isn't enough trouble, without messing with stuff like *that* as well."

"Oh," Peter said, not able to find much to add.

"Oh, go on," Jonah said, glaring at him and gesturing away between himself and Robbie. "I'm tired of looking at you. You just don't have any imagination, that's the problem. And as for *you*," he said, turning to Robbie.

Robbie winked at Peter as Peter slid by. For his own part, Peter was glad enough to escape. When Jonah got on one of these rolls, there was no stopping him. He would blame Spider-Man for the federal budget deficit, global warming, and World War II if he kept going long enough.

I wish I understood it, Peter thought as he made his way down the hall. *It's not as if Spider-Man ever really had it in for JJJ.* Maybe he was just one of those personalities, like the old king in Thurber, who thought that "everything was pointed at him" to begin with. That Spider-Man should be as well would only help him make more sense of the world. But who knew?

In any case, JJJ had long since made up his mind and no longer had any desire to be confused by facts. Peter doubted any fact concerning Spider-Man was big enough to do anything but hit Jonah and bounce at this point.

At any rate, he had other things on his mind right now. First, that voucher. He took himself downstairs to the accounting offices, and took his turn standing in line at the cashier's armor-glass window. Maya smiled from behind the window, and said, "Long time no see!"

It was her constant tease, one she used with all the freelancers. "Yeah," Peter said. He handed her the voucher.

She widened her eyes appreciatively at the sight of it. "That'll buy some cat food," she said.

Peter chuckled. "We don't have cats."

"I know," Maya said. "Which makes you the perfect home for one of the new kittens!"

"Maya," Peter groaned. "Don't tell me you still haven't had her spayed!"

"I just hate interfering with nature," Maya said. Her beautiful Persian had struck up a nonplatonic and extremely fruitful relationship with a handsome black tom from several buildings over, and periodically escaped, the result being litter after litter of gorgeous, long-furred, mixed-color kittens, with which Maya had populated half the *Bugle*'s employees' apartments. "No, thanks," Peter said gratefully. "We're a no-pets building."

Maya *tsk*ed, handing him the cash. "Terrible sort of place to live," she said. "You should move out."

Peter just sighed, but thought, *We may have to if Venom finds us again.* . . . He headed off.

"I've got a real cute one!" she shouted after him. "Black longhair!"

Peter just waved at her and kept going. He had a lot more than cats on his mind.

He took the elevator back up to the second floor to the *Bugle*'s morgue. These were the archives where earlier editions of the paper were kept. Once upon a time, they had been kept in their original paper format; later, the archives had gone over to microfilm, but over time, even that had proved too bulky. Now both new paper and old microfilm were being stored on CD-ROM, able to be called up instantly from any terminal at the newspaper. At least, that was the plan. Everybody would be able to do that when the new system was completely installed, but at present the installation was only half done and the staff half trained. And there would always be those who preferred to go down to the morgue as a break from being stuck at their desks. Many claimed that this new system was in fact intended to keep them at their desks, where keystroke-activated "smart" productivity monitoring systems buried in the software would keep track of who was working and who was slacking off. Peter had heard of such things at other companies, but he personally doubted anything like that would be brought online at the *Bugle*. He suspected strongly that JJJ was too cheap to pay for such stuff, preferring to go stalking into people's offices and bug them about their productivity personally.

Peter sauntered into the big airy room. There were only a few people at the scattered workstations. Off to one side, the big mainframe computer sat, making no noise except that of its private air conditioners. The rest of the place, too, was pleasantly cool, the computer's own aggressive air-conditioning keeping the temperature down.

Bob the computer maven wandered over to Peter as he stood looking around. Bob was a big, rugged-looking, handsome Irish guy, another one gone prematurely silver, with a mustache to match, and a big engaging smile. He looked less like a software nerd than anything you could imagine. "You need some help?" he said to Peter.

"Just a spare terminal. I could use a look at today's edition, too," Peter said.

Bob grinned at him. "Why not just pick up a paper?"

"What," Peter said, "and get newsprint all over me?"

Bob snickered. "We could make a software jockey out of you eventually," he said. "Come on over here."

He showed Peter to a spare terminal and handed him a photocopied booklet. "There," he said. "This is the idiot's guide. Control-F1 gives you the main menu. Just page through it and pick the day you want."

The screen in front of Peter was a big handsome one, the size of a full tabloid page. Bob hit the keys for him the first time, and the menu came up on screen: a numbered list of dates, starting with today's and proceeding backwards. "Morning edition okay?" Bob said. "Evening's not out of comp yet."

"Morning is fine."

Bob brought up the page. It appeared in black and white. The front page had a quite well composed but not terribly illuminating photo of the shattered wall in the warehouse, a few canisters still scattered about, all rather dark. *A little hurried*, Peter thought. *If I were him, I would have waited and gone up a couple more f-stops—gotten a little more light.*

He pushed the arrow key to turn the "page," looking for the rest of the story. "Give a shout if you need anything," Bob said, and strolled off to see about something else.

Peter read on through the continuation on page three. The language was straightforward enough. Venom was indeed accused of the murder of a homeless man by his friend squatting in the warehouse, the man whom Peter had seen early that morning on the news. The story gave a little more detail: the address of the warehouse; its owner, Consolidated Chemical Research Corp. in New Jersey; and some detail, rather garbled, about what Venom had looked like to the man. The description mostly focused on the tentacles the man saw. That was accurate as far as it went: the symbiote's tentacles looked like strands and long flowing lines, tendrils that came alive and reached for what they wanted.

But the part of it all which still left Peter most confused was that Venom did this at all. Venom had settled in San Francisco and was supposedly protecting homeless people there. The idea that Venom would kill a homeless person, much less any innocent bystander, was hard for Peter to imagine. One of his few redeeming qualities was his belief that the innocent were to be protected at all costs, that life had given them a hard enough run as it was, and that somewhere they needed a protector.

Something, though. . . . Peter paged forward to see if there was anything more about the story but filler. Nothing.

He paged back again. *Consolidated Chemical Research*, he thought. *I could have sworn that CCRC had a sign on that warehouse where I was last night.* He pulled out the contact sheet from his portfolio, studied it. Yes, on that photo near the front of the roll, the lens had just caught it. Three letters out of four: CCR. . . . Right, he thought. And the likeness between the canisters, which MJ had spotted: she had been absolutely right.

And here, that weird detail which the homeless man reported in today's story, that he had seen Venom drink the radioactive toxic waste. Peter sat there and shook his head. *Is this some weird new taste the symbiote's developed?* he wondered.

"How's it going?" Bob said, materializing at his shoulder.

"Not too bad. Is there a way to scan for a specific word or phrase in this thing?"

"Oh, sure. You want to scan for a string? Just take it out of graphic mode. Here." Bob tapped the control key. The screen went mostly blank, except for a C:> prompt up in the corner. Then Bob entered something which didn't echo to the screen—a password, probably. The screen went dark and showed another menu. One option highlighted on it was "string search."

"There," Bob said. "You get, I think, up to sixty-four characters. There are ways to sort for two or three phrases at once, if you want. Just hit this one here and it'll show you the sample screen, with examples of how to enter the stuff so you get what you want."

"Hey, this isn't so bad," Peter said. "Why's everyone complaining about it?"

"Because it's not what they had the last time," Bob said, resigned.

Peter grinned. "That's okay. In five years they'll get used to this, and then Jonah will bring in something newer."

Bob moaned. "Don't tell me," he said. "I know damn well."

Peter turned back to the screen and had a look at the help menu. Carefully, because he knew how relentlessly stupid computers were about typographical errors, he typed, "CONSOLIDATED CHEMICAL RESEARCH."

"One Moment Please," the screen said. "Processing Your Request."

The cursor sat there and blinked at Peter for a little while. Then, up came a list of locations in the text archives where the computer had spotted the name. There weren't that many of them. The company was a newish one, as Peter found from reading the articles, mostly from the financial pages: a small company specializing in radioactive materials of various kinds, tailored isotopes for radioimmunoassay, and the medical equipment and so forth needed to handle them. None of the articles contained anything particularly interesting.

The last two entries on the main menu were: (8) Crossindex to Yellow Pages and (9) Crossindex to White Pages. Peter chose the second. The New York phone directory came up, with a long listing of addresses—corporate headquarters in the city, some other office addresses, and then their warehouses. There were four. One was the warehouse Peter had been in last night. The other one was the warehouse into which Venom had supposedly broken.

He backed up to the main menu again, and this time carefully typed, "VENOM."

"Age Of Story?" the computer prompted.

Peter thought. "THREE WEEKS," he typed.

"Incorrect Entry! Please Try Again," said the computer.

Peter frowned. "21," he typed instead.

"One Moment Please," said the computer. "Your Request Is Being Processed."

Peter waited. At least it didn't play music while processing.

Finally, "ONE REFERENCE," the computer said.

Aha! Peter thought. He hit (1).

The screen filled, and the byline made him catch his breath. "San Francisco—A revolutionary breakthrough in snake-farming techniques means that for the first time, the antidote for rattlesnake venom will not have to be given in multi-vial doses, over the course of days, but in a single injection—"

"Oh, phooey," said Peter. He backed out of that story, went back to its menu and the one before that, and studied the search criteria a little more carefully. But there seemed no way to differentiate between snake venom and the Venom Peter had most in mind. *What this thing needs is a proper name filter*, he thought.

He paused, then typed, "VENOM + SAN FRANCISCO." The computer asked him for days again, and he told it "21."

"ONE REFERENCE," the computer screen said. Peter asked to have that displayed, feeling sure that it was going to be the same snake-venom story.

It was. Peter sat back and looked at the screen. *At least, I think I know what this means. He hasn't been sighted in San Francisco at all. At least—* He backtracked through the computer's menus to the point where one choice offered was, Crossindex To Other Newspapers/News Services. Peter chose that, and when the program asked him again for search phrases, once more typed VENOM + SAN FRANCISCO.

"ONE REFERENCE," it said, and once again, it was the snake-venom story.

Not a peep out of him, then, Peter thought. *No one's seen him or heard from him—not the wires, not the papers.*

Which means he really could be in New York. . . .

Or anywhere else, of course. There was no telling, with this dearth of data.

I still don't get it, though. Radioactives. . . .

He sat still and thought for a moment. Radioactives. There was not a lot of radioactive material loose in the city. The stuff in the hospitals—gamma sources for radiotherapy, blood isotope material and so forth—was too developed, too single-purpose, for much criminal use to be made of it. *What a crook would want,* Peter thought, *would be less refined nuclear material, or nuclear material in bulk, or both. And there are only a couple of places in the city, really, where you could get such stuff. . . .*

Peter put that aside for the moment. It was simpler to deal with the facts as he understood them. He knew that two CCRC warehouses had been hit in one night, by different people—or entities, he thought—and possibly for different reasons. Both perpetrators had been interested in those canisters of waste for reasons Peter couldn't yet understand. In the case of the warehouse where the homeless men had been sleeping, who or what the perpetrator had been remained unproven. Peter still couldn't believe that Venom was involved.

As for the Hobgoblin—what would he want with nuclear material? Hobby's motivations were something he had studied in the past. They seemed generally to come down to one thing—money. Either he would steal money directly, or he would steal something which he could ransom or sell to get a lot of money, or he would hire himself out as a mercenary for money. *Nuclear waste, though?* Peter got up from the terminal and hefted his portfolio. It was all very peculiar.

Then an idea, a sort of doomsday scenario, leapt to his mind. *A bomb?* Plans for atomic bombs were not hard to find: high school students had made them. The Freedom of Information Act made it possible to get all the data you needed except for a few crucial bits of information about critical mass and so forth, but those could be worked out by someone with, in one case, no better than high-school physics. The problem, of course, was the size. A bomb of any real destructive power could not be made very small. But small enough. You could hide a fairly damaging nuke in the trunk of a car, a much worse one in the back of a truck. There was certainly no question that, if he felt like it and had the time, Hobgoblin could build such a thing himself.

Even if he didn't want to, there were enough terrorists, cranky underpaid scientists-for-hire, and disaffected high-school physics students whom Hobby could get to do such a job for him. *But why now? It can't be that the idea just occurred to him.* Such do-it-yourself bombs had been in the news for years—either the possibility of them or the actuality. If Hobby were in fact building a bomb, or masterminding one, why right this minute? Why not a long time ago?

Either the talent he needed had just become available—or something else had just become available.

What?

Peter shook his head and waved to Bob, heading out of the morgue. There were still too many pieces missing from this puzzle. What he was sure of, though, was that Venom was not involved in this.

Peter was equally sure, though, that Venom did not like having his name used behind his back. If you mentioned him often enough, he had a way of turning up. And when he did . . . all hell broke loose.

Just what we don't need right now, Peter thought. Bad enough to have Hobby messing around with some kind of unspecified nuclear material. All we need is old Chomp-'n'-Drool showing up at the same time.

Still, there were at least two very obvious places where nuclear material, in raw and refined forms, was kept and worked with, sometimes even stockpiled. One was Empire State University, where Peter was working on his doctorate. Half the doctoral candidates in the place were working in some aspect of nuclear physics, having sought out the labs there, widely thought to be the best-equipped on the East Coast. The other place— about which he had heard enough complaints over time, from people who didn't care to have nukes so close to New York City—was the Brooklyn Navy Yard. Nuclear subs came there, docked, and were refuelled and defuelled. A visit over there as Spider-Man would not go amiss.

Peter chuckled a little as he walked out of the *Bugle* offices. *The Hunt for Web October, huh?* he thought—

Preoccupied with all this information he'd just processed, he blithely stepped off the curb. The blare of the horn practically in his ear shocked Peter almost out of his skin. He jumped back, almost fell over, reeled to one side and clutched a lamppost to keep himself from ramming into it. "Why don'cha watch where you're going, ya dummy!" shouted the voice of the driver of the truck which had almost turned Peter into paté.

He stood watching the truck roar away. *My spider-sense should have warned me—* But of course, it was gone, still gone, for another eighteen hours at least.

Peter muttered under his breath. *I'm going to have to be a lot more aware of my surroundings until this clears up.* He ostentatiously looked both ways, and crossed the street.

ary Jane Watson-Parker sighed, settled herself in front of the bathroom mirror, and started putting on her makeup. Her thoughts drifted to the apparent reappearance of Venom. Once, long ago, in one of those earlier apartments she and Peter had shared, she encountered Eddie Brock standing over her. Because he knew Spider-Man's real identity, it had been easy for him to track them down. She found herself wondering whether they were going to have to move again, and if so, how the heck they were going to afford it. First-last-and-deposit on anyplace decent was really out of their reach at the moment, unemployed as she was and with Peter's employment on the sporadic side. *But if we have to, we'll manage it. Somehow.* She refused to tolerate the idea that a costumed villain—or, in Venom's case, a villained costume—was going to start invading her and her husband's personal space again. If there was something Peter deserved, it was a quiet place away from the bizarre and dreadful people and creatures with whom his work brought him into conflict.

She got out the mascara, fiddled with the brush to get the usual huge blob off the end of it, and began working on her lashes. MJ had become more philosophical about Peter's work over the last couple of years. There had been a time when she thought perhaps married life would steady him down to the point where he wouldn't need his "night job" anymore, where his family life would be enough to make him renounce those long dangerous nights out. Now she smiled briefly at her own old naïveté. Peter's commitment to what he did was profound, though he covered that commitment with glib, good-natured street talk most of the time as a distraction. Once MJ had come to realize this, life had become both simpler and more difficult. Simpler, because she stopped waiting for something which was never going to come; more difficult, because now she had to struggle for two. They were a team.

The issue of support came up sometimes with some of the women she knew from her television and modeling work. It wasn't that the men weren't trying, holding down menial jobs while struggling to make it. The women, meanwhile, would gather in one of their occasional kaffeeklatsch sessions, in the back of some studio or off to the side of some photo shoot, nodding and grinning a little ruefully at one another as they compared stories.

"It could have been worse," June, one of her cohorts on *Secret Hospital,* told MJ dryly over their last lunch, "you could have married an artist." *She* was married to one, the kind of wildly creative "conceptual artist" whose idea of a meaningful installation was to cover the inside of a plain-walled room with slices of bread stuck to the walls with peanut butter.

At such times, while sympathizing with June, MJ knew that her situation was worse, and there was no way to explain it to the others. So she let them console her on the rising price-per-credit at ESU and the cost of textbooks, and otherwise held her peace on the issues which really concerned her, like patching her husband up after he came home badly messed up following yet another brawl with some intransigent caped kook.

Now, while she knew that one of the worst of them

was seemingly in the neighborhood, she had to concentrate on other things, and specifically, work. It was hard enough for Peter to be out and about his personal quest against evil without him having to obsess about the rent as well. That concern, at least, she had been able to keep off his mind while she'd had the job with *Secret Hospital*. But that job was gone now, and it was her responsibility to get employed again as quickly as possible, to leave Peter once again free to concentrate on his work.

MJ checked her face over one last time. Theoretically, she was just going down to the store for the trades, but if she saw something likely in one of them, MJ had to look good enough to walk straight off into an interview or a cold reading with confidence. *Not too bad*, she thought, *for a woman who was up half the night wondering if her husband had fallen off a tall building.*

She went back through the living room, where Peter was still snoring under the quilt, and paused a moment to look at him thoughtfully. *I don't like those circles under his eyes. But then his hours have never been exactly what you'd call regular.*

She picked up her keys and her purse, and headed for the door, locked up, and went down in the elevator.

Their street was still fairly quiet, this time of morning. MJ didn't hurry: there was no need, and the weather was too pleasant. This was the only time today when it was likely to be: the weather report claimed it was going to get up in the high 90's again, and with the humidity they'd been having, the climate would be no joke later.

The thought kept her sighing down to the open door of the store at the corner.

"Morning, Mr. Kee," she said as she passed the owner at the counter.

"Morning, MJ," he said, glancing up from behind the lottery tickets and the chewing gum. "Got your papers in, today."

"Thanks." She paused by the rack, picked up *Variety* and the *Hollywood Reporter*, and turned to the back to have a quick look at the classifieds. There was nothing much in the *Reporter*, and she tucked it under her arm.

"Hey, MJ, you gonna buy that?" Mr. Kee called from the front of the store.

"Oh, no," she said, "I was just planning to stand back here and bend all the pages." She grinned. Mr. Kee was not above teasing her as if she was one of the comics-reading ten-year-olds whom he claimed were the bane of his existence.

That was when her eye fell on the boxed ad almost at the back of *Variety*.

OPEN CALL
Young-looking females, 22–25, for episodic work:
reading & look-over. August 12, 445 W 54th St,
10 AM–2 PM.

MJ blinked and looked up hurriedly into the mirror to see if she looked 22–25. Then she smiled at herself, but the look was wry: these days, it seemed, 22–25 meant "just out of the cradle" to some of the directors she had auditioned for, and despite the fact that she was between the ages in question, the odds were no better than fifty-

fifty that she would manage to be cast as such. *Still—nothing ventured, nothing gained—*

She made her way up to the checkout, still staring at the copy of *Variety. Ten o'clock . . . there's plenty of time to get back up to the apartment, pick up a couple of eight-by-tens and a CV or so . . . then get down there. . . .*

"Going to walk into a post or something, reading like that," Mr. Kee said, eyeing the two papers. He tapped at the cash register for a moment. "Mmm . . . three forty-five."

She fished around for the change. "You find anything?" Mr. Kee said.

MJ raised her eyebrows. "I'm not sure. Do I look between twenty-two and twenty-five?"

He shook his head at her, smiling, his eyes wrinking. "Eighty at least."

MJ grinned. "You're no help. If I'm eighty, what are you, chopped liver?"

"Good luck, MJ!" he called after her as she went out.

MJ, equipped with copies of her résumé and publicity stills and dressed in interview clothes, got on the subway. A half-hour later, she was at the address where the open call was being held.

It looked like any other somewhat-aging office building in that part of the West Side: no air-conditioning, grimy linoleum, broken elevators, windows that appeared to have been last washed around the time the Mets won their first World Series. The only clue to anything interesting was the hand-scrawled sign taped to the elevator which said AUDITIONS—SECOND FLOOR.

MJ found the stairs and climbed them slowly: it was already getting warm, and she didn't want to get all sweaty. She could hear a soft mutter of voices upstairs. *Not too loud, though. Maybe not too many people. That would be good luck for me.*

She pushed open a fire door at the top of the stairs, and the wall of sound, about a hundred voices, hit her. *Well, so much for* that, she thought, as she pushed her way into a hall full of women twenty-two to twenty-five years old, or purporting to be.

A harried production assistant was pushing through the crowd. "Anybody who doesn't have a number yet," she yelled to the assembled actresses, "take a number, will you? Numbers over on the table, ladies."

I am not a number, MJ thought, somewhat ironically, pushing her way over there through the crowd, *I am a free woman.* She grabbed a card, one of only a few remaining on the table. *Free woman number one hundred and six. Oh, joy.* There was no hope of finding anywhere to sit; she resigned herself to leaning carefully against the cleanest piece of wall she could find, and pulled out her much-thumbed copy of *War and Peace*.

An hour and a half later it was about twenty degrees warmer, and all around her the remaining thirty or so women were wilting. MJ was not exactly cool herself, but the combination of images of a Russian winter and the likelihood that absolutely nothing would come of this interview were helping her somewhat.

"One oh four," came the voice from the next room. One oh four, who was certainly no more than eighteen and dressed in the most minuscule possible shorts and a halter, vanished into the room and came immediately out again, looking morose. This had been happening with increasing regularity over the last while, MJ had noticed. The heat, she thought, was beginning to tell on the interviewers as much as on the interviewees. "One oh five," the voice said, and no question that the PA at least sounded weary of the day, if not of life.

One oh five raised her eyebrows at MJ and went in. The door closed. About three minutes later it opened again, and she came out. "One oh six," said the tired PA's voice from inside.

MJ slipped her paperback into her bag and strolled into the room, looking around. The room was bare, except for a table which held the first PA and two other people, a middle-aged woman and a younger man, all of whom looked at her with various degrees of loathing.

Except the middle-aged woman, whose expression changed abruptly. "You were on *Secret Hospital*, weren't you?" she said.

MJ smiled. "Was, yes."

Glances were exchanged at the table. The young female PA held out some sheets of paper. "Would you mind reading from this?"

Cold, MJ thought, not losing her smile in the slightest. *I hate cold reading.* But she took the pages, and started reading after no more than a glance.

It was something to do with social work, some dialogue about homeless people. *Typecasting*, MJ thought, *do I mind? I should think not!* She threw as much feeling into it as she could, recalling the compassion in the voice of one of her friends, Maureen, who had been doing some volunteer work with the homeless and had told MJ some dreadful horror stories about the situations they got into these days. When she finished, the three were looking at her with interest.

"Can you come back Thursday?" the young man said.

"Certainly," MJ said.

"Do you have a CV?"

"Right here," MJ said, and handed it over, along with her still.

And a few minutes later she was out on the street again, staring with mild bemusement at a five-page premise for something called *Street Life*, which was apparently intended to be a dramatic series with a comic edge, and involved a starring role for a female actor who was to play a crusading social worker. There were three more sets of dialogue and half a script to study as well. On Thursday she would read for real.

What happened to the interview? MJ wondered as she walked down the street, trying to recover her composure after the abrupt excitement of the past few minutes. Never mind: she hated interviews. She preferred job tryouts that seemed to actually have something to do with her acting ability, rather than her life experience.

She stopped at the corner, waiting for the light to change, while traffic streamed by in front of her. *This*, she thought, *could* be *something. Now, is that a phone over there? Okay—*

She crossed hurriedly, pulling out her address book. By the time she reached the phone, someone else was using it already, but the guy in question was mercifully brief. A few moments later, she was dialing.

The phone at the other end rang, picked up. The first thing MJ heard was a yawn.

"Mau-*reeeeeeeeeen*," MJ said, very amused, for this sound she had heard often before. Maureen liked to sleep in.

"Oh, MJ," her friend said, "what's your problem? Where are you, anyway? It sounds like a parking lot."

"Nearly. Seventh Avenue, anyway. Look, are you still working at that soup place?"

"The shelter? Yup." Another yawn. "I have a shift this afternoon."

"That's great. Can I come with you?"

Another yawn, mixed with an ironic laugh. "Having a sudden attack of social conscience?"

"I should, I know. But no. Listen, this is what it's about—" She quickly told Maureen about that morning's job-nibble. "It would be real smart if I went into this reading Thursday knowing what I'm talking about as regards homeless people, anyway."

"Stanislavsky would approve, I guess. Listen, no problem. How's your cooking?"

"My *cooking*? Not bad."

"Good. I can always use another hand in the kitchen. Come on by and I'll take you in to the shelter with me, and you can help me out while I'm getting ready. Then you can do your research while we're serving."

"Sounds great. Maureen, you're the best."

"You just keep telling me that. See you in a while."

About two hours later MJ and Maureen were walking in the front door of the Third Chance Shelter on the Lower East Side. MJ had had a mental picture of a dreary, spartan kind of place, but Third Chance totally overturned it. The outer brick wall was blind, true, but inside the front door MJ found herself in a courtyard full of green plants with an open skylight, and beyond that lay several stories' worth of meeting rooms, workrooms, a cafeteria, bedrooms, game rooms, and offices.

"We don't have a lot of beds," Maureen said, leading MJ into the kitchen area of the cafeteria, where people were finishing the cleanup after lunch. "Mostly we're about feeding people, and after that, teaching them new job skills—office work, computing, things like that." She paused a moment by one of the big stainless-steel industrial stoves, tying up her long blonde hair. Maureen was small, with one of those faces that people usually called "severely pretty," and her gorgeous hair went almost down to her knees, causing envy in everyone who saw it.

"That was how you got into this, then?" MJ said. "The job part."

Maureen nodded, pulling out a long apron and handing another to MJ. "They brought me in as a consultant on the computer end. Came to teach, stayed to serve." She chuckled. "Here—"

She pulled a paperback down from the shelf, handed it to MJ. "Potato soup today," Maureen said.

MJ turned the book over. "Alexis Soyer. Why is that name familiar?"

"He was the founding chef of the Reform Club in London. Also the last century's greatest expert on nutrition on the cheap—he got started working in the soup kitchens in Dublin during the Great Famine. 'A Frugal

Kitchen' there is still one of the best sources for recipes designed for maximum nutrition and minimum money."

MJ smiled as she put on her apron. "Better than macaroni and cheese?"

"Much. There's the potatoes. Let's peel."

For at least an hour, they did just that, potato after potato, hundreds of them, until MJ didn't want to see another potato for the rest of her life. Then they started making the broth—chicken broth, as it turned out, using stripped chicken carcasses donated by one of the local places that did "fast-food" roast chicken. Herbs went in, and both sliced and pureed potatoes, and when the soup was done about two hours later, MJ could hardly stay out of it. "Old Alexis," Maureen said, "he knew his stuff. You've got time for just one bowl before the customers start arriving."

MJ was almost drowning in sweat from working over the hot stove in this humidity for two hours. All the same, her stomach growled assertively, and when Maureen handed her the bowl, MJ grabbed a spoon and finished it right to the bottom.

Maureen looked up approvingly. "It's just four-thirty," she said. "First shift will be in shortly. Help me get that pot onto the trolley. We'll take it up front by the serving window."

Together they handled the big twenty-gallon pot onto the low trolley and trundled it forward. As they passed the serving window, MJ saw that there were already a lot of people gathering out on the cafeteria side. She shook her head slightly. "Why do so many of them have their coats on?" she said. "In this weather—!"

Maureen looked, shook her head. "Some of them are just old. Others—you can't carry the stuff in your hands all the time, and most of them don't have anywhere they can leave things. Simpler to wear them—even though in heat like this, they get so dehydrated sometimes that they pass out. We go through a lot of bottled water here. Come on—here comes the first shift."

The two of them grabbed ladles and started filling bowls and putting them out on the cafeteria side of the serving window. Other workers were filling water pitchers, or putting out pitchers of homemade Gatorade-type drinks. "Electrolytes," Maureen said. "This weather, you can sweat all your salts out before you even notice, and die of it."

The soup quickly vanished. MJ lost count of how many shabbily dressed people came up to the counter, took a bowl and a spoon, nodded, said a word or two, and went off. She knew that there were a lot of homeless people in the city, but had never had it borne in on her so straightforwardly how *many* of them there were. She started feeling somewhat ashamed of herself for not having noticed. The single lone figures on a streetcorner, in a doorway, you could ignore, turning your head as you went by. But not these.

When she realized there wasn't any more soup, MJ found herself suddenly not having any idea what to do. She looked up into the face of the person standing outside the serving window with an empty bowl, and could only stammer, "Uh, I'm sorry, we're all out—"

The man nodded, walked off. MJ almost felt like crying. "Maureen—" she said.

"I know. Take a break. There's some iced tea out here. Then we'll go out and have a chat with people."

"Do they mind?" MJ said a little shakily, sitting down with the iced tea.

Maureen looked at her with a small quirk of sad smile. "You mean, do they think you're patronizing them? No. Do they know that this hurts, on both sides? Yes. But it's better than doing nothing. Drink the tea."

She drank it. Then they went out into the cafeteria.

It *did* hurt, talking to people who had had busy lives, and proud ones, and who now spent most of each given day working out in which underpass, tunnel, or doorway they would spend that night. But Maureen's example made it easier to listen to them. By and large, though there were angry people in the cafeteria, and sullen ones, most of them were curiously and consciously kind to the first-timer, as if they were more embarrassed for their predicament than for MJ's.

A few of them were people she felt she would have been pleased to meet socially, and the knowledge made her ashamed, considering that had she today met them in the street, MJ knew she would have looked away. *The least I can do is look at them* now, MJ thought, and concentrated on doing that.

Three of the people finishing their soup at one table had waved at Maureen, calling her over: she and MJ sat there, and Maureen made the introductions. "Mike," she said, indicating one big redheaded, broad-faced man, "our newest computer nerd. He's learning C++ during the days. Marilyn—" This was a little old lady of about seventy, from the looks of her, well wrapped in coats and sweaters, thin but apple-cheeked and cheerful. "She's a few months ahead of Mike. Writes the fastest code I ever saw."

"Only problem is," said Marilyn, "to get me employed, we're going to have to pass me off as a twenty-year-old."

"On-line," Maureen said, "who'll know the difference until it's too late? And Lloyd." Lloyd was a young handsome black gentleman with a face that reminded MJ of something from Egyptian monumental art, noble and still, except for when the rare smile broke through. "Lloyd is still seeking his *metier*. Typist, possibly. He's got good speed."

The chat came easily enough after that. MJ was instantly recognized and teased about her own job loss: the others seemed to think it made her more accessible, and shortly she found herself talking to them about the difficulty of getting an apartment and keeping it, the fear of losing it, how tough it was to hang on.

They told her how they did it. All of them used shelters when they could: all of them wound up in the occasional favorite doorway or tunnel. Lloyd favored the tunnels under Grand Central. "They keep trying to clean them out," he said, "trying to get rid of us and the cats. Us and the cats, we keep coming back."

"Not so many of us, lately," Marilyn said. "I've been hearing stories—"

Glances were exchanged. "Not the transit police again," Maureen said.

Marilyn shook her head. "Something else. Something big and dark . . . down in the train tunnels. A couple of people who usually sleep down there haven't been seen, last couple of days."

Lloyd's eyebrows went up. "Not George Woczniak?"

"George," Marilyn said. "Rod Wilkinson, you know Rod, told me he saw some big black guy—not black like you: *black* black—down there on the lower level, not far from the Lexington Avenue upramp where the maintenance tracks are. Saw him the other night, over by where George usually sleeps. Then, the last couple of days—no George. And you know how George is: predictable. This isn't like him."

Mike looked up and said, "Now, you know . . . that's funny. Jenny McMahon, you know her, the blond lady who stays around 49th and Ninth—she was telling me she'd heard somebody telling some kind of story about something in the sewer tunnels under Second—you know where those access tunnels are—"

"Alligators again," Marilyn said.

Mike shook his head. "Nope. This was going on two legs. Teeth, though. She said whoever told her the story said the thing had teeth like a shark's happy dream. Lots of teeth."

MJ's eyes opened a little at that, but she kept her thoughts to herself for the moment.

Lloyd said, "Some of the regulars told me they didn't want to come up topside now, because of the chance that while they were leaving, they might run across . . . whatever it was. Makes you wonder whether above-ground might be safer for the time being."

Mike shrugged. "After those two guys got aced in the warehouse last night? Naah. It's just that there's noplace safe in this city, not *really* safe. Not an apartment, not the top of Trump Tower, *no* place. The crime rate's a disgrace."

The conversation started to take the same kind of mildly complaining tone to be heard sooner or later from every citydweller anywhere: things are going downhill, the place is a mess, it wasn't like this ten years ago, the city really ought to do something. . . . MJ was having trouble concentrating on it. She was thinking about someone in black, someone with big teeth, someone around whom people vanished. "And the worst of it," Marilyn was saying, "is that all their hair is falling out."

"All of it?" Mike said, unbelieving. "Maybe it's bad water."

"Helen told me Roedean's hair was coming out in handfuls, in patches. And a whole bunch of them over there were coming out in weird splotches on their skin."

"This is over by Penn?" Maureen said curiously.

"Yeah," Marilyn said. "Roedean just moved over there a couple of weeks ago, and it started. Other people took longer, but they're doing it too. Some have moved already—they say they don't care how comfortable the digs over there are."

Maureen shook her head. "Are they all getting their water from a common source?"

"I don't think so—"

"Can't be that, then."

Lloyd shook his head. "Lyme disease, maybe? There was just an outbreak of it up in the Park last year."

Marilyn shook her head. "Takes longer, doesn't it? . . ."

The conversation wandered on again, and MJ found herself thinking, *Hair falling out. Patches on the skin. Sounds more like radiation.* It was hardly a revolutionary concept for her, or any great leap of imagination. She had married a man who was very interested indeed in the effects of radiation on human beings, for very personal reasons. She had heard more than enough dissertations on the subject. And her thoughts went again to the huge dark shape with the teeth. . . .

Peter, she thought. *Peter needs to know about this, as fast as I can find him. Wherever he is.*

Peter was not available for comment just then. But on the top of a fire-hose drying tower at the southeastern edge of the Brooklyn Navy Yards, Spider-Man crouched and looked out over the place, thinking.

Hard to know where to start. Even the military doesn't routinely paste big signs all over the outside of buildings saying, RADIOACTIVE STUFF, GET IT HERE! But all the same. . . . He looked over the expanse of the place, considering. *You wouldn't leave it at the outskirts, routinely. You'd put it as far inside the installation as you could—making it as difficult as possible to get in and out without detection.*

Or, alternately, you would keep raw fissile material close to the subs. That's one of the most secure parts of the base. He had seen the anti-dive nets below the surface of the entry to the Yards as he swung in. Those would routinely be moved only when a sub was about to enter or leave. *Keep the fissiles near the missiles.* He grinned under the mask. *And the vessel with the pestle has the brew that is true. . . .*

He shot out a strand of web and began swinging in closer to the heart of the Yards, where the subs would dock. There was only one of them present at the moment, and he intended to take his time approaching it. His reconnaissance was a friendly one, but he wasn't sure the Base security people would immediately recognize it as such.

The Yards were not as easy to swing around in as, say, midtown: there were fewer tall structures, most of the buildings being one- or two-story jobs. Still, you had to work with what presented itself. Dusk was coming on—that much help he had. He busied himself with avoiding lighted windows, staying away from routes passing doorways from which people might suddenly emerge—say, people with guns.

On top of one middle-sized office-type building nearest the docks, he paused, eyeing the local traffic. Not many people were in the narrow streets that went between the buildings. *Dinner time? Staff cuts? No telling.* He pulled out the camera and its tripod from a web pouch slung over his shoulder. This was as good a spot as any—

It was the sudden faint whining noise in the air which brought his head up, not his spider-sense. *That* was still absent. He tracked with the sound, then glanced away and hurriedly turned the camera on too. It tracked as well, following the faint gleam of brightness as something fell down from where the sun still shone between the shadows of the skyscrapers falling across the water. The sun's brightness left the tiny shape, but not before Spider-Man saw it and knew it for the angular arrowhead-shape of Hobgoblin's jet-glider.

My hunch was right, he thought. He watched the shape arrow downward, heading right for the sub. *Don't know what good that's going to do him—*

But a closer look at the sub told him. Its biggest hatch, the one used to service the missiles back at the rear end, was open. And anything big enough to install a missile through, was big enough to let the jetglider through as well.

He shot out web and instantly threw himself in Hobgoblin's direction as fast as he could. It was no simpler a business than getting across the base had been, but this time at least he wasn't going to worry about avoiding attention. Hobby was already attracting enough: he could hear shouts below him, and at least once, the sharp crack of a warning shot. *If I can just keep from getting caught in a crossfire. Well, my spider-sense—*

He felt like swearing. *Won't do a thing.*

Never mind!

He swung toward Hobgoblin's plummeting sled. For once luck was with him. Hobby was so intent on the sub that he didn't hear or see Spider-Man coming at him. *I am* not *going to let him just waltz in there*, Spidey thought. *The thing is as full of nukes as a subway car's full of commuters.*

But how to stop him?

Hobby was dropping lower, was certainly no more

than a few hundred yards away. *Now here is a truly
dumb idea*, Spidey thought, *whose time has come*.

He took the best aim he could manage, and shot a line
of web straight at the sled. It caught—

He was yanked off the building with dreadful speed in
Hobgoblin's wake. At first he had entertained some wild
hope that his weight would slow the glider down, maybe
even make Hobby fall off, but that was too much to hope
for. The thing was fast, overpowered, and adaptable, and
it just kept flying. Hobby staggered briefly, turned, noticed what sudden unwelcome cargo he was suddenly
dragging behind him like a towed dinghy, and turned
hard, so that Spidey was whipped hard to one side at the
end of his line of webbing, like a kid at the end of a line
of skaters playing snap-the-whip. He hung on desperately, thinking, *This is not a good place to fall off. A
hundred fifty feet above land, a hundred fifty feet above
water, it's pretty much the same result from this height.
Splat—!*

"You just can't keep out of my business, can you?"
Hobby yelled at him, curving around so sharply in the
air that for a moment Spidey was still going in the original direction while Hobby was going the other way, and
they passed one another in the air. For that brief moment, the effect was comical.

It stopped being funny as the snap at the end of the
whip caught Spidey again, harder this time. *About 3 g's,
if I'm any judge*, he thought, his jaw clenched and his
fists locked on the webbing. He thought the jerk as he
came around again would break his wrists, but somehow
he hung on, even without his spider-sense to warn him

of exactly when the most dangerous stresses would come. "Let's just call it civic duty, Hobby," he yelled back. "This is government property—"

The second bullet went *wheet!*, just the way bullets were supposed to go, through the air right past his ear. It had been fired at Hobgoblin, but Hobby had banked hard around again, laughing hysterically. And here came the snap of the whip—

Spidey hung on, eyeing the buildings under him for one tall enough. If he could snag one of them with a webline and mate it with the one attached to the jet-glider—*without being pulled in two pieces first like a Thanksgiving wishbone, that is.*

But he didn't have time. The next thing he saw, again without his spider-sense giving him the slightest warning, was a pumpkin-bomb flying straight at his head.

Spider-Man let go the web and dropped, spread-eagled—he had learned long ago from watching real spiders, and from experience, that this was the only way to buy yourself a second or two in free fall. Behind and above him, the bomb went off. More rifle fire laced up past him toward Hobgoblin as Spidey looked around desperately for something to web to. One building had a radio mast on it, VHF from the look of it, and fairly sturdy. He shot web at it, felt it anchor, hauled himself in hard, managing to slingshot around it with enough speed and effort to keep himself from crashing into the roof of the building.

He looked up and saw Hobby heading straight down toward the open hatch of the sub. He had just enough time to see some sub crewman look up out of the hatch open-mouthed at the noise, take in the spectacle above, and duck hastily out of sight—but not fast enough to close the sub's hatch. Down the hatch Hobby went, and there followed several seconds of horrible silence.

And a BANG!

Oh God, no, Spidey thought, and swung straight down after him. It was a long shot for the hatch of the sub. He let go of the webbing, casting off as hard as he could to get those last few feet of distance.

He came down hard just at the edge of the hatch as the smoke came boiling up. *Not one of the high-explosive pumpkins*, he thought. *Maybe he's not feeling homicidal today.*

He dropped through the hatch and realized that the lack of spider-sense had betrayed him one more time. The first billow of smoke had been an ignition artifact from the bomb, nothing more. Down in the body of the sub, everything was drowned in a thick fog of gas: people were struggling in all directions, falling over each other. This gas Spidey knew from old experience. At high enough concentrations it paralyzed, even killed— and the bombs usually went off in two stages. He stopped breathing and made his way hurriedly along the way to where the cloud was thickest, squinting through his mask, which gave him some protection. *There— looks like—* He fumbled along the floor, and after a moment his hand came down on the round shape of the pumpkin bomb. Spider-Man leapt back up the ladder to the hatch in two great bounds, reared back and threw the bomb up and out of the hatch. In midair it detonated again, letting loose its main dose of gas, the one meant to flood the whole place and kill, but the breeze off the bay began to take the big noxious green cloud away immediately.

Not that this solved the problems of the men down in the sub. Spidey dove back down that hatch and started grabbing men any which way, upside down, right side up, a double armful of them. Up the hatch he leapt again, making harder work of it this time, but if a spider could jump around while lifting such proportional weights, so could he. He dropped the men in a heap on the upper hull and dived down the hatch again. A second load, men choking and coughing with tears streaming down their faces, cursing the gas and trying to find out what was happening to them. He leapt back up into the clean air, dumped them by their buddies, took a great lungful of breath and dived back down—and was slammed sideways into the opening of the hatch by Hobgoblin, still laughing, as he rocketed back up into the open with his arms full of something metallic and bulky. He soared away.

Spidey clung to the edge of the hatch and shot a webline at Hobgoblin, furious at one more failure of his spider-sense, desperate not to let Hobby get away. But Hobby veered to one side and was off across the river, heading for Manhattan at high speed, his laughter trailing away as he went. The web fell, useless, not being much good at changing direction in mid-shot.

Spider-Man clambered up out of the hatch and went over to check out the men lying around on the upper deck. They were still coughing and rubbing streaming eyes, but none of them were dead, which was something. "Hey," one of them said, focusing on him when his eyes were working again, "thanks, buddy. Maybe I'll do the same for you some day."

Spider-Man looked around him at the dark elegant bulk of the sub. "You've been doing it for a long while," he said. "I'm just returning the favor."

He heard clanking footsteps on the ladder from the big hatch, and turned. A tall dark man with eyes still wet from the effects of the gas, and wearing a sidearm, had come up out of the hatch and was eyeing him coolly. He said, "Captain wants to see you, Mr.—"

"Your friendly neighborhood Spider-Man will do," Spidey said, trying to sound as cool. "My pleasure. Lead the way."

The sergeant-at-arms went down the ladder: Spidey followed him. Blowers had been activated inside the sub, and the gas was slowly clearing, so that off to his left Spider-Man could see something he would have missed the first time: a large door labeled DANGER— RADIATION, and bearing the radiation-warning trefoil. *Now that's interesting*, he thought. *Hobby never gave that a second glance, if I'm right. Very strange indeed . . .*

"This way," the sergeant-at-arms said, gesturing Spider-Man rightwards. Spidey went. Around him, in the corridor, men were being helped to their feet by others wearing anti-gas equipment. The corridor ended in what seemed like the bridge of the ship—or, at least, *a* bridge—and standing there was another man wearing an expression entirely too calm for the situation, and triple stripes on the short sleeves of his shirt, which accounted for the expression.

"Spider-Man, I presume," the Captain said. "That'll be all, sergeant-at-arms."

The officer saluted and turned away.

"Permission to come aboard, Captain—"

"LoBuono," the Captain said, and held out his hand. They shook. "Granted. My medic tells me you saved the lives of the men who were stuck aft."

"I think so, Captain."

"Thank you," the Captain said. "We seem not to have sustained any serious damage. But there has been a loss."

"Not of life—"

"No. Your friend there—"

"No friend of mine, sir. Hobgoblin."

"He deserves the name. And worse. He broke into one of the missile silos just forward of the hatch—" A young officer came hurrying up to Captain LoBuono at that point. "A moment," he said. "Report?"

"He got at number three, Captain," said the officer. "Pulled the upper actuator right out."

"Damn him straight to hell," the Captain said, again quite calmly. "Anything else?"

"No, sir. He tried number four as well, but seems to have decided not to bother."

"Doubtless one was enough," Captain LoBuono muttered. "Very well, start decommission procedures on that silo, and notify shoreside and Omaha by the usual procedures. And check number four out. Dismissed."

The officer saluted and went. "Actuator?" Spidey said.

The Captain let out a long breath. "The device that triggers the atomic reaction in a fired missile," he said. "Certainly something which could have other applications."

"For someone like Hobgoblin," Spider-Man said softly, "no question whatever. And over the last day or so, he's been involved with the theft of some nuclear material."

Captain LoBuono looked at him thoughtfully. "Nuclear. . . . Would you come with me?" he said.

Spider-Man followed him. Further into the body of the sub, air-tight doors had closed and the air was still clean. They went through several of these until they came to the door which led to the Captain's office. The Captain closed the door behind them, gestured Spider-Man to a seat.

He sat down himself, across the desk from him, and paused a moment to run his hands over his face and through his hair. For that second all his dignity didn't so much fall away as relax to reveal beneath it a very tired and upset man. Then he straightened, everything in place again. "I want to thank you again," Captain LoBuono said, "for saving my people."

"Hey," Spidey said, "otherwise I would have kept tripping over them."

The Captain's smile was thin, but amused, that of a man used to seeing people conceal what was going on in their minds or emotions. "We have had some other unusual occurrences here over the past day or so," he said, "and in the light of this, I think perhaps you should know about one of them."

His spider-sense might not have been working, but Spidey could still get that sensation described by some as A Very Bad Feeling, and he was getting it now.

"We had an unusual passenger aboard," the Captain said. "We made pickup—I'm not at liberty to say where—and were to deliver it to a safe location in Greenland. However, our passenger parted company with us very shortly after we docked here."

" 'It,' " Spider-Man said.

Captain LoBuono nodded, folded his hands. "You have been to some unusual places," he said, "and you have a reputation for dealing with—unusual people—so I feel safe about imparting this information to you. There are no guarantees that our, uh, passenger, stayed on this side of the river. It may turn up in your bailiwick, as it were."

"What actually *is* your passenger? Or was."

The Captain's face wore a curious expression. "I can't say."

A moment's silence. "Meaning 'shouldn't'?" Spider-Man said.

The Captain nodded. "This much seems plain: it is of extraterrestrial origin."

"It was in that chamber—and broke out—"

"Through the hull of my boat," Captain LoBuono said, for the first time looking annoyed. "Though perhaps I should be grateful."

"Did anyone see it?"

"No. Not from the beginning of the cruise, and not when it left us."

Spider-Man thought about this. "Was it radioactive?"

"Not in itself, no. But its habits require that it stay in a chamber containing radiation."

"And now it's loose," Spider-Man said, "in a city with enough radioactive sources to feed on."

The Captain nodded. "I would say so."

Spider-Man nodded. "Captain," he said, "precisely what am I supposed to do about it?"

Captain LoBuono was silent for a moment. "Watch out for it," he said.

"Just that?"

"Just that. I doubt I have the right to ask much more."

Spider-Man restrained a sigh. "Okay."

"Very well." The Captain stood up. "You can find your way out?"

"Yes, sir."

"Good day to you, then. And, Spider-Man—thank you again."

Spidey nodded, caught between feeling abashed and profoundly confused. He made his way out of the sub to the applause and cheers of the men who saw him go. But it was not until he was away from there again, and had recovered his camera and was web-borne on his way back to Manhattan, that he was able to deal in much detail with the confusion. Plainly the Captain had given him classified information—though not much. A thing that no one had seen, something that could go through the hull of a sub—something fond of radiation, but not radioactive itself—was loose in the City.

He thought suddenly of the warehouse wall he had seen on TV, crumbled or melted, and of the homeless man's story of something lapping at the radioactive waste. *Drinking* it.

Spider-Man headed home in a hurry.

FIVE

t took Peter several hours to process that evening's film. The photos weren't quite as good as the last batch had been: too much swinging and jumping around, he thought. From the look of things, the camera almost suffered some sort of electronic nervous breakdown as it tried to follow their wild gyrations through the air.

It had, Peter noticed happily, taken an excellent shot of Hobby zooming out of the hatch of the sub with his arms full of equipment, knocking Spider-Man on his butt in the process. Peter felt certain Jonah would feature that shot prominently on the front page, if only to show his old nemesis getting taken down a notch.

He was still fuming over the way he had been unable to stop Hobgoblin from getting into the sub. *The problem*, he thought, hanging up a finished print and eyeing it critically—the composition on some of these was nowhere near as good as it had been on the last batch— *the problem is that I've been depending too much on my spider-sense and not enough on my brains.*

It was useful to have a sixth sense watching his back while he was fully occupied with matters in front, that warned him of dangers and stresses ahead of time. The spider-sense had saved him many times—from unpleasant surprises, from severe or fatal injuries, from the elaborate forms of sudden death his opponents were capable of handing out. But suppose Hobby *had* managed an improvement in the gas that caused this loss of his special sense. The thought of having to do without it permanently gave Peter the creeps. Suppose the loss was irrev-

ocable? Suppose that he was going to have to go through
the rest of his career this way . . . ?

He sighed. Right now there was nothing else to do but
go about his work as usual, and do it the best he could,
and keep himself as far out of harm's way as that work
allowed. He had too much going on to be incapacitated
due to a sense that wasn't there.

While he worked, he listened eagerly for the sound of
the phone going off. It was unusual for MJ to be out so
late without checking in.

I wonder if she got *that job*, he thought. Desperately,
he hoped the answer was yes. But there was no use getting your hopes up about these things. Too often MJ had
stumbled onto what had seemed to both of them a sure
thing only to come home afterwards very depressed
when it didn't pan out. They had both learned from bitter
experience not to raise one another's hopes unnecessarily, for there was never any way to tell when luck was
going to strike and too many ways to be mistaken about
it.

All the same, I wish she'd get home. I miss *her.*

There was that other thought in the back of Peter's
mind as well. *Venom.* Often enough in the past, Venom
had put pressure on MJ in order to flush Spider-Man out
into the open, where the two of them could tangle. On
days like this when she was late and Venom was known
to be in the area, he could never quite get rid of the fear
that somewhere, in some dark alley or quiet spot where
no one would hear her yell for help, that dark shape was
looming over her, smiling with all those teeth.

He wouldn't hurt her, Peter thought. *She is an innocent. Isn't she?*

That was the question he couldn't answer. As far as Spider-Man was concerned, it was a good question whether Venom considered anyone associated with him to be truly innocent. All the same, Peter's resolve was clear.

If he touches her . . .

The difficulty with Venom was that the odds were stacked against him. They had fought some desperate battles in the past, and though on some occasions a flash of genius-under-pressure—or just plain luck—had intervened on Spider-Man's behalf, once or twice those capricious dice had fallen favoring Venom, and the result had almost been fatal for Spidey. All the free-flowing hatred of someone who thought that Spider-Man was responsible for the destruction of his career and his life made Eddie Brock and his symbiotic suit a very dangerous adversary.

He hung up the last print and looked at it closely. It showed an enlarged view of Hobgoblin shooting out of the hatch, and Peter looked carefully at the shiny metal box with what looked like some circuit-boards and exposed contacts sticking out of the back of it, and a couple of lights and switches on the front. *Probably just yanked it right out of a console. So much equipment has gone modular these days. Easy to remove for repair or replacement, and just as easy to remove for robbery. But if I was suspicious about him building some sort of bomb, this seems to clinch it. First radioactive material, now a trigger. What the devil is Hobby up to this time . . . ?*

He picked up MJ's borrowed hair-dryer and started fanning it over two of the prints to dry them faster. The part of the theft giving Peter the most trouble was the radioactive material itself. Even if you *were* going to build a bomb, you needed the so-called "weapons-grade" fissionable material that thriller-writers were so fond of. You couldn't just make off with a barrel of nuclear waste, hook a fuse and a trigger to it, and hope that the end result would be *boom*. A barrel of gunpowder, yes. But not this stuff.

It would have to be refined. The refining was an expensive, slow, and above all, obvious process, as some countries, never mind crooks, had already learned. Refining uranium ore, or even spent low-grade reactor waste—where part of the process had already taken place—into metallic U-235 needed a linked series of massive heavy-metal separation centrifuges. Such equipment took up a great deal of space and consumed an equivalent quantity of power.

You couldn't build such a facility in a populated area without someone noticing, no matter how much you tried to disguise it. The power drain on the local grid whenever the separation system was running—and it would have to run almost constantly—would tell even the most unimaginative electrical engineer that something out of the ordinary was going on.

Later, Peter thought, *when I have some time, I'm going to look into the thefts at the two warehouses in a little more detail. I want to find out exactly what was in those canisters. More to the point, why is someone storing nuclear waste—nuclear material of* any *kind—in Manhattan?* Offhand he could think of about six environmental groups that would blow their collective stacks if they found out about it . . . and were perhaps already doing so. *That's for later*, he thought. *Right now . . .*

He checked the six best of his prints to make sure they were dry, put them in his portfolio, put the negatives in as well, and headed for the door. As he went, he threw a last look over his shoulder at the stubbornly silent phone. *MJ . . .* he thought, then shook his head and smiled a bit to himself at his own nervousness. *She's a big girl, she can take care of herself.*

He headed for the *Bugle*.

"Your long lens again?" Kate said, looking over his shoulder at the prints as he put them down one after another on her desk. "That one's not too bad." Critically, head on one side, she studied the shot of Hobby coming up out of the sub. "A little underexposed, though."

"They can push it in Comp," Peter said. Kate nodded. Another shadow fell over the desk. Peter turned, and saw J. Jonah Jameson standing there, scowling down at the photos.

"What are these?" he said, picking up the shot of Hobby, the sub, and Spider-Man. "Not again?"

"Why, Jonah," Kate said dryly, "I'd have thought you'd be delighted. We're having a good news day. Look at that; there's your headline. 'Hobgoblin Strikes Again.' "

"Who cares about that creep?" J. Jonah growled. "It's

Spider-Man I'm wondering about. What's he doing inside a nuclear sub in the Port of New York? He could have been doing anything in there!"

"Uh, Mr. Jameson," Peter said gently, "it was Hobby who was doing the 'anything.' Seems he grabbed a trigger for a nuclear missile out of there. You can see it in the shot."

"Maybe," JJJ said, frowning. "But I'm still sure Spider-Man wasn't there just for the good of his health."

Peter thought of the noxious green cloud of gas that had enveloped him inside the sub and silently agreed.

"There's got to be some connection," J. Jonah said. "Hobgoblin and Venom and Spider-Man all in the same day. Are you trying to tell me they're not involved with each other somehow?"

Peter agreed with that too, but not in the way that JJJ thought.

"Look, Jonah," Kate said, "that doesn't matter at the moment. We've got the best picture in town for the *Bugle*'s front page, and we've got time to run it for the first evening edition. I don't care if those two were getting together for their weekly pinochle game, this picture's going to make *us* look good tonight! You have any problems with it?"

Jonah glowered at Kate. "Well, not *that* way, but—"

"Good," she said with satisfied finality. "That wording sound all right to you?"

"Well, it'll do for the moment, but—"

"Good," she said again, even more satisfied, "then we're set." She bent over the shot of Hobgoblin. "Just let me decide how I want to crop this—"

Just then Harry Payne, one of the junior editors on the City Desk, stuck his head around the edge of Kate's door. "Hey, Kate," he said, "something on the scanner you might find interesting."

"Oh? What is it?"

"There's something going on in the rail yards over by 11th Avenue," he said. "I think it's Venom!"

"*What?*" all three of them said, turning, the photographs forgotten.

"That's what it said on the scanner. 'Unidentified person, big, black, huge teeth, drooling slime.' That sounds like Venom to me . . ."

Kate shook her head and grinned. "This is my lucky day," she said. "Peter, don't you move until I can find—" She put her head out the door, looked around for a moment, then shouted down the hall. "Ben? *Ben!* Saddle up! You're needed!" She turned back to Peter. "You go with Ben," she said. "Grab a cab. Go!"

"Let me know how it comes out," Jonah muttered, and stalked off down the hall towards his own office.

Kate watched him go, then glanced at Peter. "You know, I wish I could yell 'Stop the presses!' But it's kind of a problem when you haven't started them yet . . . And what are you still here for? Go *on!*"

Ben Urich was one of the most experienced reporters on the *Bugle*. Peter was uncertain exactly how long he had been in journalism—it might have been thirty years or longer, but there was no telling by looking at him. Ben's age seemed to have frozen at forty-five, a hard-bitten, cool-eyed forty-five that Peter

suspected ~~would hold right where it was until Ben was~~
ninety.

By the time Peter got down to the *Bugle*'s front doors,
it was dark out. Ben was already pacing and looking impatient. He had a cab waiting at the curb. "Come on," he
said, "time's a-wasting!"

Peter jumped into the cab. Ben followed. "Go!" he
told the driver, who took off and went racing through the
traffic.

Ben glanced down at Peter's camera, then pushed his
thick-framed glasses back up the bridge of his nose and
looked at Peter. "That all loaded up?"

"Yup."

"Nervous?"

Peter looked at him sharply. "If what we think is down
at the rail yards is actually there, I'd say we have reason,
wouldn't you?"

Ben raised his eyebrows. "*If* it's what we were told."

"You don't think so?" said Peter.

Ben leaned back in the seat and stretched. "Kind of
hard to tell at a distance. All we've had so far is hearsay,
and extremely odd-sounding hearsay at that."

"Odd-sounding how?"

Ben looked at him, causing his glasses to slip down
again. "As I understood it, Venom isn't much the type
for killing people who don't need it. These days, anyway."

"That's what I'd heard, too," Peter said. "Still, you
don't suppose he could have had a change of heart?"

Ben's mouth quirked, and he pushed his glasses back

up. "People change their minds all the time," he said. "Their hearts—not so often."

"If you can call Venom 'people.' "

"Oh, I don't know," Ben said. "There is a human being in there somewhere."

"There's a lot of difference," Peter said, "between being a human being, and being a man."

Ben raised his eyebrows, looking skeptical. "Semantic difference, mostly," he said. "Anyway, we'll soon find out. Assuming—" and Ben looked even more skeptical "—that the man, creature, or whatever does us the courtesy of hanging around until we get there."

Ben leaned forward and gave the cab driver instructions. They pulled into the pickup and delivery entrance for the rail yards. Overhead, the rail yard's huge yellow sodium lights cast a harsh glare on everything, making the buildings look unreal, like a movie set. The red-and-white strobe of several police cars added to the effect, making the whole place seem like a kaleidoscope.

"Now, then," Ben said, and launched himself out of the cab.

"Your friend meeting somebody?" the cabbie said to Peter, as they both stared at Ben's hurrying back.

"I hope not," Peter said sincerely. Sighing inwardly, he paid the fare and got a receipt. He'd have to put in for reimbursement the next time he was at the *Bugle.*

Then he followed Ben into the guard's shack, a long low building full of file cabinets, a couple of ancient formica-and-aluminum tables, and numerous very upset railroad personnel, many of whom were talking to cops.

155

Ben already had his pocket recorder out and was speaking to one of the supervisors who wasn't giving a statement to the police. "It was this tall," the big blond man was saying, indicating a height at least two feet higher than his own head. "And this wide—"

Peter studied the distance in question and wondered if Venom had put on a great deal of weight. Then again, the costume could change shape. . . .

"Where did you see it first?" Ben said.

"Down by the siding," the foreman said, pointing. "At first I thought it was a cat, moving in the shadows down in the mouth of the tunnel. We have a lot of cats down here, they run in and out all the time. But then it came a little closer, and I got a better look at it—and cats don't get that big. It came sliding out of the tunnel, all black—"

"Black," Ben said. "Did you see any designs, any patterns on it?"

"It had these big long arms—"

"Patterns. Did you see any color on it?" Ben said.

"No, I don't think—that is—" The foreman shook his head. "It moved too fast. That was the trouble. It just came storming out of there all of a sudden, you know? And then there was this train coming down the line at it, and it looked at that, and it roared. It didn't like that—"

"It roared?" Ben said. "It didn't say anything?"

"It just kind of yelled—"

Peter, taking pictures of the man for the "our-witness-tells-us" part of the story, had quite vivid memories of that particular roar. It was usually followed by a statement that Venom intended to have some portion of your anatomy for lunch. "So it roared then," Ben said. "*Then* what did it do?"

One of the other rail workers, a small sandy-haired man who had just finished giving his own statement to the NYPD, said, "He jumped. He jumped away from the train that was coming at him—it was heading into the tunnel—and yeah, like Ron says, he roared at it. But then he stood still. He kind of hunkered down and just looked—"

"Yeah," said a third man, small and dark. "He just looked around him."

"Could you see his eyes?" Ben said.

The three men shook their heads. "Just these blank spots," one said. "Pale," another said. "All white. But when he was in the shade, they glowed a little, you know? Kinda fluorescent."

Peter concentrated on taking more pictures of the three storytellers, while thinking that that odd, faint glow was something he had seen or seemed to see before in the costume—possibly a function of its being alive. He wasn't sure. "It was smelling," the foreman said. "Sniffing."

"You heard it?" Ben said.

"No, no," the three men said, shaking their heads, waving their hands. "It was just the way it looked like—with its head, it sniffed, you know—" One of them put his head up and mimicked something smelling the air, looking alertly from side to side, seeking. "Yeah, and pieces sort of came off it, and swayed around—"

"Came off it?" Ben said. "Came completely off?"

"No, just stretched out, you know?"

"You mean it put tentacles out?"

"Like an octopus, or something like—that's right. They sort of waved all around it, like that, as if it was smelling with them. Like a jellyfish, an octopus, yeah. Do octopuses smell with those?"

"I couldn't help you there," Ben said. "Then what?"

"Well, then," said the sandy-haired man, "another train came up out of the tunnel."

"And it smelled at it," said the small dark man, stretching out his arms and wiggling his fingers at Ben in what Peter assumed was an octopus or tentacle imitation. "And it jumped at it—"

"And it knocked the train over," they all three said, more or less simultaneously.

Ben blinked. "The train. It knocked it *over*?"

"Come on," said the foreman, and he led Ben and Peter out the back door of the building. Behind it was a rust-stained concrete platform, littered with stacks of railroad ties, coils of wire and cable, and some small stacks of track rails further down. From one end of it, to their left, tracks ran down to the railbed. Six tracks ran in parallel here, with two sets of siding on each side.

Between the number one and number two tracks, slewed over on its side, lay the train. Its engine, one of the big Penn Central diesels, had been knocked furthest off the track and now lay diagonally across it, on its right side. The other cars of the train, four of them, had derailed. It looked, Peter thought, as if some giant child had lost patience with his Lionel train set and had given it a good kick between the second and third cars. He started taking pictures as fast as he could, walking down the length of the train, while the railroad workers stopped near the engine with Ben.

"At first we thought it was gonna jump," said the foreman. "But it didn't. It held still, and it crouched down, kinda, and it put out a lot of those arms, tentacles, whatever, and it grabbed the engine—"

"About how fast was the engine going?" Ben said.

The foreman shook his head. "No great shakes. This is restricted-speed track. You can't really open up until you get across the river. About ten miles an hour, maybe."

"Even so. . . ." Ben said. "So a train weighing—how many tons?"

"These diesels are rated for twelve," said the foreman. "It just sort of grabbed the front of the engine—"

"It sort of shied back, shied away a little, when it did that," said the sandy-haired man. "The bell, you know the bell on the diesel goes constantly under fifteen miles an hour—it was going right in front of the guy's face. I don't think it liked that."

Peter's eyebrows went up at that as he continued down the length of the train, snapping images of the huge exposed undercarriages, the wheels in the air. He turned to get another shot of the gesturing men, small beside the huge overturned engine.

"I don't know about that," said the foreman. "I didn't see that. But then it grabbed the engine, and it just hunkered down and"—he shrugged—"wrestled it off the track. Threw it down."

"The engineer's all right?" Ben said.

"Yeah, he climbed out the window when it went over on the other side."

"So it grabbed a twelve-ton train," Ben said slowly, "and pulled it off the track."

"Right," said the small sandy-haired man. "So it stood there a moment, and it smelled around a little more— and then it went straight back to the third car—"

"Ripped the door right off it," said the foreman. "Like cardboard. And then it climbed in, and came out with a little drum of something. An oil drum, I thought at first."

"But not oil," Ben said.

"Nope," said the little sandy-haired man. "It had the 'radioactive' sign on it."

"I pulled the shipping manifest," said the foreman. "Here it is." He reached inside his bright orange work vest, came out with some paperwork.

"Now what's this—" Ben said, pointing down the list. "Uranium hexafluoride—"

Peter came back from down the length of the train and looked over Ben's shoulder at the manifest. "It doesn't go in toothpaste, that's for sure," he said. "It's a by-product from the uranium-enrichment process." He looked up at the foreman. "What did it do with the canister then?"

"It tried to bite it, first," said the foreman, sounding understandably puzzled. "With those teeth, I thought we were going to have a spill right here on the tracks. But it looked like it was having trouble. By then, pretty serious noise had started up—the yard sirens and all—and the warning loudspeakers in the tunnel, all that stuff. It looked around, like it didn't like the noise, and it grabbed the canister in some more of those tentacles and ran off."

"Which way?" Ben said.

The foreman pointed down into the tunnels, into the darkness. "Thataway."

"I take it no one followed it," Ben murmured.

The rail workers looked at him, and all shook their heads. "Hey," one of them said, "we've all got families. I know theft from the rail network is a felony, but—no paycheck's worth *that* much."

The small sandy-haired man looked from Ben to Peter, and back to Ben again. "It was him, wasn't it?" he said. "That Venom guy."

Ben looked at his little pocket recorder, switched it off. "Boys," he said, "I'd be lying if I said it didn't sound like it." The three exchanged nervous glances. "But I want to be sure about this. You didn't see any markings on it? Any white in that black?"

The men shook their heads. "Just the eyes," one said.

"And the teeth!" another said, shivering.

They all stood there in silence for a few. "Well, gentlemen," Ben said, "is there anything else you need to tell me?"

They all shook their heads. "Don't want to see him again," one of them said, "and that's a fact."

"I hope you don't," Ben said. He turned to Peter. "Pete, you got enough pictures?"

"More than enough." He handed Ben the film he'd already shot and unloaded: his camera was whining softly to itself as it rewound the second roll. "Will you take this stuff back with you?" he said. "I've got an appointment tonight that I can't blow off."

"No problem," Ben said. "I see you've had a long day, what with one thing and another. Your photos got page one and two today, Kate tells me." He grinned. "Well," he said to the rail workers, "thanks for your help, gentlemen. If I could get your names and phone numbers for questions later on if we need to ask them?"

They spent a few minutes sorting that out. Then Ben and Peter made their way back up through the guard shack and up onto the street again, where they waited to hail a cab.

"This should make interesting reading in the morning," Ben said, tucking his recorder away.

"What's the headline going to be, you think?" Peter said.

" 'VENOM,' " Ben said, "with a big question mark after it."

"You're still not convinced," Peter said.

Ben shook his head. "I am not. There were a lot of the right signs there, but not all."

"The costume?" Peter said.

Ben nodded. "Partly that. But also—" He shrugged, looking down the street for any sign of the light at the top of a cab. "Venom has always been a very verbal sort. Not the kind to do something and then just leave without saying anything, let alone bragging a little. Every report I've heard has made him out to be a talker. I just don't know. . . ."

Peter nodded. It was good to hear his own thoughts being substantiated this way. Ben was a sharp thinker.

Peter had learned from Daredevil, one of the local costumed crimefighters, that Ben had worked out for himself Daredevil's secret identity from fairly minimal information, when others had had much more and had never made the connection. "Well," Ben said, "J. Jonah may not like it, but I'm not going to construct a story that's not there. I'll report the news as it was reported to me, and let it do the work itself."

Peter nodded. "When you get back in," he said, "if you want to call Alicia down in Comp, she'll take care of the developing—"

Ben snorted. "I know what *she'll* do—she'll send your film around the corner to the one-hour place! You let me take care of it—I'll see that they're properly developed." He smiled slightly at Peter as a cab pulled up in front of them. "Got a hot date with MJ tonight?"

"That, and other things," Peter said. "Thanks, Ben! I appreciate it."

"Have a good evening, youngster," Ben said. He climbed into the cab and was gone.

Peter watched him go, and then made for the shadows, for somewhere private, where he could change into something more comfortable.

Before too long, he was web-slinging along through the dark city streets, making his way from building to building and thinking hard.

Mostly he was turning over a thought which had occurred to him belatedly, after recovering from the craziness last night. He really did have to find out what that radioactive stuff in the warehouses had been. Taken together, those two thefts raised a nasty question: what was Consolidated Chemical Research Corporation doing keeping radioactive material on Manhattan Island, in such insecure circumstances, in two different places? Environmental groups, when they heard, would go ballistic. So would the Environmental Protection Agency, for that matter. Normally, he thought, so would the city. There should be no storage facilities for such stuff within the city boundaries. The material stolen from the train, on the other hand, had been completely aboveboard, destined for the legal storage in one of the deep disused salt mines down south, where nuclear waste was now kept under controlled conditions and federal supervision.

He was determined to take a closer look at CCRC, from the inside if possible. If a little discreet poking around turned up no evidence of wrongdoing, that was fine. But this whole thing smelled pretty fishy to him.

He crossed the city carefully. His spider-sense showed no sign of coming back yet, which made him twitchy. He tried, as he went, to keep watch in all directions. If there was any time for Hobgoblin to hit him and take him unawares, this was it. *Unless Hobby is off busy somewhere this evening*, he thought, *playing with his newfound toy.*

He shook his head. If Hobby was holed up building a bomb. . . . *Something else to look into tomorrow at the paper*, he thought. *Check the database again and see if there have been any other recorded thefts or losses of nuclear material elsewhere in the country. Hobgoblin wouldn't necessarily have to be there himself to steal the stuff. He's not above having it stolen for him. And then*— He frowned under his mask. He would have to sit down and work out exactly what critical mass was when you were working with uranium isotopes. It was not a piece of math he could do in his head, unfortunately. The physics of military fissionables was something he paid little attention to, on general principles. Some of his classmates spent happy afternoons working out engineering solutions and materials criteria for battlefield nukes. But Peter was not one who found such work enjoyable. *I'll take care of it when I get home*, he thought.

Right now, though, the warehouse building from which the radioactive material had been stolen loomed ahead of him, and next to it, the office building which housed CCRC's New York City offices. CCRC's headquarters looked a little seedy, but in good enough repair. The police had the street in front of it and the warehouse cordoned off. Yellow "police line" tape rustled slightly in a slight warm breeze coming off the river, and the cops standing out on the street fanned themselves with their hats. This late, there was little traffic. They looked bored.

All their attention was toward the street, so it was no particular problem for Spidey to swing up from behind the building, let go of his last webline, land against the upper part of the outside wall, and cling there. He held still for a moment, waiting to see if anything had been dislodged by his impact, waiting to see if the police had noticed. They hadn't. Faintly he heard a voice come floating up: "So a guy is crossing the street, and he sees this duck—"

He smiled inside the mask. *A bored cop makes a happy Spider-Man*, he thought, and wall-crawled down the building, testing window after window as he went. Only the lower ones had protective grilles over them. The upper ones were all locked, except for one. *Always some careless person*, he thought, *who doesn't think that Spider-Man might visit their building tonight*. He pushed the window open—it was an old-fashioned sash window—and swung in through it.

His feet came down on thick carpeting. He looked around and saw a heavy walnut desk, with matching office furniture all around. *Very nice*, he thought. *That explains the window, too. Some executive who doesn't want his view spoiled by bars—President's office? Vice-president's? Hmm.* President's, or CEO's, probably; it was a corner office. He looked the place over for signs of alarm systems, saw none. *Very lax—especially when you're involved in* this *industry*.

Silently, Spider-Man stepped up to the door of the office, touched it. No contact alarms, either. No wiring on the door betraying a "reed switch" which would be broken when the door opened. He turned the knob: the door opened, and he found himself looking into an outer office, a secretary's office from the looks of it—nearly two thirds of the size of the office he had just come from, lined with file cabinets all in walnut, more of that thick carpeting on the floor, a big wall unit with a television, sofas, glass tables— a somewhat executive-level waiting room, it seemed, for people seeing the boss. *Now let's see—*

He went over to the file cabinets. These, at least, were

locked, but over time he had become fairly expert at lock-picking. Shortly he had the master lock on the first cabinet open, and was rummaging through the drawers, hunting for anything that seemed interesting.

Several drawers down, he came across what, to judge from the thickness of it, must be the incorporation info for the company itself. He pulled the file out and riffled through it thoughtfully. CCRC turned out to be fairly young. The names of its members of the board could have been from anywhere in New York, but he was interested to note that the majority shareholder was not an American citizen: he was Ukrainian.

He worked backwards to the date the company was formed. *The Soviet Union would have just fallen—*

After turning up nothing else of great interest, he put the file back where he had found it. But ideas were stirring in his mind, nonetheless. *One of the things they've been having trouble with in that part of the world*, he thought, *is radioactive material being smuggled out and sold cheap. What was that one report I heard?— how two guys took a near-critical mass of U-235 out of Russia in the trunks of two cars, and wound up abandoning them on the Autobahn in Germany because they misjudged the distance to Berlin, and ran out of gas?* He shook his head. Not everyone dealing in radioactives from behind the former Iron Curtain was that stupid.

He started going slowly and with care through drawer after drawer. There were a lot of file envelopes with English labels, which, when he opened them, he found contained pages and pages of stuff typed in Cyrillic. He *tsk*ed at himself. MJ had been teasing him for some time now about getting so singleminded about the sciences that he was letting the humanities pass him by, the languages especially. Russian was one of the languages she suggested he take—"Because it's one of the hardest," she had said, looking at him as if the sense of that reason should be obvious. Now he wondered whether he should have taken her advice. But Cyrillic or not, digits were the same. Some of the files he looked at, as he went through the drawers, were plainly shipping manifests of some kind: lists of figures, amounts in rubles and equivalent amounts in dollars—that much he could make out plainly. A lot of currency transactions, in fact, and a lot of changeovers from rubles to deutschemarks, and here and there a document turned up in what looked like German.

He was only marginally better at reading German than he was at Russian, but at least here the alphabets were mostly the same. More amounts in deutschemarks appeared, along with references to weights and masses, always in tens or hundreds of kilograms. And here and there, the German word for "nuclear," which he had come to recognize during his doctorate work, having seen it often enough in the titles of dissertations and articles in journals. The names of the transuranic elements were also just about the same in German as in English, and he came across repeated references to U-235, U-238, and the German word for "enriched" U-235—

Each time it was mentioned, somewhere nearby was a column of figures which made it plain that money was changing hands. But nowhere in all those documents did he see anything like a customs stamp or a bill of sale authorized by any government—and governments had to authorize such sales, as far as he knew.

This place, he thought, *is a front, almost certainly, for smuggling the stuff around. The conditions under which they've been keeping it downstairs seem to confirm it. Those canisters had the barest minimum of labeling. They were being kept clandestinely—*

He shut the files, tidied up after himself as best he could, and looked thoughtfully at the computer on the secretary's desk. *Not networked: a stand-alone. Might have some interesting files in it.* He moved toward the desk.

From downstairs, in the body of the building, he heard a single, hollow booming sound. A door shutting? He froze, listening hard.

The sound repeated itself, just once. *Boom.*

I think I'm just going to look into that. First of all, though, I want a look at that wall next door.

He stepped to the outer office door, silently let himself out, looked up and down the hall. Nobody.

He started looking for a door exiting to a stairwell. At the end of the corridor, he found one, opened it, slipped out, anchored a webline to one of the stair railings, and let himself down, slowly and silently, as far as the well reached: about six stories. When he let go, he found himself looking at a door with a large letter L on it. *Loading?* he thought, holding still, listening. Somewhere in the building, that soft, low *boom* sounded again, much closer—

This level? he thought. *Well, let's have a look.*

Softly he pulled the door open and peered through it. Nothing: a dark first-floor loading area, as he had expected, pillars supporting the ceiling, plain bare concrete floor—and, off to one side, a hole in the wall, with slumped, crumbling-looking edges. Much nearer to him, though, was a big hole in the floor. Its edges had the same look as those of the hole in the wall, and of the picture he'd seen on TV of the warehouse's wall. That hole would be just across the alley from this one, he thought, glancing up.

What the heck are they up to in here?

That booming noise came again. *Might be the police,* he thought. *Might be a good time to excuse myself.* But that hole in the floor, the size of it, the look of it, drew him.

He stepped carefully to its edge and looked down. It gave directly into a big brick-lined sewer tunnel which ran beneath this building. A faint smell of sewage floated up out of it. *Radiation,* he thought, *could definitely cause a hole like this—if it was tremendously intense, tremendously confined—causing the material to come apart out of sheer fatigue. A good push would break it at after such treatment.*

Boom.

It is *the police, I bet. Well, I'm going to get out of here.* He went hurriedly to the hole in the wall, looked hastily up and down the alley. The yellow police tapes fluttered a bit down at the far end. Being inside them, he had no one impeding him. The coast was clear, so he slipped hurriedly across the alley, through the hole in the far wall, and into the warehouse where the homeless man had died.

The place stank of blood. It was drying, but not fast enough in this humidity, and the place had a dark, desolate feel, very much like the lower level of the next building over. There was nothing to see here.

Boom.

Not in the other building: in *this* one. Possibly a door opening and shutting in the wind? He turned—and saw the dark shape loom out of the shadows, almost directly behind him. There would have been no warning from his spider-sense even if it had been working at the moment. The dark shape, tall, broad-shouldered, fangs like a shark's dream of heaven, splitting in a grin of unholy glee, and the white stylized spider-shape splashed across the chest.

Spider-Man launched himself at Venom and was astounded a second later when Venom merely backhanded him away. The backhand by itself was more than powerful enough to slam Spider-Man into the wall near the big hole, and leave him reeling for a moment.

"We might have thought," said the low, menacing voice, angry but also oddly amused, "that you at least might have learned never to judge by appearances."

Spider-Man leapt again, and this time Venom's dreadful fangs parted in a smile that went so far around the back of his head, the top should have fallen off. Two-handed, he clubbed Spider-Man sideways again, and this time he stepped back. Spidey flew ten feet or so through the air, came down hard on the concrete floor, but rolled and sprang up again. There he crouched, taking a breath to get his composure back.

"I don't care about the smooth talk, Eddie," Spider-Man said, looking for the best place to attack. "Whatever else may be going on, you're a fugitive—"

"Whatever else," Venom said softly. "Then you have some odd suspicions, too."

"Suspicions? About what?"

"That we would never be involved in such as what happened—here." Some of the awful grin faded as Venom looked around him with distaste. "Someone," he said, "did murder here, in our name." He looked sideways at Spider-Man. "And we are not amused."

"Now why should I believe you?" Spidey said.

Venom simply looked at him, folding his arms. "Because you know us?"

Spider-Man breathed in, breathed out. "You've got me there," he said.

"So," said Venom, "you will forgive us for the moment if we choose not to permit your infantile attempts to apprehend us." He chuckled nastily, and the symbiote for its part took the opportunity to wave that horrendous slime-laden tongue at Spider-Man, *wuggawuggawugga*, in straightforward mockery. "Later on we'll have leisure to joint you and nibble the bones. But right now, we have other matters to attend to."

"Is 'we' you or is 'we' us?"

Venom paused a moment, then chuckled again. "A college education just isn't what it used to be, is it? 'We' is us—I think. At least, any information you can share with us will be welcome. Someone here," Venom said, looking darkly around at the spattered walls, "someone here is trying to frame us for the deaths of these innocents—and when I catch them, both for the attempted framing, and for the murders, we shall certainly eat their spleen."

Spider-Man sighed in brief annoyance. "Listen," he said, "hearts, livers, even lungs I could see. But spleens? Have you ever even *seen* a spleen? I bet you don't even know where it *is*."

"We could find out," Venom said, looking at him speculatively, and that grin went right around his head again. "It would be fun."

"I thought you said you didn't want to do that right now."

"Don't tempt us. Part of us still desires to make peace with you in the most final manner. But that's going to have to wait. We have done some preliminary research on the firm which owns this property and the one next door. Its clandestine associations make us very uneasy."

"The smuggling, you mean," Spidey said.

"You deduced that? Very good."

"Nothing as fancy as deduction," Spider-Man said. "I just went through their files. Their paperwork is lousy with deutschemark and ruble transfers."

"Yes," Venom said. "That would seem to argue a busy trade across the former East German border. Possibly also the hiring of old East German scientific talent for some purpose. There is a lot of that going very cheap now, I hear. Russian as well."

"And Ukrainian," Spider-Man said.

Venom nodded. "The owners." He glowered back at the hole in the wall. "A sordid business, but one with which we would not normally concern ourselves. In our normal haunts, we have other concerns these days."

"You mean that cave under San Francisco?" Spidey said.

Venom eyed him. "It is an underworld," he said, "though not the kind that's usually meant by the term. People who've taken refuge in a part of the city buried and abandoned in the earthquake eighty years ago. We protect them." For a moment there was just a tinge of pride in the voice.

"It's always nice to have a purpose," Spider-Man said, "besides eating people's spleens."

Venom sighed. "You are an insolent puppy," he said. "But you're right about the purpose. There is worthwhile work to be done, down where the innocents have taken refuge from a world too cruel for them. Noble work, building them a better world than the one they've fled."

"I won't argue that," Spider-Man said.

"You'll understand, then," Venom said, gazing around him coldly at the spattered walls, "that all this—" he gestured around with several tendrils "—will sully our image. Whoever is masquerading as us will be unmasked, swiftly, and will pay terribly for the crime."

"Look," Spider-Man said, inching closer, "I understand that this makes a sort of image problem for you. But a lot of other people have had problems with you and that suit. A lot of them haven't survived them. So you'll understand if I have to cut short the chat, and at least try to take you in—"

That was when they heard the voice from outside. "Charley? Charley, is that you down there, or Rod?"

"Nope, Rod's down here," came another voice.

"Then who's in the building?"

Spider-Man and Venom looked at each other, shocked. It was the police this time.

"You'll forgive us," Venom said, "if we don't wait around for whatever it is you're planning to try now. If you cross our path again, Spider-Man—don't cross *us*. We're on business." And he leaped out the hole in the wall and upward into the darkness.

"Rod, you see that?" came the voice from down the alley. The sound of running footsteps followed it almost immediately.

Yeesh, Spider-Man thought, and shot a webline to expedite his departure and chase down Venom.

"There's another one!" the cry went up. "Get him!"

In the alley, Spider-Man looked and saw cops coming at him from both left and right. He shot a line of web up and out, and went up it just as fast as he could, shooting another line across to the CCRC building and then swinging out past it, around a corner and away, just as fast as he could. As he went, he scanned desperately for any sign of Venom, but there was none to see. *Of course*, Spider-Man thought, *he's immune to my spider-sense— even when it is working—*and *he can make himself look like anyone. I could be staring right at him and not even know it.*

Reluctantly, he started making his way home. The lights were on in the apartment when he got there. He found MJ just dropping her purse on the front table, and bending over the answering machine to get the messages. She looked up with delight at him as he swung in one of the windows which she had just thrown open. "Hey, tiger," she said, "how was your day?"

He pulled off his mask and shook his head, went to her and hugged her. "Not like yours, I bet."

"I bet," she said, stroking his hair. "Listen—get changed and get something to eat inside you. We've got to talk."

He was tired enough at the moment not to argue with her. He changed, and made a sandwich, and ate it—and made another, and ate it. Then they sat down and she told him about her day.

When she was finished, Peter was still blinking from the news that radiation sickness was being reported in the city. While trying to put this together with other facts, he told her about his day, in some detail. MJ's eyes widened considerably when he told her about his conversation with Captain LoBuono, and they widened more yet when he told her about the hole in the sub's wall. Afterwards, his tale of meeting Venom in the warehouse seemed almost anticlimactic.

"Wow," MJ breathed when he had finished. She looked at him, shaking her head. "There's our riddle for today, then. What goes through walls, and likes radioactive stuff, and isn't Venom . . . and is loose in New York? And comes from another planet."

"It's the first stuff that's our problem," Peter said, leaning back on the couch. "In this town, who cares if you're local? But now we have to figure out what to do next."

SIX

T
hey stayed up late that night talking. There was a
lot to be gone over; a lot more news than a few
minutes' worth of conversation could hope to deal
with. And additionally, just because of business,
they hadn't had a lot of time to see each other over the
past few days. So there was a prolonged period of hug-
ging, snuggling, smooching, and general touchy-feely
before they got back on the subject again.

"Slow down with the sandwiches, tiger," MJ muttered, amused, "save some for me." She headed into the
kitchen, Peter close behind her. His stomach growled.
"You've *been* eating!" she said. "I can't believe you can
still be hungry!"

"You haven't had the day I've had," Peter said again
and smiled slightly.

"Oh, haven't I? I may not have been swinging all over
the city, but boy, do I feel grateful for food right now.
And a place to sleep." She cocked an eye at him as she
started rummaging in the refrigerator. "Which is something *you* should start thinking about fairly soon. Look at
the bags under your eyes!"

"Bags or no bags, I couldn't sleep right now if you hit
me with a hammer. I've got too much on my mind."

"That's the problem with you," said MJ. "You wouldn't
know what to do if you didn't have something on your
mind. Just imagine it for a moment." She shut the refrigerator door and looked at him challengingly. "Imagine a
twenty-four-hour period when everything's working.
When the rent's paid, and the phone bill's paid, the elec-
tricity's paid, and you've got a credit balance in your

checking account, and no checks have bounced, and the credit card company is happy—"

Peter opened his mouth.

"Hush," she said, "I'm on a roll." He shut it again. "Where was I . . . ? Oh yes. And there are no super-villains tearing the joint up, and no crime—"

"Are you sure this is Earth you're talking about?" said Peter, raising his eyebrows at her. "Gimme that mayonnaise."

"Nothing for you until I'm finished," she said, standing with her back to the refrigerator door, blocking his way. "Think about it. Just—" She put out one hand and pushed him back, then waved a finger under his nose. "Go on, try it. Stand still for a moment and imagine it. One whole day, just one, when everything's all right."

He stood still, and tried, and found it a bit of a strain. "All right," he said. "So?"

"Well, don't just imagine the events. Imagine how you'd *feel*."

Peter looked at her and shook his head. "I have to confess," he said, "that I don't have a clue. I don't believe that it's ever going to happen."

MJ sighed and moved away from the refrigerator. "You'll never get there," she said, "because you can't— or won't—see all of that as something worth imagining. My money says that if it ever actually got that quiet, you'd go nuts. I'd give it about an hour, and then you'd go out into the street and shanghai the first super-villain you saw and beg him to start a fight with you."

"I'd do no such thing," Peter said. "I'd sleep. For about a week, and not get up. I presume this wonderful world we're imagining means I don't have to go into work?"

MJ shook her head. "Oh, no. I know you better than that. Work? If you didn't have to do it, if money didn't drive you to it, you'd *dance* into it. You'd be all over this town, taking pictures of everything that moved—and everything that didn't. The film bill alone—"

"A-*ha*!" Peter said triumphantly. "Something to worry about. Now give me the mayonnnaise."

"Here," MJ said in a lordly manner, stepping away from the fridge and getting a loaf of bread. "Take your mayonnaise." She handed him the jar, which hadn't been in the refrigerator after all. "Listen to me, tiger. You're missing my point. I really think sometimes that the way you keep yourself busy, the way there's always something or somebody to run after, always something important to do, is just that. A way to *keep* yourself busy so you don't have to stop and think about things."

"Like what?" Peter laughed. "Is that bologna still in there?"

"Forget the bologna. . . . it looks like a science experiment."

"Let me see."

"I wouldn't, if I were you," said MJ. "Certainly not just before you eat."

"All right then. What is else is there?"

"No more salami. We've finished that. Some sliced chicken?"

"Okay." He rooted around for it, noted the bologna in passing, rolled his eyes, and shut the fridge again. Then he went over to the counter and started constructing his sandwich. MJ got out a cup, filled it with water, and put it in the microwave to boil. She spent a silent moment rummaging in the cupboard and then said, "I'm thinking about the creature on the sub."

Peter nodded, spreading mayo on the bread. "So am I."

"They wouldn't tell you where they found it?"

"Nope. The captain said it wasn't dangerous." Peter laughed. "Well, not in so many words. He implied it, or at least let it be implied. I don't know about you, but I would normally call something that could go straight through the hull of a nuclear submarine close enough to 'dangerous' to make no difference. I think they're worried. And if it was in that warehouse, and if it killed that homeless guy, then it's already meeting my usual definition."

MJ paced in front of the microwave. "He did say that the thing wasn't radioactive."

"So he *said*."

"Then how did it make that hole in the hull? And in the wall of the warehouse, and in the floor there."

Peter had been chasing around those questions as well. "I don't know," he admitted. "Radiation alone can crumble concrete like that after a few years."

"But how can this—whatever it is—do that *without* being radioactive?"

Peter shook his head. "I'm thinking that Captain LoBuono's higher-ups were economical with the truth when they briefed him on what he was carrying. It may not be radioactive all the time, just under certain circumstances—and I can't even begin to guess what those might be." Peter's voice trailed off as he tried to put the jumble of theories into a coherent form. "Maybe it's immune to radiation, the way snakes are supposed to be immune to their own venom."

MJ raised her eyebrows. "Not my favorite word just at the moment," she said. "He *is* here, then?"

"Oh, he's here, all right. Though he didn't seem particularly interested in me."

MJ sniffed. "I suppose we should be grateful for small favors." The microwave went off. MJ got her cup, put it on the counter and started hunting through one of the cupboards for a teabag. "What gets me," she said, dunking the teabag up and down and watching the way the hot water darkened, "is this thing looking like Venom. If it really *is* the same thing that got out of the sub."

Peter made a wry face as he took a bite of his sandwich. The face had nothing to do with the way it tasted. "It gets Venom, too, from the sound of it. But I suppose it's not *entirely* unlikely. From what the others tell me, there's an awful lot of bipedal, more-or-less humanoid life in this arm of the galaxy."

The others was his blanket term for the various super heroes, super-powerful beings, and all the other oddities in and out of costumes that he ran into during the course of his work as Spider-Man. One theory was that one species, many, many millions of years ago, seeded this part of the galaxy with similar genetic material. All the carbon-based planets, anyway. Some others, among them Reed Richards, said that there was no need to postulate a *species ex machina*—that for carbon-based life, the bipedal pattern was merely logical and tended to recur. Whatever the reason, the approximately upright bipedal form with bilateral symmetry was common enough that he had grown used to seeing it in the most unlikely places. And maybe he was growing used to seeing what he *expected* to see.

"My problem is, I need to know what this thing wants. And what to do about it."

"If it's the same thing that came out of the sub," MJ said, "then what it wants seems to be radiation. But why would something that wasn't radioactive itself be attracted to a radioactive source?"

"I'm not sure," Peter said. He took another bite from his sandwich. "I keep thinking of the train worker who said the first thing it tried to do was gnaw the canister open. Then there was the homeless guy from the warehouse, who claimed he saw it licking the stuff up off the floor." He caught an escaping dribble of mayonnaise with his finger and popped it in his mouth, then looked at his finger as if it held the secrets to the universe. "Biting and licking—like I'm doing with this sandwich! Maybe it wants this radioactive material to *eat*." He looked at the chicken sandwich, still dripping mayo from the two big semicircular bites he had taken out of it, and felt his appetite suddenly disappear. He put the remnants down and wiped his fingers on a paper towel, then folded his arms and leaned back in the chair so that its front legs left the floor. "It's an interesting question," he said. "What kind of creature eats radioactive material, but doesn't hold any detectable trace of radiation in its body?" He thought a moment. "*If* it doesn't. Captain

LoBuono said that it had to be kept sealed away with radiation because of its habits." He looked sideways at MJ.

MJ sat down and started dunking the teabag in her cup again. "I keep thinking of gremlins. Or tribbles. What if feeding enables it to breed?"

Peter shuddered. "Don't even suggest it. If that thing reproduces, we've got real trouble on our hands. Can you imagine a bunch of those things running around, eating everything radioactive in sight? And the most obvious place for them to start would be the hospitals, looking for X-ray isotopes."

MJ dropped her teabag onto a nearby saucer. "You're so good at imagining the nasty things," she said, "and no good at all at imagining the good ones! There's a definite problem there."

"We'll deal with that later," Peter said. "But its metabolism . . . Everything has to get energy from somewhere. We tend to think of living things getting energy from food, or from sunlight if they're plants. But what if you had a life form that started out one way and was forced to adapt? To change from what we think of as normal sources of nutrition," he eyed the sandwich again, "and resort to a direct transfer of raw energy."

He stood up, paced around the table, then sat down again. "I'm not even an ordinary biologist, never mind a xenobiologist. This stuff isn't my strong suit, and it's giving me a headache. But radioactivity I know a little about. If there was a life-form that has the physical structure of a living nuclear reactor—" He shuddered.

MJ looked at him sympathetically. "Then maybe you need to ask for advice from somebody who *does* know about that kind of thing. Try Reed Richards. He's always been able to give you some sort of answer before. Why not now?"

"Because right now I don't even know if he's in town. And there's so much other stuff to do. I've got to do some more checking into these CCRC people, and then there's Venom, and there's Hobgoblin—"

"It occurs to me," MJ said, "that if Venom runs into this whatever-it-is that looks like him, there's going to be an almighty ruckus."

Peter nodded grimly. "Yeah. Probably right in the middle of the city, as usual. And in broad daylight. Venom doesn't wait for anything if he thinks the moment's right. Patience isn't something he's good at. And then I have to go after him. I can't just stand by and watch him waltz through and not do something about it." His voice trailed off and he rubbed at his shoulder, still sore from where he had gone crashing into the wall earlier on.

MJ saw the gesture. She walked around behind him and started rubbing his shoulders. "Do you know," she said conversationally, "how many tubes of Ben-Gay we've gone through since we got married?" Peter looked at her, completely confused. "Eighty-six," she said. "Deep Heat, Mentholatum, you name it. Every time I go to the grocery store, I have to buy more. The guy in the Gristede's asks me if I put it in my tea or something."

Peter's only reply was a groan of ecstasy as his wife rubbed the kinks out of his shoulders. He poked at the sandwich, decided not to waste it, and demolished it in about three or four bites.

MJ ceased the shoulder rub and said, "Your spider-sense still isn't back, I take it."

"Nope. It's possible I just got a really heavy dose of whatever Hobby was using last time."

MJ looked at him sadly. "You think that it's gone for good," she said. "At least, that's what's worrying you." He looked at her and she smiled a little, one-sided. "Do you seriously think you can hide that kind of thing from me at this point? I can recognize your 'brave face' at fifty paces. Wait a little longer and just watch your step. That sense is so much a part of your powers that when everything else is still working fine, I can't imagine it's going to be gone for long."

Peter smiled back at her. "It doesn't necessarily follow," he said, "but for the moment, I like your explanation better than any of the ones that I've got. And as for Hobby, he *will* strike again. If he doesn't do it tonight, it'll be tomorrow. And I can't do anything about tonight, because if I don't sleep, I'm going to fall over."

"You got *that* right," MJ said. "You are not leaving this house, no matter *what* happens between now and 8 A.M." Her eyes glinted. "I have plans for you."

"Oh, boy!" Peter said, and meant it, even though he was still somewhat distracted. "Anyway, as for Hobby. I really doubt that he's going to get any more stuff from any more warehouses. Anybody who's running an illegal trade in radioactives in this town will have noticed what's been happening, and they'll have slapped extra security on whatever they've got. So I think we can rule out CCRC or anyone else like them. Which leaves the legal sources." He frowned slightly. "They'll be raising their security levels too, but increased security hasn't stopped Hobby in the past. And I doubt it'll stop him tomorrow. Or the day after. So I'm going to have to do some patrolling myself."

"Do you have a good guess as to where he's going to be?" MJ said.

Peter nodded. "The only big *legal* nuclear research facility in New York right now is at ESU. There's enough material of the kind Hobby will want on campus for him to try making a grab. There's always somebody on the inside who'll talk about where things are for money, or fear . . . Hobby has a gift for finding people like that. If he doesn't know already where something is, he's going to find out soon."

"And what kind of luck are *you* going to have at finding out where things are?" MJ said.

He yawned, and stretched until his joints went click, then grinned at MJ. "Oh, I'll do all right. Tomorrow I'll stop by the lab, chat with some people, pick up on the gossip, hear what's going on."

"And do a little judicious inveigling of information?" MJ said.

"Oh yeah. I'm sure I can find out what I need to know. Because Hobby will turn up. I'm sure he will."

MJ was sipping her tea again, and looking thoughtful. "What about Venom?" she said.

"One thing at a time, please! I don't think it's a headache at all. I think my *brain* hurts."

"That's it," MJ said, pushing the teacup to one side. "A nice hot tub for you, and your sore head, and your sore muscles. And I'm getting in with you."

"Ooh!" Peter said, grinning at her. "Lucky me!" He got up, wincing at the bone-deep aches he had been trying to ignore, and followed her down the hall.

Next morning, after checking the papers and the news to make sure that nothing untoward had happened during the night, Peter betook himself to the groves of academe.

Empire State University was located in Greenwich Village. The main building was an old structure, full of little rooms tucked off into odd nooks and crannies. One tiny broom closet into which Peter had found his way looked down through a small window over at the Science Building. There were endless ways for a Spider-Man, or other unauthorized person, to sneak into or out of ESU's campus, if that person knew where those ways were. And if you were expecting someone who didn't know the ins and outs, you could make their welcome a very interesting one, indeed.

The new annex out back was not nearly so architecturally inspiring as the main building, built as it was during a period when being functional was deemed more important than being stately, but it too had its advantages. Over his years of study, Peter had had plenty of leisure to observe where its ducts went, which grilles led into which part of the air-conditioning system, what roof spaces gave onto rooms through utility traps or openings to attic storage space. A clever and determined person could stay out of sight and out of mind for a long time up in those empty spaces—moving from place to place, keeping an eye on things. That was what Peter had in mind for Spider-Man. But first, he had some things to take care of which Spider-Man couldn't manage with impunity and Peter Parker could.

He headed up the big marble steps, through the front hall and the body of the main building, finally on out the back door to the little square which separated the main building from the annex.

The annex was all very sixties-academic—plate glass, aluminum, and solid blocks of color. Somebody with a strange taste for modern art had erected, in the middle of the square, something which purported to be a stainless steel Tree of Life. The science students claimed that, on moonlit spring nights, coeds danced around it scattering ball bearings. At most other seasons of the year, the thing was festooned with toilet paper. Everyone hated it.

Peter went up the shallower set of steps by the science building, paused by the bulletin board inside the front doors, and looked to see if anything interesting had been posted. This time of year, between the active semesters, there was nothing much to be seen but some outdated flyers about parties, and a university directory of Internet e-mail addresses that had probably been out of date by the end of the week it had been posted. Far down on one page of it, someone had scribbled, FOR A GOOD TIME, CALL PI 3 -1417. . . .

Peter went off to the right, where a stairwell led to the classrooms on the second floor, and a door in the wall stood underneath it. This was where the Nuclear Physics department was, for the simple reason that most of the equipment was too heavy to be put any higher.

The door under the stairs was not a swinging door, like most of the others in the building, but required a key to open. Peter pulled his key out of his pocket and let himself in. All the instructors and doctoral and degree students working in Nuke had the keys: they weren't exactly difficult to lay hands on. But that door was a boundary of sorts. Here the construction of the building changed, got abruptly heavier and more solid. Walls were thicker, and in the hall behind the door a wall jutted out into the corridor, covering two-thirds of its width from the left side out. About five feet further on, another wall did the same from the right side. It was good old-fashioned radiation safety. Should some kind of accident occur inside, radiation couldn't just stream through the door and out. The construction and look of it was very fallout-shelterish, and every now and then it brought back Peter's childhood memories of crouching under his desk at school with his hands over his head during atomic war drills. What was the old song? "Duck and Cover?" *A lot of good it would have done us at ground zero*, he thought as he went past the baffle.

He headed on through to the classroom and lab area. The place was utterly quiet. It felt that way even in mid-semester. The machinery here didn't need heavy air-conditioning: most of the machines had few or no moving parts. But the whole place, clean and light and bright as it looked, held a slight edge of threat, of silent power, usable by some, misusable by others, waiting to see which way it would go.

The door at the very end of the downstairs hall was the one Peter was heading for. It, too, was locked. The same key opened it as had opened the outer door.

He put his head in. As he'd hoped, lights were on,

shining on the big closed cabinets, the blocky silent machines. "Hello?" he said.

"Yo!" came a familiar woman's voice from the back. "Who's that?"

"Peter Parker."

"Good lord, the wandering boy returns!" the voice half-sang from the back of the room. A cheerful face with blonde hair drawn tightly back in a ponytail peered at him around a room divider.

"Dawn," Peter said. "How're you doing?"

"Not too bad," Dawn said. "Catching up on work—" She put unusual emphasis on the word as she grinned wickedly at him. Peter was hoping that Dawn Mc-Carter—no, Dawn Luks her name was now; he kept forgetting she was married, though it had been more than a year—would still be around working on her dissertation. She was a doctoral candidate in Nuclear Physics, and had one of the quickest, brightest minds he had ever seen, able to move within a second from a learned discussion of supercollider physics to going "ooji-ooji-ooji" at her new daughter. Speaking of whom, he noticed Dawn's baby girl sitting in her carrier on the floor, waving a pink-and-white star-and-heart chew-toy in front of her face, and occasionally giving it a good gumming. "I see you got stuck with the baby this time," he said.

"Ron's deep into work-on-the-computer mode. The kid could drop dead in front of him and he wouldn't notice. Since I'm just polishing off the dissertation work, I figured I'd take her in here for the next week or so. God knows we can't afford a sitter on our stipends. How's MJ? What's she up to, these days?"

"Just fine. She's doing the audition circuit right now."

"What brings you in?" she said. "Didn't think I'd see you until the fall."

"Oh, well, I'm supposed to be meeting with my advisor, but he's running a bit late."

Dawn laughed. "So what else is new?"

Peter wandered around the room. There was a lot of big, bulky, expensive, and difficult-to-move machinery in here. One large installation on the side, a glove-box with three sets of waldoes for working with sensitive material behind leaded glass and concrete. Next to it, a big lead safe for storing radioactive material, with a smaller one beside it; various light sensing equipment here and there; and over in the far corner, about twenty feet away, the thing he was most concerned about, and which Dawn was working with: the casings and materials fabrication unit. After all, you couldn't just carry nuclear material around in a lunchbox, you had to build containers according to the requirements of the sample in question, to handle its specific level of radiation, and to suit the application for which it was to be used. It was a combination isolation box and machine shop, all very compactly made. The whole thing was no more than four feet square, and it had occurred to Peter that, if Hobby were going to steal something at this point, this might very well be it. It would be difficult to move, but far from impossible.

Dawn was busy inside it at the moment, putting the final touches on a small lead-lined carrier box. "For sushi, right?" Peter said, looking over her shoulder through the leaded glass.

"Idiot," Dawn said affectionately. "Here, amuse the rugrat while I'm working on this."

"Hey there, gorgeous," Peter said, hunkering down beside the baby, "how ya doing?" The baby took the chew-toy out of her mouth, looked at it thoughtfully, and offered it to Peter.

"No, thanks," he said, "I'm trying to cut down." He let the baby grab his finger in her fist and shook it around a little. She gurgled.

He turned back towards the blond. "So how goes the dissertation, anyhow? It was something to do with transuranic superconductors, wasn't it?" As he stood up from beside the baby, he palmed one of the spider-tracers from his pocket and stuck it unobtrusively near the bottom of the fabricator unit.

"Yeah," Dawn said, not actually looking at Peter, engrossed as she was. "Most of the papers were saying the lanthanide connection wasn't turning out to be very productive . . . so I decided to try some of the higher transuranics, and see if sandwiching them together with one of the higher-temp superconductors would produce any results."

"Which one were you playing with?" While he spoke, Peter wandered away from the box and headed over to the safes.

"Americium, mostly."

Peter grinned. "Why don't you just try holding water in a sieve? As I recall, that stuff has a half-life shorter than your kid's attention span."

Dawn grunted. "This *is* a problem. With a ten-hour half-life, you might well invent a revolutionary superconductor compound, but if you go to lunch at the wrong time you miss it, and the results are dang near impossible to replicate. Oh, well, if that doesn't work"—and Peter saw her grin—"I might try something simpler, like cold fusion."

Peter chuckled. "I can see your point. Well, I hope it works out," Peter said. "You've got to graduate from this place before *she* starts her freshman year, or people will talk. Anything new in here?"

"Not that I've seen," Dawn said absently. "They took out most everything but the project stuff in there."

"So I see," Peter said, his eye falling on a series of little lead canisters all labeled "americium tetrafluoride." There were enough canisters that Dawn wasn't likely to miss one of them, and each was small enough that it would get the attention of anything that liked radiation. Fighting down a twinge of guilt, he palmed one of the canisters, and tucked it in his pocket without Dawn seeing.

Then he leaned over and placed two more tracers on the shelf containing the canisters and on the bottom of the bigger safe. "So, Dawn," he said, "when are you going to come have dinner with us?"

"Oh, Pete, you know how it is," she muttered, still intent on what she was doing in the fabricator. "It's all I can do to drag Ron away from the computers—or his baby daughter." She smiled. "Maybe you ought to make a date with *her*."

"Better not," Peter said, straightening up. "MJ would get after me for chasing younger women. Listen, if I don't see you before then, I'll see you when classes start again, huh?" He waved at the baby. "Bye, gorgeous!"

"Urgle," she commented as he shut the door behind him.

A short while later he was changed into his spider-suit and entered the ducts of the science building. He had leisure to think about a lot of things as he moved stealthily from place to place, checking the ducts to see that they were as he remembered them, peering into this room, out that window. How he really needed to call Aunt May, how he had forgotten to pick up the Woolite again, about many other things. But none of them could quite take his mind away from the little lead canister webbed at his waist. The skin under it itched.

He knew, of course, that there was no possibility of the substance in the canister causing the itch. The canister was solid, the radioactivity inside was fairly low. Nonetheless, he imagined he felt it.

Very slowly, afternoon shaded into evening. Offices started to be locked, lights began turning off, and people went off to dinner. Thinking that a view from outside might be wiser than a view of the inside, Spider-Man took this opportunity to make his way cautiously out of the ducts and back up into the main building, into the little broom closet that looked down on the annex. Its grimy window, when you pushed the sash up, would be more than big enough to let him out. Inside it, he couldn't be seen. He waited there, while the shadows lengthened and leaned toward dusk—

—and something twinged inside him, just faintly, just once: the taste of danger coming.

The chemical has worn off, Spider-Man thought happily. His pulse started to pick up. *My spider-sense is returning!* He didn't even mind that the faint tingle meant trouble was coming.

Outside the window, he heard that faint telltale whine of very small, very sophisticated jet engines.

He couldn't even wait for it to get completely dark, he thought. *Impatient cuss.*

Spidey leaned forward to watch the jetglider settle into the courtyard, with the eerie shape of Hobgoblin standing on top of it. His back was to Spider-Man.

"It's showtime!" Spidey said softly to himself as, very gently and very quietly, he eased the little window open.

Now this is going to be interesting, Spidey thought. While the Nuclear floor of that building had windows, they were very few and small. Most of the light came in via glass brick. Hobby, though, seemed undaunted. He jockeyed the jetglider around to the rear end of the building, where the least important equipment was sited, and very straightforwardly flung a pumpkin-bomb at the outside wall.

A tremendous explosion shook the building, and the rear wall fell away in ruins. Alarms started ringing, but Hobby obviously didn't care about those. He zipped in through the opening.

Just as I thought, Spider-Man thought as he leapt from the open window and swung across the courtyard. *Somebody told him where things were. What to worry about damaging, what not to care about.*

Hurriedly, Spider-Man began webbing almost the entire outside of the building, except for the opening

Hobby had blown in the back side. The webbing was in the garden-spider tradition, a fairly fine-meshed network anchored to the ground all around. Spidey leapt and bounced from place to place, very glad that he had restocked his web-shooters earlier in the day. When all the rest of that side of the building was covered, he went to the hole and threw a similar webbing across it. He was barely half done when Hobgoblin appeared on his jetglider. He hovered behind the web mesh, staring at Spider-Man with a look of shock on his face.

Spidey was slightly shocked, too, for Hobby had cabled the bigger safe to the bottom of his rocket sled, and to Spidey's astonishment, the jetglider was actually managing to lift the thing off the ground.

"All right, Hobby," Spider-Man said as calmly as he could. "Put it back where you found it."

Hobgoblin's incredulous expression didn't last long. A nasty grin spread over his face. "Surely you jest, Spider-Man," he said, laughing. He pulled out another pumpkin-bomb and lobbed it casually at the nearest wall.

There was another huge explosion. Brick and broken pieces of equipment flew in all directions, and Spider-Man felt a moment's extreme unhappiness over how much it was all going to cost to replace. "Ta-ta, bug," said Hobby as the smoke cleared, and without hesitation, he and his jetglider zoomed straight at the hole he had made.

He should have hesitated. As soon as Hobgoblin came through the hole he'd made, he ran into Spidey's trap full tilt. The webbing caught and held him. Spider-Man moved in fast to finish the job, parting his webbing and leaping through the first hole. From behind, he webbed Hobby up like a neat package. Hobgoblin thrashed and swore, but it did him no good. Within a few seconds, all he could do was glare mutely at Spider-Man, so tightly webbed from toes to mouth that there was nothing he could do. He couldn't reach a bomb to throw, nor deliver any shock from his energy-gauntlets that would do anything but fry himself. The jetglider, tethered now, thumped to the floor with its leaden cargo.

"Now then," Spider-Man said gently. "You and I have things to discuss."

"Perhaps," said a deep voice from behind him. "But we think *our* conversation with this—thing—takes precedence."

Spider-Man turned. There, silhouetted against the webbing and the opening Hobby had made, stood Venom. The symbiote slowly grinned, his terrible snake-like tongue reaching toward Hobgoblin.

"We've got to stop meeting like this," Spider-Man said, annoyed, "or people will talk. This is just a good old-fashioned garden variety theft of nuclear materials. Nothing for you to concern yourself about—"

"We think not," Venom said, stepping slowly toward Hobgoblin, who was so thoroughly wrapped up that he couldn't even speak. Instead, he made nervous, placating-sounding grunting noises.

"The very fact that he is thieving nuclear material," Venom said, "makes plain what he's been up to. The other 'us' that we've been hearing reports of has also been thieving such material, has he not?" Slowly he drew closer to Hobgoblin. "So you kill two birds with one stone. You fulfill whatever nasty mercenary criminal scheme you're working on at the moment, and you also throw the blame on someone else. And they eat it up, don't they? The media." Venom smiled his awful fangy smile, and the symbiote drooled in anticipation. "No one has ever dared try anything quite so audacious with us. Such action on your part would seem to argue that you are weary of your life. That being the case—"

Tendrils from the symbiote streamed off him, grabbed Hobby, webbing, glider, safe and all, picked him up, and shook him as another man might shake someone by the lapels of a jacket. "Before we julienne the flesh off your bones and tie it in bow-knots while you watch—we want to know *why*?"

Hobgoblin made muffled, desperate noises. Venom's dark tentacles begen to edge themselves like razors. They descended on the webbing—sliced it, ripped it, shredded it away.

"Hey, wait a minute," Spider-Man cried. "It took a little doing to get him that way!" He leapt at Venom to pull him off from behind.

Venom's hands were occupied. Some of his tendrils whipped around to deal with Spider-Man—still razor edged, deadly as any knives. Spidey ducked away from them, and managed—but only because Venom was distracted—to throw some of his own webbing around Venom this time.

The struggle that followed was a chaotic sort of thing—Venom tearing at the web, his tentacles wriggling and streaming out from between the strands, trying to reach Spidey, Spidey throwing more web over it all, desperately hoping he wasn't about to run out after all he'd just used on the building. The two of them danced to and fro, spraying webs, cutting webs, tendrils clutching, being tangled, freeing themselves and being tangled again—

—until the whine of the jetglider stopped them both where they stood.

It was a pitiful-looking package which was soaring slowly, but more and more quickly every second, up out of the shattered building. Shreds and rags of web hung off Hobby, the jetglider, and the safe—all ascending as Hobby put on speed.

"Oh, no," Spidey moaned. He dashed out and shot web desperately at the receding form, but the jetglider kinked suddenly sideways, rose over the walls of the college, and was gone.

Glaring terribly, Venom rid himself of the last few rags of Spidey's webbing. "You utter fool. Now he'll get away and finish whatever awful thing he's started! Not to mention going back to impersonating *us*. And there's no telling where he's heading now—"

Spider-Man said nothing. He had seen, as the safe ascended, that his tracer was still on it. When his spider-sense came back fully—which he hoped would be soon—he would be able to track him well enough. He turned to Venom. "You're serious about this. It really *wasn't* you down there."

"You still don't quite believe us," Venom said, his voice a low, angry growl. "O ye of little faith."

"Yes, and the Devil can quote scripture to his purpose," Spider-Man said. *Still*, he thought, *I've been giving him the benefit of the doubt all this while. And now when he comes to me and tells me I was right—I can't believe him?*

"You're telling me that you didn't knock over a train last night?" Spidey said.

Venom's smile was grim, but just a touch more humorous-looking than usual. "Someone who could knock over trains," he said, "would not have had the trouble with your webbing that we just did." He frowned. "We must see about a more effective remedy."

"Let's leave that aside for the moment," Spider-Man said.

"I think we had better. That creature can't continue impersonating us—"

"I'm not so sure it was Hobgoblin," Spider-Man said. "And it would be dreadful to eat his spleen for the wrong reason, wouldn't it?"

"If he's doing what we think he's doing at the moment," Venom said, his tongue flickering in shared rage, "there's reason enough to rip him limb from limb, even leaving personal business out of it. Hobgoblin is almost certainly building a bomb of some kind, wouldn't you agree?"

Spider-Man could only nod at that.

"And the only reason one builds atomic bombs is to threaten other people with their use. And sometimes . . . to actually use them." Venom glared at Spider-Man again. "We, for one, though we consider this city a Hell for the innocent, and the den of every kind of injustice and crime, would prefer not to see it blown up . . . it, or any other like it. That Hobgoblin is even willing to threaten to do such a thing, or to help someone else to do it, merits him death. If he would do more—if he would actually detonate a bomb and end millions of innocent lives—then he merits death millions of times over. And we promise to make that death as prolonged and painful as he would make the deaths of many of the people here!"

"Look," Spider-Man said, "I'd agree, but—"

"No buts," said Venom. "We are going after him. This wretched creature has been brought to 'justice' enough times—with what result? *This*. We swear to you, we will find him before you do. By the time we are done with him, he will bewail the fate that kept you from finding him first."

Venom turned and leapt out the blown-out end of the building.

Spider-Man leapt after him.

SEVEN

MJ had seen Peter off that morning in a somewhat mixed state of mind. She had the pleasure of knowing that he was rested, not aching too badly (for a change), he'd had enough to eat, and most important, he'd actually had enough time to digest and consider what had been happening to him for the last couple of days. MJ watched her husband with considerable concern. She was afraid that, if he went out one time too many unrested and without his plans in order, he wouldn't come back.

She knew what he was planning for his day at ESU. She couldn't say she was overwhelmingly happy about it, but he was as well-prepared as he could be; he had a plan. So, there was nothing much more to be said about it. That being the case, she made tea and toast, sat down at the dining room table with the sun coming in through the window, and paged through the trades she'd bought the other day at Mr. Kee's. There wasn't anything much of interest that she hadn't already seen. News of mergers, buyouts, movie deals— *I'd love to have anything happen to me,* she thought, *that had lots of zeroes after it. . . .*

She made a second batch of toast, buttered it, and sat down when the phone rang. She debated letting the machine take it, then got up and went over to the phone table. "Hello?"

"Ms. Watson-Parker?"

"This is she."

"This is Rinalda Rodriguez, over at Own Goal Productions—"

"Yes," MJ said, and her heart leaped. It was the people who had offered her the audition.

"Listen, I'm sorry to trouble you so early, but we've had a change of plan—"

There it goes, MJ thought. *The whole thing's off.*

"My partner and I have to leave for LA early tomorrow morning—"

I knew it, it was too good to be true.

"—so is there any chance that you could come up to do your audition today?"

"Today?" MJ said, swallowing. "Certainly. I don't see why not. What time?"

"Would after lunch be all right?"

"After lunch—"

There was some babbling in the background. "Oh, no, wait a moment—" The phone was covered, and some words were exchanged. "Actually, three o'clock. How would that be?"

"Three o'clock. Fine. Same place?"

"No, we're moving uptown for this one." The AP gave her an address on the Upper West Side.

"That's fine," MJ said. "I'll be there."

"Sorry again to change plans on you like this."

"Oh, that's all right. It's nice of you to tell me this early," MJ said, meaning it. Some producers she'd known would change plans without warning and then make it sound as if it was your fault somehow when you couldn't meet the new requirements. "I'll see you this afternoon, then. Bye!"

She hung up. *This afternoon. Ohmigosh!*

She had planned to spend a leisurely afternoon, studying the material she'd been given, reading to feel what the material did for her, and working to the mirror, making sure that her expressions were doing what she thought they were doing. Well, it was going to have to be mostly mirror work today, and in a hurry, too. As always, when a crisis like this came up, she was all nerves, all at once. She scooted over to the window, leaned against the windowsill and looked out across the rooftops, twitching slightly. *Peter . . .* she thought.

But Peter could take care of himself. He had proven that often enough in the past, in one set of clothes or another. Now she was going to have to get out there and do the lioness thing. She would make him proud of her.

She let out a fast, excited breath, then went to get those script pages.

The time until two o'clock, when MJ needed to leave, flew by. How to read young Dora, the social worker character—that was the main problem. She was young: if the producers were casting actresses 22–25, they meant it. Surely they didn't want Dora too experienced, too knowledgeable. Yet at the same time, someone coming out of school that age could have considerable expertise—and the series bible did emphasize the character's sense of humor. That, MJ thought, was the key. When the character knew for sure what she was talking about, she would be all business and certainty, but when something happened with which she'd had no previous experience, she'd cover with humor while trying to figure out what to do.

As time to leave got closer, it got harder for MJ to

concentrate. *I wonder how many other people are auditioning?* she thought. She had trouble dealing with cattle-calls like the one the other day. But surely most of those people had been shaken out. All the same, she didn't like watching a lot of readings before her own— the fear dogged her that she could accidentally adopt someone else's approach when her own would really work better. And at the same time, she was usually forced to see a lot of other readings, because her name began with "W." So she did her best to ignore what was going on around her—but the long wait always made the nervousness worse. *Sometimes I think it would be less stressful to go out and have a fight with a super-villain.*

As two o'clock inched closer she read the pages one last time, putting some extra emphasis on the set of lines about hunger, letting the feeling out. There was a lot of it: her close look at the shelter yesterday reminded her how easy it was to forget about the homeless problem completely, and the anger and frustration came up in the reading, she thought, to good effect.

Well, she decided at last, *this is as good as it's going to get. Let's get dressed and head out.*

She had showered and taken care of her hair and makeup earlier. Now she went into the bedroom and hunted through the closet for the right thing. Something attractive, but appropriate for a young social worker. Fawn linen skirt, just barely below the knee; medium heels; white silk shirt. She thought for a moment and pulled out her one and only Hermes scarf, the one with the tigress on it, a present from Peter. She twined it around her neck outside the shirt collar and left it hanging down casually. *There*, she thought, looking herself over in the mirror. *A touch of class.*

She went out, grabbed her purse and keys, the script pages and audition pack, and her copy of *War and Peace*, and headed down to catch a cab. Normally, MJ had cab luck. Rain or shine, all she had to do was go out to the curb, stick her arm out, and a cab would materialize from nowhere. Today, naturally, the luck deserted her for all of five minutes, so that she stood there twitching impatiently, thinking, *What if I don't get a cab at all, what if I'm late, what if there's a traffic jam . . .*

Peter . . .

She let out a breath, then smiled at herself. At times like this, her free-floating anxiety fastened on anything it could find. Peter was quite probably happily and coolly ensconced at ESU somewhere, biding his time.

A cab finally pulled up. She got in, gave the driver the address, and let him whisk her away. From Peter, her mind jumped again to the homeless people she had met. While she and Peter had been in the tub, they had talked about the radiation sickness—for so it seemed to be— that some of these people were suffering from. *The submarine captain said*, she thought, *that the creature itself wasn't radioactive. And Peter mentioned the hole in the bottom of the warehouse, leading down into the sewers. If that thing's been down in the sewers, and in the train tunnels where some of the homeless people are, doesn't it have to be the cause? But if the captain's right and it's not affecting them, not the cause of their radiation sickness—what is?*

She turned the problem over in her mind, but could

find no obvious answer. *Could there be some kind of radioactive waste leaking down into the tunnels and sewers? Could someone be disposing of the stuff illegally?* She knew that toxic waste got dumped in landfills where it didn't belong. Sometimes, tankers full of it just sprayed their contents out on the side of some lonely country road, or into common sewerage, where it just flowed out to sea, untreated. Suppose someone was doing something similar with radioactive waste here in the city?

It would be easy enough to do, and there would be reasons for it. Disposing of nuclear waste safely was expensive: companies that used the legal methods of disposal were charged a lot for it. Why not save the money and just dump the stuff somewhere?

She was too nervous to think clearly about it. There was something nagging at her—the image of people, hungry and homeless to start with, now having to watch the blotches and sores form on their bodies, their hair falling out, feeling themselves getting more ill and weak every day. It didn't bear considering. She hoped somebody—Spider-Man, or the police, or even Venom—would find the creature, if it was the cause of this, and end its threat. *Those poor folks*, she thought and was surprised to find her eyes stinging with tears.

She got a tissue out of her purse and dabbed herself dry again. *Nerves*, she thought. And then, after a few seconds, she shook her head ruefully, catching herself in a lie. Nerves was not what it was about, feeling was what it was about—and there was no need to be ashamed of that.

The cab pulled up in front of a tall old brick building. She paid the cabbie, put herself in order, tossed her hair back, and strode into the building's lobby, smiling and ready.

Two hours later, she felt a lot less ready, but the smile was still there, mostly.

The reception area was typical: full of comfortable, sleek furniture, big sofas curving around to match the lines of the room, gorgeous modern art on the walls, two separate televisions showing two separate channels, and a busy, expensive-looking receptionist working behind a massive and politically incorrect desk of polished teak that MJ estimated would have cost about a year's rent on their apartment.

The audition room where she and the twenty-three other actresses all gathered to meet the production staff was more of the same: state-of-the-art sound and video equipment all stashed away in absolute tidiness behind a floor-to-ceiling glass wall, not a loose cable or wire in sight. Next, the AP ushered them into a big, bright, clean, carpeted rehearsal space, everything brand-new. There was serious money here and MJ was determined to be part of it, one way or another.

The competition daunted her. She looked good—she knew that—but some of these women looked spectacular, with the kind of effortless beauty that suggested they didn't have to do anything to themselves in the morning but wash their faces and toss their hair back out of their eyes. It was not in MJ's style to be jealous—not after a first flash of emotion which usually simply translated as,

"It's not *fair*!" and then melted away into rueful and slightly forlorn admiration. At least ten of her fellow auditioners looked like this. The others were all at least extremely good-looking, and possibly better actresses than she was. And here she was, enduring the Curse of the W's, watching them go in before her, one after another. Why the producers would want to look at her in the face of this competition, she couldn't imagine.

She sighed and determined to raise her mood somewhat. How, though, she wasn't sure. She had already read every magazine sitting out here on the Italian glass-topped tables. *War and Peace* did nothing for her today. The smell of hot coffee in the pot off to one side had been enticing when she came in. Now she was getting sick of it.

She leaned back and looked at the televisions. One of them was showing a large, purple, blunt-faced dinosaur, which was at that moment dancing clumsily and singing a song about how it wanted to be someone's friend. MJ gazed at it and had a sudden bizarre but very satisfying image of herself introducing it to Venom: taking the dinosaur by its pudgy purple hand, turning, and saying very sweetly, "Here, make friends with *this*."

The other television was in the middle of a commercial for a used-car dealership, car after car and license-plate number after license-plate number flashing on the screen, followed by the image of the dealer, a man with one of those faces MJ would *never* buy a used car from. *I don't know how he does it*, MJ thought. *Maybe I'm just suspicious. Must come of having super-villains running in and out of Peter's life all the time.*

The screen went mercifully black, then suddenly MJ found herself looking at a card that said, "SPECIAL REPORT." The card was replaced by the image of a newswoman sitting at a desk, an "Action News" logo and the network "bug" in the lower-right-hand corner of the screen. "Reports are coming in of an explosion on the ESU campus in the Village," the reporter said. "Emergency services are responding. Witnesses report substantial damage to the ESU science facility—"

And whatever composure MJ had managed to recover went right out the window.

Peter!

Across town and downtown, Spider-Man was swinging between building and building, scanning the streets frantically for any sign of the dark shape which was his quarry.

That boy really can move, he thought again. One of the most annoying things about having to tangle with Venom was how closely they were matched, in terms of their powers and abilities—and when it came to physical strength, while Spider-Man's strength was proportionally that of a spider his size and mass, the strength the symbiote lent Eddie was another matter entirely. The symbiote's job was to do, literally, whatever its host wanted—and it frequently seemed to bend various physical laws to make it all happen. Having worn the symbiote himself for a little while, he remembered the astonishing feeling of something as light as silk but as strong in its way as a steel exoskeleton—something that flowed around you being as hard or soft, as edged or

smooth as it needed to be for the moment's requirements. It looked like whatever you wanted it to look like
and *became* whatever you needed. Without thought,
without hesitation—just doing it. Wearing that symbiote,
you didn't need a weapon. You *were* a weapon.

Going through walls would be no problem for Venom.
If he wanted to claim he couldn't knock over a train,
well, perhaps that was true—but watching him try would
be worth the price of admission, and if bets were being
taken, Spider-Man wasn't sure he wouldn't put a five on
the symbiote, just to be safe.

In the meantime, there was no telling where Venom
had gone. Theoretically, since they were both chasing a
flying target, Venom should still be out in the open the
way Spider-Man was. But if Hobgoblin had gone to
ground, there was nothing to prevent Venom from going
right through walls, or the ground, for that matter, to get
at him.

Either way, Spider-Man's only chance to find them
both was to get some height and cover as much ground
as he could as quickly as he could. *So head for the tall
timber and start looking*, Spidey thought. There was a
good cluster of skyscrapers just west of him, near
Columbus Circle. He would go up the old Gulf-Western
building, have a look around, and decide his next move
before the trail got too cold.

Spider-Man hared off along 57th Street, high up,
swinging from building to building, surprising office
workers and window cleaners and the occasional pere-
grine falcon. As he headed westward, he got another

twinge, the slightest buzz, from the spider-sense. *Trouble ahead*—

The sense was vaguer, more prolonged, and more directional than usual, possibly a side-effect of its slow return. *This is the right direction, then*, he thought, and didn't bother stopping when he came to the area south of Columbus Circle. He just kept going west. The sense twinged him again, more sharply, as he continued, and Spider-Man kept heading that way, as much for the pleasure of the returned feeling as anything else.

He paused near the corner of one building, and swung out in a partial arc, like a pendulum, to see in which direction the "buzz" was strongest. Straight west—okay.

He continued that way. The buildings weren't as tall here—mostly apartment buildings, pretty nice ones, with rents he didn't even want to think about. At Eleventh Avenue he swung out again, looking all around him—

The spider-sense jolted him, hard. He looked down toward the West Side Highway. At the end of Fifty-Second Street was a horse corral, and near it he saw something black moving, heading for the street. Something two-legged, shining, dark, heading toward a manhole cover.

Not Venom! he thought in triumph—Venom would not have triggered the spider-sense. Instantly he let go of the present line of web and dropped down, cannonballing, his arms wrapped tightly around himself so he would fall faster. A couple of stories above ground, he shot out another webline, caught a streetlight pole, and swung across toward the fleeing figure. He dropped to the ground just in front of it.

It was black. It shone. It looked humanoid, but not

quite. The blackness was total, except for the pale, moonlike patches on its head, very much like the eyes on his or Venom's mask. That blackness was not a suit or clothing of any kind. It was the creature's skin, gleaming in the late sun like ebony polished to a high gloss, and it was actually very beautiful. It was bipedal and had arms, but there was something tentative about the hands. The fingers were lithe like tentacles, but sharp-looking like claws.

For only a second it crouched there, looking at him. Then it leapt, to tackle him—

Spider-Man jumped sideways, leaping for the nearby streetlight pole. The creature came down hard where he had been, but not as hard as Spider-Man had expected. From its body, tentacles erupted, slapping the ground hard and absorbing the shock as expertly as any judo enthusiast would. It bounced to its feet again, casting around it to see where he had gone, lifting its blank-eyed head with the kind of "sniffing" motion that the railroad workers had described.

Its eyes may not be so good, Spider-Man thought. *Could that be one of the reasons it prefers the dark? It doesn't need to see, so much? Or maybe—if it's radiation-sensitive, maybe the presence of the normal background radiation from sunlight and so forth, at ground level, bothers it—*

It leapt at him again, and this time came at him with tentacles and talons both, aiming right for his middle. Spidey jumped straight up this time, pulling his legs up hurriedly as it shot by underneath him. He shot a webline up onto the nearest building and gained himself some altitude, watching his frustrated adversary hit the ground again, roll, and come up to its feet again, "looking" to see where he had gone.

I'm really not sure it's not blind to visible light, Spider-Man thought. *Or else as far as it's concerned, there's so much ambient light, even this late in the day, that whatever it uses for optics are overwhelmed.*

His spider-sense stung him hard, so hard that he simply let go of the webline he was holding and dropped. This was just as well, for right past Spider-Man, whizzing through the air, the creature came plunging past him in a superb and unlikely leap from ground level. Whipping tentacles and claws both lanced out at his waist *en passant*. In midair he twisted aside, cannonballing again to fall faster, then shot out web and caught another light pole. Recovering, he saw the creature slam into the wall of the nearest building, clinging there a moment as if stunned.

Three times was too frequent a hint to miss. *It wants the canister*, Spider-Man thought, leaping away from the light pole again. *It must be really sensitive to the isotopes I'm carrying to be able to pick it out right through lead with all this background radiation.*

The creature dropped down from the building, "seeking" him again. *The thing's a living Geiger counter*, Spider-Man thought. *What on earth are its insides like—or off Earth, rather.* He peered down at it thoughtfully from his light-pole. *And more to the point, now that I've got it, what do I do with it?*

Its head turned blindly toward him, and it started for him across the street. Traffic, which until now had been crawling by at the easy pace New Yorkers use while rubbernecking, now screeched to a halt as the shining black creature scuttled across the road. Horns blew, and the creature threw its head up and produced a high, piercing soprano roar, a bizarre sound to come from inside a chest so big. It threw itself at the foremost car, a cab, tearing at it with tentacles that suddenly flew from all parts of its body. Pieces of bodywork came off—fenders first, then the roof of the cab, and the hood—and from inside the cab came the indignant yell of the cabbie and the scream of a passenger.

Uh-oh, Spider-Man thought, and leapt down from his streetlamp perch, shooting web two-handedly. The webbing settled over the creature, wrapping it—or trying to. It reared up from the cab, roaring again, and shredded the web all around it, turning and twisting to try to see where the stuff was coming from. Spidey danced around, keeping the webbing coming, and yelled to the people in the cab, "It's a write-off, folks, better get out while you can!"

They did, erupting out opposite sides of the cab, front and back. The elegantly dressed lady in the back, seemingly unhurt, vanished down the nearest side street at high speed, without wasting a second. The cabbie, though, stopped nearby and yelled, "What am I going to tell the insurance company?!"

Spidey shook his head as he kept laying webbing over the creature, which was shredding and shedding it as fast as he spun it. "Don't think they'll buy 'act of God'," he said. "Listen, just get away, this thing's—"

The "thing" abruptly spun into a whipping vortex of

activity, throwing off web faster than Spider-Man could lay it down, and at the same time reached out to the cab again with a whole new batch of tentacles, longer and thicker than any it had produced so far. It wrapped these around the cab, and without any apparent effort at all, simply picked the car up and looked around for something to fling it at.

That blank gaze fixed on Spider-Man. The creature heaved—

Spider-Man needed no hints from his spider-sense this time. He simply leapt the biggest leap he could manage off to one side, grabbing the distraught cab driver as he passed, hitting the ground and bouncing again. Behind the two of them, the cab hit the side of the nearest building with a tremendous crash, shattering into enough pieces to stock an auto parts store. The cab's gas tank ruptured in the process, spraying gasoline all over the place, and the gas promptly caught fire.

The honking and beeping and shouting from the backed-up traffic further on down the street got louder. The fire spread over the asphalt of the street, though mercifully not very far, and burned enthusiastically. In the midst of all this the creature stood, some of its tentacles clutching its head, others whipping around it, as if the noise and commotion were all simply too much for it. It "looked" at Spider-Man, and some of the tentacles reached out toward him indecisively.

"Uh-oh," he said, putting the cab driver down. "Mac, you'd better get out of here—I don't know what my buddy there's going to do next. There's a phone down the street. You'd better call 911 before this spreads—"

"No problem," said the cabbie, and got down the street in a hurry, looking glad to get away. Spider-Man turned his attention back to the alien creature. It was staring all around it, and "smelling" as well. Several times, its pale gaze came back to him, but it made no immediate move.

The noise of horns got louder, and the creature looked more distressed, twisting and turning. *It really doesn't like it out here*, Spidey thought. *Maybe the noise. Maybe the background radiation. And it* really *wants the isotopes, too. But it seems to be learning from experience. It can't just take them by frontal attack—*

The creature turned and headed uptown, away from the noise and the flames and smoke. Spidey went after it cautiously, not wanting to lose it, not wanting to let it do any more damage, but wanting to see where it was headed without himself influencing its decision, if possible. It looked over his shoulder at him, then stooped to the ground, produced more tentacles, and used them to heave open the manhole cover it had been approaching when he first saw it.

That's the ticket, Spidey thought and headed after it in a hurry. He didn't want to lose it in the sewers, either. At least down there it was less likely to endanger innocent bystanders.

The creature vanished down the manhole head-first, its tentacles helping it go. Spider-Man followed it down, though not too closely—he was acutely aware of the danger of the thing turning suddenly, in a tunnel too tight for him to maneuver in, but in which it would have its tentacles to help it. He could still clearly hear the rustling sound of it as it made its way downwards and onwards.

As he entered the manhole and headed down the ladder along its side, he heard more scuffling as the creature headed off southward along the connecting tunnel which the manhole met. Spider-Man followed, listening hard, letting his eyes get used to the darkness, and waiting to see if his spider-sense warned him of anything.

No warnings, nothing but the faint sound of the creature making its way downtown. Down here, where the city sounds didn't wash it out, he could hear another sound, a sort of soft moan, repeating itself at intervals of several seconds, and decreasing with increasing distance. *Is that it breathing?* he wondered. *Or doing something else? I don't have any proof that the thing's metabolism cares one way or the other about oxygen— or any other kind of atmosphere, for that matter. And with its fondness for radiation—*

At the bottom of the manhole, Spider-Man stopped and looked around. This wasn't access to a sewer line, as far as he could tell. Among other things, it didn't smell like it. This was a general access tunnel, one of the "utility" tunnels that honeycombed the island just ten or twenty feet under the sidewalks and streets. They carried all kinds of utilities, sometimes several kinds together in separate conduits in one tunnel—steam, electric, cable TV, phone lines, water mains—never giving away their presence or location except by occasional plumes of steam. This tunnel, as far as he could tell, carried phone and cable. Bundles of waterproof-sheathed cable conduit ran down the sides of it, with occasional "spurs" vanish-

ing upward through the ceiling of the tunnel, to buildings that they served. Here and there, very occasionally,
were faint lights meant to guide the utility workers who
toiled down here, in case their own lights failed. Down
toward the southward end of the tunnel, he could hear
the faint scrabbling sounds of his quarry hurrying away.

He followed a long way. The creature seemed unwill-
ing to let him get too close. When he sped up a little, it
did too, increasing its pace until he was hard pressed to
keep up with it. The creature took its turns at great
speed—right, left, left and down, down again, right,
right—and Spider-Man quickly lost any sense of direction. All he could do was follow. *I'm never going to be
able to follow my path to get back out*, he thought. *I
should have brought a ball of string, like the guy in the
fairy tale.* But he doubted he could have gotten a ball of
string big enough—he'd have to head upward, instead,
and pop out of a manhole cover somewhere else.

I hope, he thought, for the creature was heading
deeper and deeper, going down a level every few minutes. *I think it knows where it's going*, he thought. *And
that may mean something bad for me. It's a bad move to
fight on ground of your enemy's choosing.*

Ahead of him, dimly seen down the dark length of the
tunnel, the creature paused, looking both ways. *Confusion?* he thought. *Or is it tired? Or*—It was making that
"sniffing" motion again, hunting something. Down
under his feet, Spidey started to feel something: the faint
rumble of a train. They were near one of the subways.
We've come a long way east, he thought. Maybe south
too.

He headed for the creature, trying to be stealthy about it—running along, half-crouched, on the ceiling of the tunnel rather than on its bottom.

Then his spider-sense hit him like a club in the back of his head just as the tentacle came slithering out of the shadows at the bottom of the tunnel, reached up, snagged him by the leg, and pulled him down.

The next few minutes were like a nightmare of being attacked by an octopus—except that once you've webbed up eight of an octopus's tentacles, theoretically the nightmare is over and you can leave. *This* creature produced more tentacles each time Spider-Man webbed up the ones attacking him. It had apparently decided that cutting the webbing was a waste of time and was now simply working around it instead. The tentacles swarmed over him. As fast as he could throw them off or web them down, more emerged to hold and pull at him—and at the canister webbed to his waist.

And he realized all of a sudden that he couldn't move at all: the thing had him thoroughly tied. It shredded the webbing on its imprisoned tentacles, and then one tentacle flashed in, developed an edge, and slashed down—

The webbing holding the canister parted, though not completely: for a moment the canister dangled. Another pair of tentacles snatched at it, and the canister, not designed to take such stresses, fell apart, clattering to the tunnel floor. One of the little packets of americium isotope fell out.

Somewhere nearby a train's rumble began, got louder. The creature roared too, that high piercing roar again, released Spider-Man, and leapt on the fallen canister.

Not with Dawn's science project, you don't! thought Spidey. He jumped straight at the creature's face. The fangs parted—though not to bite, to roar—and then more tentacles whipped around and hit Spider-Man broadside.

It was like being hit by a train: Spidey was lifted off his feet and flew straight across the tunnel. His head, side, and right leg crunched into the far wall and bounced off. In a blaze of pain, Spider-Man slid down to the floor, unable to stop himself or do anything but lie there, wheezing, and in agony from trying to breathe, *having* to breathe.

The creature clutched at the isotope packet, bent over it and stuffed it into its maw. *Get up, get up, get up*, Spider-Man could hear one part of his brain ineffectively exhorting his body.

He managed to lever himself up onto one elbow, then wavered to his feet. The creature froze in what might have been a moment of after-dinner digestion and paid him no mind. Spider-Man shot a quick line of web at the first half of the canister, then at the second half, and pulled them to him. Then he shot one last line of web at the remaining packet of isotope just as the creature turned its head slowly, beginning to come out of its moment of assimilation.

He quickly sealed the isotope back into its canister, rose unsteadily, and fled down the tunnel, not sure where he was going, not caring, as long as it was away from *that.*

The soprano roar went up behind him again, but Spider-Man kept running. The sound of trains grew louder, drowning out the roar behind him. He plunged through the dimness, every breath a stab in his side, stumbling, clutching his ribs. *Broken. Has to be at least one broken.*

That roar sounded behind him again, closer. Desperate, Spider-Man ran for the trains. *Can't let it get the rest of this stuff. If it gets it—if it finishes it—it might just go on with* me—*as an hors d'oeuvre—since I was so close to the radioactives.*

The roar seemed to be fading in the increasing roar of the trains. He could hear no sound of pursuit. He fell down once, got up and staggered on, but not far. Then he fell again and couldn't get up, no matter how the back of his mind yelled at him. His whole side, from head to foot, was one long line of pain, which washed the thought out of him, left him sitting, then lying, helpless, on bare cold concrete, in the dimness, which grew darker . . .

. . . went black.

EIGHT

MJ stared in horror at the TV screen. It cut to a game show, in which a well-dressed woman turned over letters in a row, while contestants tried to guess the words of the phrase they spelled. Normally MJ was of the opinion that this game was intellectually challenging only to those with IQs lower than that of a banana slug. Now, though, she stared at the impending words and couldn't make head or tail of them. *Peter!* she thought.

She hoped for some kind of continuation of the bulletin, but nothing came. An explosion at ESU—she knew what the science building there looked like. Maybe not as solid as the main building, but solid enough. Not something you could blow up easily. *He was right,* she thought. *He knew Hobby was coming. Sometimes I wish he didn't have to be so—*

She looked around nervously. There were fewer women in the reception area now than there had been before, but not that many fewer. Obviously a lot had been asked to stay, possibly to do a second reading, maybe even to read for some other part. That happened sometimes. It might happen to her. She couldn't leave now. She hadn't even read for the first time yet.

At the same time, even if she was free to leave now, what could she do? There was no telling exactly what had happened over there at ESU, and nothing was to be gained by her shooting off in that direction without a good reason or a plan. She would be much smarter to sit still and bide her time. Peter would be annoyed with her if she just ran out of an impending audition because—

"Ms. Watson-Parker?"

"Here," MJ said, standing up, the mask of the professional falling into place—though not with the usual assured slam. She followed the AP toward the audition room, feeling a lot less excited about it all than she had been just a few minutes before. *I wish I'd never seen that bulletin*, she thought—then smiled at herself, a little ruefully. *If he can be a hero*, she thought, *you can too, even if only by staying at your post.*

Head high, she went in.

It was a good reading. She had always been able to memorize quickly, even at school, and her work on *Secret Hospital* honed that talent to a fine skill, especially since lines changed even as they filmed episodes. Several times they had even broadcast live, with several of the staff writers scribbling hectically away on the sidelines to cover up mistakes made by actors, or by another writer who had somehow slipped out of continuity. At such times, you had better be able to plaster the words onto your brain while four thirty-second commercials were airing. To actually have lines that *weren't* going to be changed was something of a luxury.

So MJ stood up in front of them confidently enough. The older woman producer, Rinalda, was there; the younger woman, the AP; the young male AP; and a suit, a handsome enough man with gray hair and a weary look. *Executive producer*, MJ thought. At least, that seemed most likely. Her résumé, duplicated, was on the table in front of them. They had her still, and they were looking at MJ speculatively.

"Please, sit down," the woman AP said, and there followed the usual two or three minutes of pleasant chatter about what she'd been doing recently ("job-hunting"), had she had any other work since *Secret Hospital* ("no"), her schedule for the next year—it was hard to throw caution to the winds and say, "Empty," but she did it.

"There's a little more modeling work coming free this year," the young female AP said thoughtfully.

MJ simply sat back and said, "I like this better."

Then they asked her to read. MJ went into the ten-page excerpt they had given her without pausing for more than a breath or two—delivered the first few lines of it sitting, as the social worker in the script might have. Then she got up and began to work with the lines moving—pacing a little, playing to Rinalda as if she were the other character in the scene. She let herself fall into feeling like Maureen as best she could: that passion and compassion, clear-eyed, a little humorous, a little edged when it needed to be, letting the anger come out at the hopelessness, the hunger. Hopelessness—that was accessible right now. MJ couldn't get her mind off what she had seen on the TV in there, even while she was in the middle of the part. Maybe that was all right. It gave the reading a bit more edge than it had had at home, when she was comfortable and unworried.

She didn't usually look at the rest of her audience while she was reading, but once she stole a glance and saw the rest of them looking at her with much more lively and intent expressions than they'd had when she'd first come in. The young female AP was smiling slightly as she scribbled something on her legal pad. The smile was not a nasty or bored one; it was genuinely pleased.

That was more than MJ often saw during a reading—too many producers prided themselves on being poker-faced—and it encouraged her oddly.

As usual, when she finished, no one told her whether they thought she'd done well or badly. Rinalda simply paged through a script in front of her, curled the pages back at one spot, and said to MJ, "Would you read this?"

MJ took the script, swallowing. Her character's parts had been highlighted in pink. That was a courtesy on the producer's part—some liked to make it harder by just letting you cold-read the part as best you could and see-ing whether nerves would trick you into reading some-one else's lines under pressure. "Both parts," MJ said, "or just the one?"

"Both, please."

The dialogue, as she instantly saw from scanning just the first page, was between her social worker and a young, inexperienced doctor who obviously thought very well of himself—the tone of his dialogue was pompous, the vocabulary unnecessarily complex. MJ thought she could see where this was going. She read the social worker's dialogue as patient, at first, then a little annoyed. The doctor was using heavy medical vocabu-lary, and MJ rocked forward on her feet a little as the so-cial worker explained to him that he didn't need to use long words to intimidate her, and that if shorter ones like "caring" and "commitment" were beyond him, he should practice them a little until he got familiar with them. It got to be a noisy piece as it continued for page after page—and MJ began to wonder how much they had stuck her with—as the two characters began shouting at one another. MJ felt she had some shouting in her at the moment, so that came out well too, her uneasiness inside translating itself most effectively into annoyance at the idiot doctor—at any establishment that hindered her pursuit of what really mattered.

She took the reading straight through to the act break. They didn't stop her. And when she was done, the man with the silver hair was nodding. "We have a few more to go through," he said to MJ, speaking directly to her for the first time. "Will you wait?"

"Of course," MJ said. And then added, on the spur of the moment, "I might need to step out briefly—"

"We won't be too long, I don't think," said Rinalda, looking at her. MJ tried to read the expression, trying to work out whether it was one that said, *Go ahead, step out, it's okay,* or *I'd stay where I was, if I were you.* Impossible to tell; she simply didn't know the woman well enough.

MJ smiled, nodded, stepped out into the front room again.

She sat down where she had been. One of the other auditioners, a short-haired blond woman, looked over at MJ and smiled a little. "Tough in there, huh?" she said.

MJ nodded. "Tough bunch . . ."

After a few minutes, the AP came out of the audition room and began to step around to some of the women in the reception area, one after another, having a few quiet words with each, smiling, shaking them by the hand. The message was clear: they weren't being considered for the part. MJ waited.

The AP did not come to her.

In a few minutes the room had cleared a little more. There were about six actresses left now, and MJ. They all looked at each other, and at her, with the polite expressions that MJ knew perfectly well concealed a desperate desire that everybody else in the room should be sent home except *them*. MJ was wearing the same expression herself, she knew. She tried to get rid of it, on general principles, and wasn't sure how well she was doing.

Now more time went by in which nothing happened. The game show edged toward its end. On the last commercial break she watched a trailer for the end-of-the-week episode of the network's big soap. MJ could hardly bear the banality of the characters' conflicts and troubles, their petty jealousies and rivalries, considering what was going on in the real world at the moment down at ESU.

But after a moment, even she had to laugh softly under her breath. Doubtless, to the average person in the street, *her* problems would seem fairly fantastic. "I'm worried," she imagined herself saying, "because my husband is out chasing a raving lunatic who flies around on a jet-glider and throws pumpkin bombs at things, and being chased by another nut case who's in cahoots with a sentient suit of tailor-made clothing from another planet. And they're both chasing something which appears to eat fissionables for lunch. Did I mention that *it's* from another planet too?" Any sane person would have her carted away to Payne Whitney, or some other similarly therapeutic refuge for the extremely confused. *People just have no understanding of the problems of super heroes' wives*, she thought. *Maybe I should found a support group.*

The trailer flashed on from confrontation to confrontation. MJ looked at her watch. It was pushing five o'clock: the network was about to start its local evening news. Maybe there would be something about whatever was going on at ESU.

After some more commercials, the news came on. MJ watched eagerly, and she tried to get control of her face as the first graphic to go up behind the newsreader was a picture of Hobgoblin.

"Just minutes ago," the newswoman said, "we received copies of a videotape from the costumed criminal known as Hobgoblin. In the tape, Hobgoblin claims to have planted a nuclear bomb somewhere on the island of Manhattan. He threatens to detonate this bomb unless one billion dollars in cash is paid to him within twelve hours—by five-thirty A.M. local time."

Everyone in the place was now staring at that TV, not just MJ, as the station began to play Hobgoblin's tape.

The tape showed Hobby sitting behind a desk, like a bad parody of a corporate executive about to give a pep talk. "People of New York City," he said, "such as you are. This being, according to actuarial figures, the richest and most successful city in the United States, I have decided it's time you plowed some of that wealth back into your local infrastructure. That is to say, me. Using that traditional American trait, good old-fashioned entrepreneurship, in the spirit of free enterprise, I have caused to be built one of the little toys with which the great nations of the world have been cheerfully threatening each other these last fifty years: an atomic bomb. It is rated at one point two kilotons and is more than sufficient to scour Manhattan Island down to its original native granite and basalt. Being that materials for so-called 'clean' bombs are increasingly hard to lay hands on these days, it will doubtless make life uncomfortable in the four surrounding boroughs and New Jersey—in fact, probably as far north as Albany and as far south as Baltimore, depending on how the winds blow.

"To demonstrate that I am not wasting your time," said Hobby, "and that I can in fact carry through with what I'm proposing, I have, at the time of this tape's airing, delivered to municipal authorities in New York a sample of the material I have acquired, which has allowed me to construct the tidy little device which at present sits so happily ticking to itself in some snug and secure corner of this great metropolis. Along with the material in question are instructions for how and where the payment is to be made. Any attempt to make the payment spuriously, or to lay a trap for me or any of my associates, will unfortunately result in the device being detonated—as will the failure to make a payment at all. Manhattan, in either case, will be history."

He folded his hands and grinned a little more widely. "About time, anyway. The architecture's been getting out of hand. Now, it may be that some of you will agree with me, especially about the architecture, in which case my advice to you is to sit back, do nothing, and wait for the fireball. Those of you who desire to put your affairs in order should feel free to do so.

"However, for those of you who might have breakfast

or lunch dates to keep, or who for whatever other reasons desire to continue your wretched mundane little lives in what passes for their normal fashion, I strongly suggest that you call your local city councilmen, your mayor, your borough councils, your Congressional representatives, and anyone else you think may be of any use, and tell them to pay me. Otherwise—" he shrugged "—those of you who have had to deal with city bureaucracy over the years will understand that, as one more person routinely oppressed by it, especially by the doings of what are euphemistically referred to as New York's Finest, my patience with such bureaucracy is rather limited—just as yours is. Therefore, I hope you'll understand when I say that no extension of this deadline will be made. The city has twelve and a half hours from the initial broadcast of this tape, which I have embargoed until five PM local time. At five thirty this morning, either I am going to go away independently wealthy, or the sun is going to come up in New York. *In* it. So please, call your representatives in Government . . . and just say yes.

"Thank you for your attention, and—" another nasty grin "—have a nice day."

The view on the screen went back to the newsroom staff. One of them said to the female anchor, "June, we have a report from the Fourteenth Precinct downtown, which states that a canister labeled as nuclear material was delivered by courier to the Precinct a few minutes ago, and that it is currently being checked by experts from City University and the New York City branch of the Atomic Energy Commission. We hope to have a reporter down there shortly to bring you news of this development. Meanwhile, the response from Gracie Mansion—"

The room erupted in a hubbub of confused and anxious voices. MJ shut it all out. She couldn't care less about the mayor's reaction—or anyone else's, at the moment. All she could think of was, *He went to deal with Hobgoblin. And now here's Hobby on the news—but no news of* him. The hair was standing up all over her. The feeling she was having now was one she had had many times before, and repetition never made it any easier to bear.

That tape could have been made just a few minutes ago, she thought, *or days ago. There's no way to tell. If it was a few minutes*—That wasn't a thought that she much liked. It would imply that Spider-Man had met Hobby this afternoon, and Hobby had gotten away from the encounter—while Spider-Man hadn't been heard from since. It would imply that Spider-Man couldn't stop him.

"Ms. Watson-Parker?" MJ turned to see Rinalda standing in the doorway with a somewhat urgent expression on her face, beckoning MJ back into the audition room.

MJ nervously followed her in. The others were all gathering their things into briefcases and portfolio packs. "Ms. Watson-Parker, we'd like to offer you the role." MJ's eyes widened. "But with what's going on here, we're flying out to LA tonight instead of in the morning. Can you come with us? We have to start shooting tomorrow."

I got the part, was her first thought. *But Peter's in trouble*, was her next one.

She bit her lip. *Do you know how many people would kill for a chance to get out of New York right now? But I can't just leave Peter—he could be hurt or dying or worse, for all I know.*

In the end, there really was no choice.

"I'm afraid I can't leave New York tonight. I'm going to have to turn it down."

Rinalda stared at her in disbelief, her mouth twitching. Before MJ had the chance to talk herself out of it, she turned and left. She did not look back.

Outside, everyone was still standing around staring at the TV, pointing, arguing—shaking their heads, not believing it, believing it all too well. Not even the receptionist saw MJ head out, take the elevator downstairs, and rush out into the street.

She stood there on the sidewalk and had no idea what to do next. The back of her brain was still shouting recriminations at her, things about making a fool of herself, losing the job, not getting out while the getting was good, being blacklisted in this town, and other nonsense which she listened to briefly and then decided to ignore. She had more important fish to fry.

Peter, she thought, *was at ESU*. That, at least, gave her a place to start. She hurried down the little side street to a public phone, picked up the receiver, and listened for the dial tone. There wasn't one. MJ slammed the receiver savagely back into its cradle and went back up to the street, crossing to where she'd seen another one.

Someone was heading for it at the same time she was. MJ practically leapt across the street, got there first, said "Sorry, emergency!" to the poor guy she pushed in front of, fed the slot money and started dialing. Normally she had trouble remembering the ESU main switchboard number, since when she called Peter there, she usually called the lab direct. But now she remembered it with no trouble.

It was busy. She hung up, dialed again. And did this five more times, while the guy waiting behind her nearly expired with impatience.

"I know, I know," she said out of the side of her mouth. "Just hang on." The sixth time she dialed, it rang . . . and rang, and rang, and rang. After a while it was answered by a harried woman's voice which said, "ESU—"

"Listen," she said, "my husband was back in the science building when— Has anyone seen him?"

"Who's your husband?"

"Peter Parker. He's a doctoral candidate in Biochem."

"Just a moment, I'll inquire." The woman put her on hold. MJ stood there practically stamping her feet in frustration and fear, while a deranged computer sang "Greensleeves" at her. "I could punch you right through this phone," she hissed at the hold music, the switchboard, and the composer of "Greensleeves," some five hundred years distant. The man behind her, intimidated by her tone, took a couple of cautious steps backward.

"Not you," MJ said. "Sorry—" The music seemed to go on for weeks. Finally the voice came back, saying, "Peter Parker?"

"Yes!"

"Sorry, no. No one's seen him."

"Oh, great," MJ muttered. "Listen, what was going on there, anyway?"

"It was just on the TV," said the operator wearily. "Hobgoblin did it." MJ suspected that she had been saying this to everyone for the last half hour. "He flew in on his little whatsis and stole one of the safes with some radioactive stuff inside it. Then Spider-Man showed up, and they started to fight, and then that other one, Venom, you know, the one with the weird suit? He showed up, and there was some kind of big argument."

"I bet," MJ breathed. "But they're not there now?"

The operator laughed shortly. "Do you think I'd be here if they were? And if I'd known they were coming, I'd have called in sick, I can tell you. No, they've all left, I don't know where for, and good riddance. You should see the science building. It looks like someone crashed a train into it."

"Did they leave in any particular order?"

The operator laughed again. "You working for the *Post* society column or something? They're just gone, ma'am. Don't ask me who took precedence. Anything else I can help you with? My phone's lit up like a Christmas tree."

"No—thank you. Thank you very much."

MJ hung up and walked away, staring at the sidewalk and thinking. *Gone, simply gone. But where would they go?*

She walked, trying to put it all together.

They were all there, she thought. *They met. They must*

have talked. She tried to imagine what the conversation would have been about, extrapolating from what Peter had told her last night. Venom wanted whoever was impersonating him, she thought. So Peter said. Hobgoblin wanted the radioactive stuff.

She stopped there. Venom knew about the radioactive waste in the warehouse and the way the creature took it. Suppose he came to ESU because he, too, suspected Hobgoblin would try to take some more radioactive stuff, or because he suspected Hobby of being the impostor?

Now, Peter's pretty sure the creature that escaped from the sub is responsible. But did he get a chance to tell Venom about it? She had no way of knowing.

But Venom has obviously made the connection between radiation and Hobgoblin. So that's why he was at ESU. *Fine. I still don't know where I'm going to find Spider-Man . . .*

She stopped in the middle of a cross street, having walked a couple of blocks while she was thinking, and stepped back to let a car pass in front of her. *I wonder if he's called home and left me a message?* she thought and walked quickly to the next phone she saw, dropped a quarter in, and called home.

The phone rang three times. She hung up quickly before the fourth ring, when it would pick up. It only did that when there were no messages. *Nothing,* she thought, retrieving her quarter. *Either he didn't think to call . . . or he can't.*

She'd go home and wait for him. If he needed her, she'd be there.

• • •

The voices were screaming again.

Sometimes Fay McAvoy thought the noise would drive her crazy. She heard things—always had—but down in the tunnels below the city it should have been better. Usually she could sleep here, bothered only a little by the rats and the trains. It was the voices she tried to escape.

Those voices were starting again, a little whisper at the back of her head. She pressed her hands to her ears. *No no no*, she thought. *You're not real. You're not real.*

Fay had been homeless for the better part of a decade, sometimes scavenging, sometimes living on charity, always just getting by. The voices made it impossible for her to work, impossible for her to hold a job of any kind. Half the time she just wanted to crawl into herself and disappear. Once, long ago, before her medical insurance had run out, the doctors had tried to help. She'd been in and out of institutions for years. Nothing had been able to get rid of the voices in her head, though.

Fay suddenly froze in her tracks. *What was that?* It had sounded like a footstep behind her.

She whirled, straining to hear. Footsteps—and they were getting closer. "Who's there?" she called.

"Well, look what I found," said a voice. And then, very low, Fay heard a chuckle.

It was not the sort of voice she wanted to hear. About six feet in front of her, she could see the tall, shadowy shape. Even under the rags he wore, she could tell he was broad in the shoulders, certainly stronger than she

247

was, possibly faster. *Don't wait*, said one of the voices in her head. *Run. Run now. Knock him down, get past him, and keep going.*

She was just taking a deep breath to start her charge at him when something brushed against her leg, quite high, from behind. She screamed at the top of her lungs. Something ran by underneath her—rats, several of them. She knew all too well the abhorrent little pitty-pat of their footsteps.

The next thing she heard shocked her even more, for the man now screamed too. Then Fay heard his footsteps running in the other direction—rat-scurry and shoes mixed together.

Not one to miss an opportunity, Fay ran. She vaulted up sideways, over the third rail, and into one of the dive-ins that led to an access tunnel. This went at right angles to the train tunnel, and then curved around to parallel it again. One dim utility light was all she could see in this stretch, but it was enough to see that this particular spot, at least, was deserted.

The voices in her head had grown quiet for the moment. Then Fay heard a sound behind her—boots, not crunching on trainbed gravel, but coming down hard on concrete. *He's behind me!* Again, Fay ran.

She kept it up for nearly five minutes. Several times Fay had to stop, holding her side as the stitch started. She couldn't keep up such a pace much longer. Between bouts of panting, she strained to hear. The footsteps seemed to be getting closer over time.

When she stopped, what would she do? Scream? Certainly, for all she was worth—and for all the good it would do down here. Fight? The best that she could. She had been successful at fighting off the occasional mugger in the past. But that had been above ground and, despite the fabled noninvolvement of New Yorkers, you always knew you had a better chance to get away, to survive, when there were other people in the neighborhood. Here she was alone.

She hurried on into a bigger, more open space, as poorly lit as the one she had left. She stopped for a second, gasping, trying to get her bearings—

—and saw a red-and-blue shape, walking towards her.

After a moment, she realized it was a man in a red-and-blue outfit. Then she recognized the outfit—it looked like it had been rubbed threadbare in a couple of places, and it was covered in grime, dirt, and sewage, but none of that mattered. He was a real super hero. She'd seen him before from the streets, and she knew he'd help her.

"Spider-Man!" she hissed. "You gotta help me!"

He looked at her. He seemed poised and ready for action, despite the somewhat bedraggled state of his costume. "What is it?" he said.

"Help me!" Fay whispered fiercely. "There's someone after me! Please, Spider-Man!"

Spider-Man threw back his shoulders, and turned toward the spot where Fay pointed.

The big, dark shape which had been following Fay came in that doorway. It was another homeless person, with long hair and a scraggly beard—and a knife in his hand.

Hands on his hips, Spider-Man glared menacingly.

The man looked back, stunned for a moment. Then a big grin split his face. "Awright!" he said. "Nice Spider-Man costume! Whadja, raid a Halloween shop or somethin'? Well, 'hero,' you gonna rescue the lady?" He moved slowly closer. "Let's see you rescue her from this." He approached Fay with the knife. Fay's mouth widened, about to form a scream.

But it was the man who screamed as the line of web shot out, fastened to the knife, pulled it out of his grip, and flung it across the tunnel.

"All right," Spider-Man said calmly, his voice sounding comfortingly strong and vibrant, "I rescued her. But who's gonna rescue *you* when I'm done with you?"

He took one step toward the man. The guy went wide-eyed, backed away stammering something that Fay couldn't make out, and fled through the entrance to the tunnel again, back into the dark.

They stood there for a moment, just waiting, but there was no sound save the receding footsteps, still running far up the tunnel.

"Are you all right?" Spider-Man asked.

"I—I think so," Fay said. The voices were still silent. "How about you? You look like you were in a real bad fight."

"I'll live," Spider-Man said. "Can you show me the fastest way out of here? I need to get to the East Side."

Fay turned slowly, getting her bearings. She'd been in this tunnel before, she realized. "That way," she said, starting out. "Follow me."

A bit less than half an hour later, Spider-Man returned

home. There he found MJ, who nearly bowled him over with a hug.

"You're all right! I was so worried!" She pulled out of the embrace. She wrinkled her nose, probably from the smell of the sewer Spidey had been lying in, but she said nothing about it.

"Good to see you, too. Just came back to restock the web-shooters."

"You're going to need them," she said gravely, and then Spider-Man noticed her look of apprehension, which he realized was about more than her husband's welfare. He removed the mask from his sweat-stained face.

"Bad news, I take it," he said, opening the drawer where he kept his spare web cartridges.

MJ quickly filled him in about what she'd seen on the news. "I was worried sick. After hearing how ESU's been torn up, and that you and Venom and Hobgoblin were all there, what was I supposed to think? And then the next thing I know, Hobgoblin is on the TV, threatening to blow Manhattan up with a bomb if the city doesn't give him a billion dollars by five thirty this morning!"

"Five thirty. Boy," Peter said softly, putting a hand to his head, "some people just can't sleep in, you know?"

"I guess he wants to get to the bank early, so he has the rest of the day free." MJ shook her head. There were times when she noticed that her husband's turn of phrase had contaminated her. "Anyway, he says he has an atomic bomb. He gave some radioactive material to the city to prove he could do what he said he was going to."

"He could certainly send them quite a bit of stuff," Peter said. "He stole two safe-fuls from ESU."

"But how did he get away?"

"Venom and I had a little, uh, disagreement about how to handle him—I guess that would be the best way to put it."

"Well, never mind that, we have more important things to think about."

"I'll say we have. When I ran into our little friend, a while back—"

"Who, Venom?"

"No, the critter from the sub."

"You caught it!"

"Um, no," Peter said, rubbing the back of his neck meditatively. "I would say offhand that it's about fifty-fifty as to who caught who."

He told her in some detail about his encounter with the creature. "No question that it looks like Venom," he said finally. "There are small differences, but you don't see them until you're pretty close up—and by then you're too busy trying to keep yourself in one piece to pay much attention to them. And it's a lot stronger than Venom. Brock's no pushover, but he doesn't usually push over trains, either."

MJ shook her head. "Where can that thing have come from? Wherever did they find it?"

"The Captain didn't tell me much," Peter said. "Couldn't."

"It's a pity he couldn't have told you how to catch it," said MJ. "I wonder how they did it?"

"No telling. And in the final analysis, even having

caught it once didn't help them much, the thing melted its way right out of a nonstandard radiation confinement when it was ready. We're going to have to think of some other way to keep it. Meanwhile—" He took a long breath, and winced. "Ouch. But I still can't get over how much it looked like Venom."

MJ looked doubtful. "Has it tried to shapechange, that you've seen?"

"No, but that doesn't mean that it can't." He turned towards her, really looking at her for the first time since he came in. "You're all dressed up. Were you out today?"

"I had an audition," she said.

"What, for the social worker thing? I thought that was tomorrow."

"No," she said. "They called this morning. They had to move it up."

"So how'd it go?"

"Not too bad," MJ said. "I'll tell you about it later."

Peter nodded and rose and put his mask back on. "Back to work," he said.

MJ glowered at him. "You are out of your alleged mind," she said. "Look at you! You can barely stand up! You're in no condition to fight anybody or anything."

"I can too." He struck a heroic pose.

MJ looked at him cockeyed, not convinced. "Look at the way your knees are trembling. And don't think I can't see you wincing when you breathe." She reached out to feel his ribs on the right-hand side, and sure enough, he sucked in breath and almost moved away from her. "You cracked them again! And after they just healed from the last time. Doctor Spencer's never going to believe that you fell down the stairs again. He's going to start thinking I'm abusing you or something."

"MJ, never mind. I have to go!"

She had had this argument with him before. She knew where it was going, but she had to have it. "Look," she said. "This is hardly fair to you. Where are all the other super heroes in this town? Let one of them take over. Call the Fantastic Four or somebody."

Spider-Man sighed. "Hon," he said, "half the time when I call there, all I get is their voice mail system. What am I supposed to do? Call and leave a message that says, 'Hi, guys, it's Spidey. Listen, I'm not feeling real well at the moment, but I just want you to know that if you haven't seen the news, you should turn it on, because Hobgoblin has a bomb, and he's going to blow the city up at five thirty this morning. I'm going home to take an aspirin; can you take care of this one for me?' It doesn't work."

"It's still not fair to you," MJ said. "And what about me? One of these days, one of these guys is going to catch you when you're hurt, and I—I don't know what I'll do."

He gathered her close. "You knew the job was dangerous when you took it, MJ," he murmured. "You having second thoughts?"

"No," she said. "I just wish there were something I could do to help."

"Can't think of anything at the moment," Spidey said. "If something occurs to me, I'll give you a call. But don't wait up for me . . . I'll be late."

"That's what I was afraid of to begin with," MJ said

dryly. "That you would be late in the funeral-parlor sense of the word."

"Well, reports of my death are greatly exaggerated. Come on, MJ, cheer up."

"It's not that easy."

"Is there anything else you can remember from the newscast that might be a help?"

She recited to him, word for word, as best she could, the text of the news report. Spidey shook his head. "I'm not sure there was anything even in the big safe that would have done Hobby any good. And he wouldn't have known that until he got it home, wherever home is, and opened it. Then he probably figured that he might as well make some use of it, and gave a batch of that stuff to the authorities as a sample."

"So he got the material for his bomb somewhere else entirely."

"That's right."

"He has to have been storing it somewhere, then."

Spider-Man nodded. "The 'where' is the problem."

"Well, I've got a suggestion. Marilyn, the homeless lady I met in the shelter the other night, told me that the place where people have been getting sick lately is over by Penn Station."

"Penn Station," Spidey said. "You know, when the critter came out into the rail yards and knocked the train over, it ran back into the tracks that would have come out of Penn."

"Interesting," MJ said.

"Well, I'll find out. I managed to put a tracer on both of the safes that Hobby took—"

"Your spider-sense is back, then!" MJ said, relieved.

"That's right."

"Well, that's good. Though, I don't know . . . it was kinda fun to see you tripping over things like a real human being. Oh well. I knew it couldn't last."

"You like seeing me fall on my nose! When I get back after all this, I'm going to tickle you until you can't breathe."

"You'll have to catch me first," MJ said mildly, but there was loving challenge in her voice. "I just want you to know that I love you," MJ said, "and I was worried for you. I want you to be real careful, and don't give me any more cause to worry, okay?"

"Okay." He pulled up his mask just enough, and gave her a long and enthusiastic kiss.

She refused to let him go for another moment. "Hon," she said, "if I don't see you by five thirty this morning—"

"You will," said Spider-Man. "Never fear."

Swinging from weblines, Spider-Man headed downtown. The buzz from his spider-tracer grew stronger all the time—its signal undiminished from being underground, if indeed it was underground as he suspected.

The alien was still on his mind. *How did they manage to capture it for as long as they did?* he wondered. *What were they keeping it in? Lead, almost certainly, if the ambient radiation around the creature had to be minimized. Probably reinforced with other substances— though maybe not reinforced enough.*

All the same, he wondered at the wisdom of sending a nuclear sub to carry such a creature. It would have been like shipping a tiger in a truck full of meat. He sighed, then. Friends who had gone into the armed forces had joked with him, telling him that the words "military" and "intelligence" appearing in the same phrase were an oxymoron, with the emphasis on the moronic side of things. *It may be that the Navy scientists really thought whatever confinement vessel they were using was sufficient. Well . . . they'll have to think again.*

Spider-Man was still bemused enough by the thing's likeness to Venom. But it was certainly nothing more than a coincidence. Though he hadn't had the symbiote-costume for very long, he'd never noticed it to have any affinity for radiation, so their resemblance wasn't a family one. He did wonder very much what kind of evolution would produce such a creature, especially one with bipedal and bilateral symmetry which also involved the ability to use those tentacular pseudopods. He would have to leave a message on Reed Richards's voice mail about it at some point, but there was no time for that right now. Maybe in the morning—assuming there was still a city with a phone system.

And the poor alien creature—he doubted that even it could survive dawn at ground zero. If it did, it would certainly get such a blast of radiation from the bomb that even *it* would get a bellyache.

Spider-Man swung up onto the top of the hotel across from Madison Square Garden and stood looking down at the entrance to Penn Station. Was he imagining it, or was the traffic a little less busy than usual this time of day? He wouldn't be surprised if people who had heard about Hobgoblin's threat might very well have decided to hurry home to their families and stay there, if this was going to be the city's last night. He wished he could do something of that sort himself, but when he could possibly do something to stop Hobgoblin, he couldn't afford such a luxury.

He swung down to ground level, and got onto one of the escalators which headed down into Penn. People stared at him with some surprise. Some waved and called his name, others just looked at him as if they saw him every day and he was just one more commuter.

He came out on the lower concourse level. His spider-sense guided him to the right . . . back and down. He went along past the Long Island Rail Road ticket windows into the main concourse, paused a moment to get his direction from the tracer. Looking up, he saw the guy who made track announcements gazing at him thoughtfully from his little glass box high up on the west wall. Spider-Man gave the guy a wave, then headed toward one of the track doors on the west wall. Its indicator light was lit, to show that the train was boarding.

Spider-Man joined the commuters crowding in through the door and headed down the stairs. Again, some looked at him curiously while others barely spared him a glance. But all of them were moving with a speed which suggested they thought a bomb might go off under their feet right now instead of later.

He left them getting into the big silver LIRR train and continued down the platform, following the buzz of his spider-sense. It was getting stronger. *Somewhere off this track and farther down.* He walked to the end of the platform, found the steps that let onto the tracks, and began to stroll down them, keeping an eye out behind him to make sure Venom wasn't sneaking up behind him.

He came to a railed stairway leading downwards between two of the tracks. *Downwards*, his spider-sense said to him, so down he went. At the bottom, he discovered another long, barren access tunnel. He followed it to another set up steps. Down he went again.

Following his spider-sense, he came to a place where half a dozen tunnels met. The spider-sense indicated that the source of the tracer was quite close. Just off to the right—downward again.

He followed the rightward tunnel. This one almost immediately deadended into a stairwell, which he took very slowly and softly in the increasing dark, for he heard voices. At the bottom he paused, looking ahead. Light poured through air vents set into the walls of the tunnel in which he now stood. The voices were louder here. He listened but couldn't quite make out the words. Then came a very familiar laugh.

Hobgoblin.

NINE

E ddie Brock's was not what one would normally consider a meticulous personality. He had been told by friends that this lack might get him into trouble one day. Sure enough, one time during his days as a journalist, he ran with a story as it seemed to be going, confident it would turn out as he'd expected. And, as his friends predicted, he got into trouble.

That, however, had been Spider-Man's fault. His career, his relationships, everything lay in ruins now because of Spider-Man. His life since then, it seemed, had been one long stroll through dark places—the sewers of San Francisco, and the basements of his soul.

At least today he had some slight hope for a modicum of satisfaction. He would catch the Hobgoblin. He would extract the last possible measure of terror and repentance from him. And, when that was done, he would disassemble him into his component parts. Nothing about Hobgoblin's life would suit him so much as ending it.

Eddie was not going about his plan in a slipshod manner. He had taken some care, while researching CCRC's connections, also to look into the Map Room at the New York Public Library's 42nd Street research library. There he had pulled the Con Edison maps for the access tunnels in the Midtown and West Side areas.

It was fortunate that his memory had always been sharp, for the whole place was a tangled warren of crawlways, passages, flights of stairs, and access holes of such complexity that anyone trying to navigate it without aid would be hopelessly lost. There were too many traps and pitfalls for the unwary—dead ends; pathways that seemed to go nowhere but led for miles, twisting, turning on themselves; old accesses added to new ones; old ones blocked up without being noted in the maps except as footnotes. It was all very complicated.

Eddie knew well enough, though, the kinds of places he was interested in. He had started, logically enough, at the CCRC headquarters.

He came after closing hours, having just had his little *contretemps* with Hobgoblin and Spider-Man. *Spider-Man* . . . All over Eddie's skin, the symbiote ruffled, a quick movement like the skin of a horse trembling when a fly bites it, a gesture of mingled disgust and desire. The symbiote's moods were clear enough to him from inside. But that gesture was diagnostic of one of the most common of its emotions. The symbiote's hatred for Spider-Man was a refreshing thing next to his: simple, straightforward, but at the same time, always tinged with longing.

His pain was always a trouble to it, and its pain to him, especially when he pitied it for what it couldn't be, for the one thing that was lacking. It had sentience—it existed, and it knew it did. But personality, it had none. A sort of a yearning toward his personality, and a sort of sad longing for something of the same kind, like the Tin Man wishing for a heart. But that was all. And when you came right down to it, sentience without personality was not enough to be *company*.

Even so, from Eddie's point of view, their relationship was better than being alone. Now, as he stood in the silence of the deserted downstairs of the CCRC building, next to the old warehouse, he got from the symbiote a sense of excitement—of interest and desire—and, very restrained at the back of that interest, the hope of something to tear, devour, consume.

That was the one danger of dealing with the symbiote, Eddie thought, as he stood gazing down into that hole. If you were careless, you could easily fall into its mind-set—to slash and feed when it desired to, rather than when prudence or necessity dictated. Its frustration that it could not subsume the one being it desperately desired sometimes drove it, hungrily, to try to consume others, like people desperate for protein who stuff themselves full of empty calories because there's nothing else. Sometimes these gorges left Eddie exhausted; other times they left him simply annoyed and enervated. But they were something he had learned to put up with in good grace. There had to be some give-and-take, after all, and his partner had plenty of positive aspects.

Now he stood looking down into that hole and said, "He's down there somewhere." The symbiote stirred and rustled all around him, starting already to send out questing tendrils that waved in the air as if testing it for scent. The symbiote had been attuned to his rage all day, reacting with eagerness and pleasure, knowing it was going to feed if they caught the one its partner was after. The symbiote wasn't picky. It had grown to like the taste of blood. Eddie's problem—their joint problem as Venom—was to make sure it got only blood that needed to be shed.

He judged the hole. No more than about fifteen feet down. Tendrils swarmed out, anchoring themselves to the edges of the hole. Eddie jumped and was let down easily.

He glanced up the length of the tunnel in which he found himself. Its bare concrete had been stained by years' passage of water, rust, and other, less healthy, things. Rats' squeaking could be heard further down. There was no light here, but far down he saw an inequality in the darkness which meant there was light elsewhere. He headed for it slowly and silently, knowing that what he pursued could go silently, too, when it pleased.

Hobgoblin . . . he thought. *Now there will be a dainty morsel for a leisurely postmortem.* Eddie confined himself to criminals, to those who preyed on the innocent. Occasionally you might find a criminal who, given the right time, the right money, and sufficient resources, could eventually have been rehabilitated. Trouble was, there wasn't enough time, and resources generally could better be used on other things. They were wasted on criminals. So often all the good intentions failed. That was the problem with life in general, from his point of view.

If there was anything Venom knew at this point, it was that justice started and ended in one's own hands, and at the business end of whatever tools you could bring to bear to enforce your power. He was justice, now. Rough justice it might be, but it worked a lot better than the milk-and-water, etiolated kind of justice that various costumed crimefighters, bumbling police, and the corrupt judiciary were trying to impose.

He paused as the light grew from a hint to a halo before him. It came from a single bare bulb set in a concrete wall where this tunnel met another. To his left, the new tunnel dead-ended. To his right, it stretched away for at least a hundred yards before either ending or turning; he couldn't see which.

That would be north, he thought. *Uptown*. "Let's go," he said.

He made his way up the tunnel, listening carefully. It was not as quiet down here as might have been expected. Even now, the incessant noise of the city managed to force its way through the layers of concrete and brick and earth: bumps and clanks from far above, as traffic hit some occasional manhole cover, the toothaching sound of someone working with a jackhammer blocks away. The low-frequency city roar didn't carry here as it did above ground, but knockings and bumpings, the hiss of steam in conduit pipes, the occasional hum of an exposed transformer box—

—and the murmur of voices.

He stopped, listened. *Nothing*. Then a sound, indistinct, but the pattern was that of someone speaking. And then, unquestionably, a cough.

Quietly, now, he thought to the symbiote. They made their way to where the tunnel did not end, but turned right again, east. Eddie was taking care to keep his directions straight; he might need to find this place again.

He headed eastward for perhaps half a long block, and then once again the tunnel turned. Now he saw the muted glow of light coming from the northward leg. This time the voices rose much more clearly.

He padded forward as quickly as he could, but took more care about being silent. Every now and then a rat bolted out from under his feet, and the symbiote stretched out a hungry tendril for it, but always Eddie would pull those reaching tentacles back. "You'll spoil your supper," he muttered. The symbiote's desires and hungers were something he had learned to exploit, and he wanted its hunger at its sharpest when they met Hobgoblin. Spider-Man had been right about one thing—he wasn't too sure where a spleen was. But he had done a little research after looking at the utility tunnel maps, and he thought Venom now had a good chance of finding it and seeing whether that particular morsel was all it was cracked up to be.

He came to the second turning of the tunnel, paused, and looked around the corner cautiously. Voices again rang out. The light ahead had a different quality than the dim, dusty-bulbed utility lights strung sparingly through the tunnel itself. It was a cleaner white, and he caught a faint whiff of kerosene.

Around him, the symbiote stirred and shifted excitedly. Eddie said softly, "Not this time. Just wait. And considering who we're going to be dealing with . . . street clothes, please."

Obediently it shifted. The spider logo across his chest faded as the black flushed into a beige shirt, jeans, boots. He looked himself over and said, "A little more used-looking."

Quickly the symbiote reshaped itself to his thought: frays and holes appeared in the jeans, a convincing patina of dirt, the collar and rolled-up cuffs of the shirt went threadbare. There was no point in frightening these people. He knew their kind: suspicious of strangers, always afraid of being driven out of their hard-won hiding places, or worse, made to live there on a new boss's sufferance. Venom had seen enough of that in the city under Golden Gate Park where he now served as protector—a portion of San Francisco buried in the 1906 earthquake and subsequently forgotten. The underground city had become a haven for society's outcasts.

He looked himself over one more time, ruffled his hair a bit, felt his chin. Well, the stubble was there, no need to do anything about that.

Slowly he walked down the tunnel, letting his footsteps echo. Ahead of him, people fell silent, listening. He was listening, too, for the sound of a weapon being gotten ready. Not that it was likely that people in these circumstances could do much to him, especially with the symbiote at hand. But all the same, he liked to be careful. "Hello?" Eddie said, trying to sound nonthreatening.

"Hello? Who's that?" came a voice from down the tunnel, fairly nearby now.

"Nobody," Eddie said. "Nobody much. I won't hurt anybody here."

"Well, Mister Nobody," said the voice, and it was female, "you just come down here nice and slow, and you keep your hands where we can see them."

Eddie did that, having no reason to disobey and hearing no overt threat in the voice, just the kind of toughness one needed to survive in these tunnels. Slowly he walked forward.

There were small "bays" in the sides of the tunnel, faired-in places six or eight feet deep. In one of these, the voices he heard were concentrated. He came abreast of the place and found himself looking at a tidy, neat little campsite, such as you might expect to find in the backwoods somewhere. Except that here they all were, any number of feet underground.

Eddie came up to the group—there were three of them—and stood there, letting them see him, keeping his hands in the open. Two women—an older one, red hair going pink as the white came in; a middle-aged one, blond, still pretty in anybody's book; and an old man, weary-looking, his face flushed with red, peppered with big broken blood vessels, some of them ulcerated. *Looks like alcohol or chemical abuse*, Venom thought, *sterno, possibly. . . .* There was no telling. It was something he had seen enough of both in San Fran and here.

"That's an old trick," the little old red-haired lady said to him, looking up at him genially.

"Which one, ma'am?"

" 'Nobody.' " She smiled, and there was some humor in the expression. "I remember another time a youngster came calling on people who weren't expecting him. They asked him his name too, and he said 'Nobody.' Then when the youngster's host started abusing his guests, and the young fella arranged to have a sharp stick poked into his host's big eye, all the poor monster could yell was, 'Oh my gosh, Nobody's hurting me!' And all his friends yelled back, 'Better pray for relief, then.' "

Eddie smiled. "A classicist," he said. "Well, the wily Odysseus we are not, no matter who else we might be."

"Who might you be, actually? Queen Victoria, maybe, with all that 'we' nonsense."

He raised an eyebrow. "To tell a name is to control the

thing," he said. "A classicist would know that. But never mind. Just call us Eddie."

"Eddie. Well, tell us, Eddie, would you be planning to stay?" said the younger woman.

He looked at her. Really very pretty, she was, with a small round face that looked sweet—until you saw something behind the eyes that belied the sweetness. A hard look. "No, ma'am," he said, "we're just passing through."

"Well, that's good," she said, but she didn't say why. Eddie noticed, though, that her hand was near her pocket, and her pocket bulged in an angular way suggestive of a small pistol.

"Can we sit?"

The older lady made a gracious gesture, like a queen offering a commoner a seat in front of her throne. Eddie slumped down with his back against the wall and looked at the trio. The man was paying no attention to him. Eddie glanced briefly in his direction and said, "Is he all right?"

The younger woman acquired an annoyed expression. The older one raised her eyebrows. "He hasn't been well lately," she said. "He's been sleeping in the wrong parts of town."

An odd way to put it, Eddie thought then. "What brings you down here?" Eddie said, looking at them.

"Usually the guest says first," said the older lady. "I'm Alma, by the way. This is Linda, that's Chuck."

"Alma," Eddie said, nodding. "We're just looking for someone. Someone in particular. A fellow we need to have a talk with."

Alma nodded. "And you'll be moving on, you say."

"That's right."

"Well, Eddie," she said, stretching her legs out, "you'll understand a person has to be cautious, talking to someone they've never seen before. But let's just say my marriage wasn't working out quite the way I thought it should. And I had nowhere else to go. The women's shelters were all full the night my husband tried to beat me to death. There was no way I could wait until there was an opening. So I grabbed my things and got out the best I could. Couldn't have stayed with any of my friends, because he'd have hunted them down and beat them too. So I took myself out of the way." The smile got grimmer. "I treated this as if it was a camping trip." She glanced around her, and Venom saw that they were well equipped: a little camping stove, one of those which give heat and light both, a kerosene lamp, hissing softly to itself, backpack, sleeping bag, foam mattress.

"Money has to be a problem," Eddie said softly.

"When isn't it?" she said. "I get by."

Alma looked over at Linda, who now looked at Eddie and said, "Family trouble. Alma had trouble with her husband. I had trouble with my uncle. Uncle Sam." She sighed. "I've been homeless for a few years now."

"Vietnam?" said Eddie softly.

She nodded. "I was a nurse. What I didn't realize was that, depending on where you worked, you were just as likely to be exposed to Agent Orange as you were if you were out slogging in the jungle. When I got sick, I knew what the problem was, but I was never able to prove it to the medical tribunal's satisfaction. So . . ." She shrugged. "I couldn't work. I lost my apartment. I went under—literally." She looked around at the tunnels. "All I can do is keep an eye on Alma and Chuck here."

Eddie looked at her pocket and nodded, knowing that she knew he knew the gun was there. "Chuck," he said. "You said he was sleeping in the wrong places. Where would that be?"

Alma jerked her head, indicating someplace up the tunnel and to the right. "Over by the Garden. Something's going on over there, I don't know what. But lately it's been less healthy than usual."

"I've heard," Eddie said. "Someone—" He was *not* going to say, *pretending to be Venom.*

"Something," Alma said. "This town is getting so full of super heroes, and super-villains, and things from other planets that it's hard to know whether you're coming or going." She chuckled. "Remember those T-shirts you used to be able to get that said 'Native New Yorker'? There's a store downtown selling shirts that say 'Native Earthling.' "

Linda smiled as well. "No, there's something down here that has a taste for people," she said, "or chunks of them. Some poor guy got his hand bit off last night."

"Over by the Garden?"

"By the Garden," said Alma. "The place is usually fairly busy because of all the traffic in and out of Penn. You can get in and out of the tunnels there without being noticed, usually. These days—" She shook her head. "A lot of the 'residents' are clearing out, heading over to Grand Central instead."

Eddie was opening his mouth to ask how things were

over there, when footsteps echoed from the other direction. Everyone's head but Chuck's whipped around. Linda's hand went into her pocket without trying to look as if it did so. Eddie sat quiet. The symbiote, without doing so visibly, was moving against him, eager. *Now calm down*, he said to it silently. *You don't know—*

But it *did* know, sometimes. He suspected it knew now.

Up the tunnel, three men came stalking around the corner, stopped, and stared. Because of the way the little bays were built into the side of the tunnel, and the way Alma and her people were tucked into the one they shared, all the three could see at first was Eddie. The men, though hardly more than shadows at that distance, looked briefly at each other, and the soft sound of snickering came down from that end of the tunnel.

It does know, Eddie thought. *All right . . . let's be ready. . . .*

The three sauntered down into the light, easy and confident. None was older than about twenty-five, and they all, to some extent, looked like a bad cross between goths and the Hitlerjüngen. They favored the present style in soiled urban camo, and black leather with as many studs and zippers hanging off it as possible. There was not much else to choose between them, other than that the first one coming along had a brush cut which appeared to have been done with a weed-eater. The second one had apparently gone for the bald look, which didn't do much for him, since he had pimples on his skull. The third had lank greasy hair hanging down so far in front of his eyes that he could have passed for a Yorkshire terrier.

"Well, well, well," said the putative leader, he of the weed-eaten hair, "what have we here?" His hand was in his pocket too, and Eddie studied the pocket for bulges. It was hard to tell, in those baggy pants, what was concealed. It might have been a gun. It might have been a knife, either for the practical reason that knives are more complicated to take away from people than guns are, or the nastier reason that knives are intrinsically more frightening than guns, and many people who can deal with being shot will nonetheless run away screaming at the thought of being cut.

"Were it not for the possibility that you're as deaf as you're possibly blind," Eddie said mildly, "we might tell you. But why waste time or breath?"

"Oh, a wise guy, huh?" said the leader. The other two snickered behind him. "A wise guy, huh, huh, heh heh, yeah—"

The symbiote was beginning to twitch with excitement, and Eddie knew exactly what was coming, but could only laugh. "My God," he said, "we've fallen into a Three Stooges movie. Not only are you three the most hopeless and pitiful excuses for human beings that we've seen in a month of Sundays, but you don't even know how to be threatening properly! We suggest you go out and try it again. Better still"—and he eyed the leader—"we suggest you just *go out*."

Now the leader pulled his weapon. Yes, it was a knife, one of the little brass-collared Italian-style switchblades. Venom smiled gently, for he had seen this particular model several times before, back in San Fran, and it had a tendency to jam. Several of them had also been jammed into him, with responses that varied from useless to amusing. It didn't matter: all those knives' owners were history.

"Man, you're gonna get slice-n-diced now," said the Little Hitler leading the group. Behind him, the bald one doing the Il Duce impression said, "Hey, yeah, slice-n-dice. . . ."

Not the Three Stooges after all, Venom thought sadly. *Nothing so high-class. More like MTV.* "Pitiful," he said. But there were certainly people up on the streets, and down here in the tunnels, who would be frightened by these idiots.

He spared a glance for Alma and Linda. The two of them wore the flat, straight faces of people trying to decide how they're going to fight to save their lives. Afraid, but resigned. The third of them, old Chuck, simply sat looking blankly at the floor.

"Well, come on, Cyrano," Venom said, grinning at the leader. "Let's see what you've got."

The leader moved, with what he probably thought was a strike as fast as a snake. But he was hardly half-wound up for what was going to be a roundhouse slash to Eddie's gut before a thick tentacle had whipped out and caught his arm, wrapping around it exactly as one of those striking snakes might have. The young man's eyes bugged out somewhat satisfactorily, then bugged harder, and he screamed at the top of his lungs. The tendril twisted and broke the arm straight across the radius and ulna, leaving two perfectly matched greenstick fractures sticking up out of the flesh of the arm, blood spurting from the torn brachial artery which the splintered bone of the radius had sliced on its way out.

All right, Eddie thought to the symbiote. But it was already flushing dark all around him again, its protective mask growing and stretching up over his head, growing all its teeth. It whipped out about thirty more tentacles, pinioning the three from elbows to knees, their arms strained behind them, a few tentacles wrapping around their mouths for best effect. Their muffled moans and shrieks that couldn't escape were music to Eddie's ears.

He turned his head quickly and ordered the symbiote back off his face for a moment, shedding the teeth and tongue again just for the moment. To Alma he said, "Look . . . I'm not going to mess up the area with this—" He gestured at the struggling three. "What's the saying? 'Pack out your trash'?"

She looked up at him, wide-eyed, and finally managed a curt nod.

"The place where Chuck's been," he said, "it's over by the Garden?"

"That's right. Listen," she said.

Eddie stopped as the symbiote lifted the three punks in its tentacles, and he prepared to carry them away. "Listen now," Alma said. "You be careful. Whatever it is over there—"

"I think I can manage," he said gently. "Thank you, Alma. You take care too."

As he lifted the punks up high, the teeth and talons and long slavering tongue settled upon him again. Venom carried the three a good way into the darkness.

He waited until he was at least half a mile further down the tunnel, and a level further down, before he allowed the screaming to start. Even then, he muffled most of it, not wanting to alarm Alma too much, or her young friend with the gun, and most of all not wanting to alarm the silent man who didn't speak or look up.

It took him a while to clear away the bodies, but he did it with some care. He had no idea how many others like Alma and her group—innocent refugees from the world above—might be down here. Those people he had no desire to frighten. The others who roved this world—the predators, the cruel ones—he didn't mind scaring them as badly as possible. But at a distance, they were sometimes hard to tell apart.

Once he was finished, Venom went on. It was slow work, finding his way. Even though his memory of the maps was good, the tunnels twisted, confusing even someone who knew where he was supposed to be going. With care he worked his way upward and over into the general neighborhood of Seventh Avenue and 34th Street.

For courtesy's sake, and in case he should meet any more innocents, Eddie returned to his "street clothes." But he met no more people. Perhaps it was early for most people to be heading underground, yet. He saw enough signs of where they had been; not everyone down here was as tidy as Alma and her group. He began to see, as well, indications that something else had been down here.

He started finding scraps of metal on the floor, and splashes of—it was hard to say what. It had no specific color, coming in dark sludgy splashes here and there on walls or floor. The metallic pieces, though, had definitely been torn from barrels or canisters.

In one long dark corridor where many of the lights were gone, he found four or five scraps of the same color—that sort of bilious yellow which marks the barrels in which toxic waste is stored. Using the symbiote's tendrils to handle them—as far as he knew, the symbiote was radiation-proof—he picked up two of these scraps and examined them as closely as he could in the dim light. On one, the edges were sliced clean, as if someone had used a knife sharp enough to cut steel. On another, though, one of the edges was jaggedly cut. *You could almost use it for a saw*, Venom thought, looking at it carefully. He knew the bite pattern of a mouthful of big fangs by now. But to see it in metal was a bit of a surprise.

He put the fragments down and continued, going very carefully and listening constantly. As he had gone along, there had been several places where two or three tunnels conjoined and ran together—different utilities, usually, phone in one, cable or steam in another. Then after a quarter-mile or so, they might part again. Normally, these multiple-joint tunnels were better lit—probably, Venom suspected, because the utility people had to be in them more often. But as he continued now, he noticed that there were progressively fewer working lights in the tunnels.

He examined several of the lights as he passed them. They were not smashed, but appeared to have been cut open cleanly as if someone had come along with a diamond-bladed glass saw, slashing both the bulb protector and the bulb itself.

The tunnel was growing very dark now. Venom came to one of those places where there were almost no lights, where several tunnels met again. Ahead of him he saw, although most dimly, walls which were further apart, a ceiling higher than the one he stood under now.

Into that space Venom came, stopped, looked around him. All the floor of the place was littered with torn and shredded metal; here and there, almost invisible, was a splash of something darker than the walls. *Not blood*, he thought, *something else*. There was a rank, chemical smell about the place.

Now then, he thought, and stood very still, and listened.

He heard a faint scraping sound—coming, not from further down the tunnel, but from somewhere nearby. He cast around him. Off to one side, he saw another access shaft, with a ladder reaching straight down into the next level.

He listened hard. With the echoes down here, it was sometimes hard to tell, but the noise seemed to be coming from down there. *All right*, he thought. *Let's not jump to conclusions. Let's just check this quickly.*

The symbiote was shivering with excitement now. It flushed dark again, surrounded him with its full complement of fangs and the flickering, slavering tongue, blazoned itself with the white spider-shape across his chest. It was eager; it wanted more of what it had just had.

Patience, he thought to it. He went over to the open access shaft and stood looking down, listening. There was only the very faintest light down there—perhaps just one of these dim bulbs left burning. And he could hear the sound of something scraping, rattling, rustling—metal against metal. Not rats—too big for rats.

This is the point, he thought to himself with a slight smile under the cowl, *in a horror movie, when the person hears those noises and goes down to see what's making them, and the audience immediately understands that the character in question is brain-damaged. But never mind. In this movie,* I *am the monster.*

Very slowly and softly, using tendrils and hands and feet, he went down the ladder. Halfway down, he reached for the next rung—and found that there wasn't any more. Air gaped under him. The tentacles let him down, but not too softly. He came down with a clang, some three or four feet further down than he'd thought the floor would be. The ladder might have had an extension once, but it was gone now.

Venom stood dead still in the near-total darkness, letting his eyes get used to it as quickly as they could. The rustling stopped abruptly, and then, very slowly and softly, started again.

Should have brought a flashlight, he thought. But it was too late for that now. He could have cursed his eyes for taking so long to adapt, but cursing wouldn't have helped and would only have attracted more attention— and he already had more of it fixed on him than he wanted.

He found himself staring at a shape so black it nearly vanished into the darkness. He gaped at it in shock.

Slowly it opened great pale moons of eyes, and by their glow he could see, though dimly.

It is unnerving enough to come around a corner in a big city, even one as big as New York, and nearly run into someone who looks so much like you that you're tempted to stop with your mouth hanging open, and stare. It's worse yet to run into such a person deep under the ground, in near-total darkness. And, Eddie discovered, it's worst of all when you are Venom.

The creature at which he was staring—and open-mouthed, for whether out of generalized bloodthirstiness, or specific jealousy, the symbiote was slavering at the sight of the thing—was bipedal, with bilateral symmetry and a head at the top. At the moment, it was crouched slightly, looking at him, and line after line of writhing tendrils wound away from it, wreathing in the air, reaching toward him. Its head was up, and the weaving motion was too swift and purposeful to have anything hypnotic about it. *Smelling*, Eddie thought. *Smelling for what?*

Reluctantly, after that, came the second thought: *It's not Hobgoblin himself, then.* Possibly some creature of his, though. "We don't know what or who you are," he said softly, moving toward it, "but you've picked the wrong person to impersonate."

Those pale eyes stared at him. Some of the tentacles, he saw, were still clutching the remnants of a torn-up canister. "Who are you?" he said. "Some new punk super-villain who doesn't have the guts to work out an identity of his own? Some kind of shapechanger? There have been some of those around every now and then.

But it doesn't matter." He stalked forward. "You have been killing innocent people," Venom said, "in our like-ness . . . our name. And for that"—the symbiote began reaching hungry pseudopodia toward its rival—"there can be only one punishment!"

He let the symbiote go. Instantly it flung a hundred tentacles at the thing, wrapping it around. Venom was not surprised when the creature wrapped as many around him. But he was very surprised when it effortlessly picked him up and threw him halfway down that tunnel, to land with a bone-bruising crash among the torn pieces of canister.

He struggled to his feet, the symbiote helping him with outflung tentacles that whirled and writhed around him now like angry snakes. The symbiote was not used to being tossed around like this. Come to think of it, nei-ther was he. The symbiote caught his rage, and after a breath or two he could hardly see his quarry for the storm of tendrils streaming out toward the fake-Venom as he headed back toward it.

"How many other innocents have you killed?" Venom hissed angrily. "People who won't be missed because no one knows that they're here and no one cares? How many—" He reached out, directing the symbiote to make the tentacles thicker, stronger this time. He wrapped them around the creature like vines around a tree, exert-ing an awful pressure to crush, and the tongue lanced out too, meaning to wrap around the head and rip the top of it off, anticipating the sweet brains inside.

Only something else grabbed his tongue, and nearly pulled it right out of the symbiote. The symbiote screamed soundlessly inside him, a feeling like a nail through his brain, a sound Venom had heard in fights before, and had learned to dread. Physical pain was something it rarely felt until it was driven very close to what it could no longer bear.

It was definitely time to worry now. The creature he was fighting still had him by the symbiote's tongue, and was pulling with such brutality that he thought his own head would be pulled off, no matter how the symbiote resisted. It was pulling him toward its fangs, fangs which had had no problem dealing with metal canisters full of nuclear waste. He tried desperately to push himself away, his bones cracking with the strain.

The creature pulled him closer and closer, its tongue flickering out, wrapping itself around Venom's head in a parody of what the symbiote had planned. The pressure began crushing in on him.

Sheer revulsion did what calculation hadn't been able to do, as the symbiote caught his terror and despair. It flung out tendrils to either side, anchored itself to the walls, insinuated other tendrils between him and the creature, and simply pushed all at once, one mighty leverage-breaking movement that shot him right across the tunnel again and into the far wall. He hit hard and slid to the floor, the tentacles unable to react quickly enough to cushion the impact.

The cure's almost worse than the disease, he thought, struggling back to his feet again. There was a roaring in his head, partly the pounding of blood vessels recovering from a moment of much-increased intracranial pressure, partly the rage of the symbiote—occasionally he would hear it this way, frustrated, angry. It pushed him to his feet and launched itself toward the creature.

He tried to stop it, preferring a more considered kind of attack, but the creature's tentacles and the symbiote's were already tangling together. Venom found himself at the far end of an increasingly violent tug-of-war—wreaths and ropes of pseudopodia knotting and pulling. The symbiote had anchored itself behind some cable conduits on the far wall. They were beginning to creak dangerously as the stress of the tug-of-war began pulling them out of the wall. *All right*, Venom thought savagely, *let's finish this!*

He began to coach the symbiote, showing it where to put the tentacles around their adversary to best advantage—head, limbs, waist. They pulled. The pains in his joints began again, and the pains in his back, and still they pulled. Venom was braced as well as he could be, as well as the symbiote could manage, but it wasn't enough. He felt the pains as his knees, helping to brace, started to bend forward the wrong way; in his arms, as his shoulders threatened to dislocate; in his neck and upper back, as slowly, slowly, the creature pulled him closer. The pair struggled, as each tried to get another grip on the other's head. *Come on!* Venom urged the symbiote. *Save us! Help me save us! Only you can do this—only* we *can do this—come* on!

Little by little he felt its desperation, its determination to be what he wanted—and little by little they pulled back, an inch, two inches, five. Pulled back toward the wall, began to pull the creature with them. *Now!* Venom said. *Now! While we can, while it's off balance!* The symbiote sprouted tendrils edged like knives, ready to tear, to rip—

The other let go. Venom reeled back against the wall again, in a clatter of torn metal and old broken glass. He fell down most ignominiously on his butt.

The creature was standing there, moving away from the wall, now, letting go of its mooring. Its head was up, all those tendrils up too, weaving in the air again, smelling. It looked over at Venom. Dazed, he looked back. The symbiote reached for the thing—

The creature looked at him, then raced away down the almost pitch-black tunnel northward and eastward, toward Madison Square Garden.

Cursing in earnest now, Venom struggled to his feet, feeling like one big bruise. He could feel the symbiote's dejection, disappointment, rage. It had wanted *that*, whatever that was.

So do I, Venom thought. *And shortly we'll have it.* He looked after the creature. *Worth noticing, though: don't attack it and it doesn't attack you. It loses interest as soon as you stop. And it can be distracted.*

Let's go find out by what. Discovering what distracts it may be the key to what will kill it. And once it's dead, then we go after its master: Hobgoblin.

With all the speed they could muster, Venom went down the tunnel after their dark twin.

TEN

Spider-Man crept slowly down the passage toward the gratings. The clear, bluish fluorescent light spilling out almost blinded him after the dimness of the other tunnels.

He edged silently over to the far wall, hunkered down, and peered through. The grating was more like heavy chicken wire than anything else, and it appeared to have been cemented into the wall. Spider-Man thought they could probably be peeled out of the concrete even by someone without spider-strength. Clearly they had been designed for ventilation rather than security.

He had a bird's-eye view of a room about eighty feet square. Three men, two wearing overalls, the third wearing a shirt and jeans and boots, were talking as they assembled a very large piece of machinery. A welter of pallets and large wooden crates surrounded them.

The spider-tracer wasn't going to be able to tell him anything more. Indeed, the buzz he was getting from the tracer was now as strong as it was going to be: he could see one of the big safes stowed over in the corner, its door pried open, the safe emptied out. Spidey's gaze went back to that big piece of machinery in the middle of the room.

Now what the heck is that? Spider-Man thought, watching them work. The men had several "passive pullers," flatbeds on low wheels, each with a handle at the front and hydraulics attached to the handle: pull on the handle and the hydraulics pushed the flatbed forward to relieve the pressure, a standard "negative feedback" device. One of these pullers held a huge, gray metal box, with wiring and power inputs showing off to one side, which one of the men was trying to maneuver into place in a bay of a much larger installation which stood in the middle of the room. The other two were working at the edges of the main installation, folding doors away from the now-open bay, tidying up cables and getting ready to make connections to the new piece of equipment.

Then Hobgoblin stalked into view. Spider-Man spotted his jetglider sitting off to one side. Hobby looked unusually nervous. "Come on," he was saying to his henchmen, "I don't have all day, here! Or all night. This thing has to be in place and running before one!" *What in the world does he want* this *for?* Spider-Man thought.

The henchmen began making placating noises, not that Hobby paid that much attention to them. He just kept stalking up and down, railing at them. Spider-Man settled on the floor of the passageway for the moment to watch the developments and evaluate that big piece of machinery.

It looked like a generator of some kind. Its side doors hung open, showing a little of its guts, and Spider-Man could see what looked like sealed housings of a shape that suggested gigantic wound coils, such as you might expect to see in a power station's generators. But he couldn't imagine for the life of him what this had to do with an atomic bomb.

It's not as if an A-bomb has to be this big, he thought, *or anything like it.* Long ago, in the days of the Manhattan Project before the birth of the transistor, an atomic bomb had to be fairly hefty. *But nothing like this. You couldn't have gotten this thing into the* Enola Gay *with a crowbar.* Nowadays, with transistors and highly compacted explosives to drive the two critical-mass components together, an A-bomb could fit in the back of a car or truck. A truck would probably be best: the uranium and other fissile components were so massive, most cars' shocks and suspension would simply give up under such a trunkload.

The man with the puller wrangled a big "add-on" box into approximately the right position, and the other two men were trying to muscle it into the sort of giant "socket" for which it seemed destined, while Hobgoblin kept stalking around the machine, haranguing them and generally getting in their way.

It's only midnight, Spider-Man thought. *I wonder what his rush is?* Silently he pulled out his camera and its little tripod out of its bag, setting them up. Later, he would move them to whichever grating he finally chose to pull away.

For the moment, a possibility occurred to him. *Could it be a hiding place for the bomb itself? This isn't something he could move easily*, Spider-Man thought. If the bomb itself is a more reasonable size, it could be hidden somewhere in this structure. *You could spend a lot of useful time taking this thing apart, trying to find where the bomb part is hidden.*

It was a possibility. Hobgoblin could be awfully clever. He might assume that he was going to be caught and made a contingency plan. He might have seen to it that whoever caught up with him would waste precious time looking for the bomb—time Hobby could use to escape, possibly with a remote-control trigger.

Spider-Man shook his head. *It might just be a hiding*

place, but I can't believe he would have taken this long to set it up. If not that—then maybe it's something else, something he's going to need later. But what?

He watched Hobby's henchmen as they started connecting a new module into the main generator, while Hobby rubbed his hands together and chuckled.

Let's say you've just held the whole city hostage, Spider-Man thought. *Blackmailed them into giving you a billion bucks. Then what? Logic says you get as far away from the scene of the crime as you can. Brazil . . . heck, Antarctica. Or the moon. Somewhere you can't be extradited from, somewhere you can't be found. But what if Hobby decided that the best place to go to ground after committing a big crime in the middle of New York City, is the middle of New York City itself? They never catch you, because you don't leave. You make yourself a nice comfy little lair with plenty of food, water, whatever else you consider necessary for life the way you like to live it—including a private generator for power. Using what for fuel, though?* And the answer immediately suggested itself: *fissiles! Atomic piles aren't the size they used to be, either. So you set up an atomic reactor for your own private use. This is the perfect place. Use a city main as the water for your reactor to heat and push through the generator's turbines as steam, giving you all the heat and power you need.*

He looked around quickly, eyeing the walls for signs of pipes or tubes. Sure enough, he spotted some in the far wall. There were enough extra pipes to reach the installation in the middle of the room. *It could be,* Spider-Man thought. *Carry out your little blackmail, get paid off, and then just snuggle down under the streets of the city, biding your time until the heat's off.* If that was what Hobby had planned, it had its points.

And if not . . . then I have no idea what that generator's about. The thing I need to do is get a good look around inside. But that's not going to happen with Hobby in place.

He looked down thoughtfully at the henchmen and then at the grilles farther down his passageway. He edged along quietly to examine the other gratings. When he came to the third, Spider-Man smiled to himself. Someone had been pulling at it—there was no way to tell when—but one corner had completely separated from the concrete, and all around the edges, the metal had rusted. It would be a simple enough matter to peel it open and slip in.

No sooner said than done, he thought, and he set to work on the wire, very quietly. That chamber below was well littered with pallets and crates and other nondescript machinery, so there would be plenty of things to hide behind.

Slow and easy, he told himself—though at this point his eagerness was getting the better of him. His anger at the sheer, calculated nastiness that enabled Hobgoblin to blackmail a whole city without even twitching made him very eager indeed to come to grips with the man. Nevertheless, he slowed himself down and concentrated on making as little noise as he could. The last thing he wanted to do was give himself away prematurely.

He began peeling the wire back, bending over a few jagged bits of metal that had broken off the grille and now stuck out of the concrete. *No sense catching the costume on the way down*, he thought.

Hobgoblin had begun to harangue his men again. "Come on, come on," he was snarling, and the nervousness in his voice was really rather surprising. *Can it be*, Spider-Man thought, *that he's finally realized that he's riding a tiger, and he's suddenly not too sure that he can keep hanging onto its ears?* That was possibly something that could be used to Spidey's advantage. Despite having made this bomb, or having had it made for him, Hobby was still nervous of his ability to handle it. *He might yet make a mistake . . . something I can exploit.* Spider-Man just hoped it wouldn't be the kind of mistake which would leave Manhattan a smoking crater.

With a final small jerk, the grating came loose in his hands. Even as it did, Hobby, muttering something under his breath, stalked off into the next room. Spider-Man smiled under his mask, got up silently, fetched his camera, and repositioned it.

The three henchmen were still wrestling and sweating at the job of fitting the new module into the generator. One of them went around the far side of the big main machine, and while the other two were watching him, Spider-Man slipped through the now-empty opening and let himself down to the floor level on a webline.

Spidey found a convenient pallet loaded with crates and tucked himself behind it, watching the men move.

"Aah, this is crap," the sandy-haired one of the pair wearing overalls said quietly to his companions. "He doesn't need this thing tonight. He's just paranoid."

The other two grunted assent, but quietly. "No use arguing with him when he's like this," said the second one, the man wearing the shirt and jeans. "Otherwise you wind up with one of those little pumpkins stuffed up your nose."

The sandy-haired man went around the far side of the machine again. "Aah," said the third one, "you know what his problem is?"

"He's a raving loony," said the sandy-haired man.

"Nah. You know what he has? A bad management style. Give him one of those executive seminars, he'd be okay."

The second man stared at the third, disbelieving. The first one was still around the far side of the machine, hammering at something with a rubber mallet. While the two discussed management technique and whether a seminar would do Hobgoblin any good whatever, Spider-Man crept closer.

The sandy-haired man in the overalls gave the installation one last desultory whack with the rubber mallet. "The contacts are in," he said, dropping the mallet on the floor. "I don't care if he does want it perfect. It's not going to fit smooth. I think they screwed it up at the factory."

"They did what?" said one of the others.

"They screwed it up, and it's not our fault, I don't care what he says." He sat on one of the crates looking disgusted.

"He'll say we did it," said the man in the shirt and jeans.

"Well, let him. He has a negative attitude," said the second man.

This might have been true, but Spider-Man didn't see any point in waiting for further analysis. He promptly stood up from behind the pallet of crates where he was hiding and jumped the sandy-haired man from behind.

There was a brief but utterly silent tussle, at the end of which the sandy-haired man was as well swathed in a web as any fly after the spider's through with it. Effectively gagged, unable to utter a sound, he lay there squirming. On the other side of the machine, Spider-Man heard the man in the shirt and jeans say, "No wonder he keeps getting into trouble at work."

Spider-Man smiled to himself, while busily webbing the first man to one of the pallets, so he couldn't squirm out into sight. Then, crouching down behind another stack of crates, he turned his attention to the other two.

Henchmen, he thought. *What the heck* is *a hench? Is it something you carry around, like luggage? Something to eat? Maybe some kind of animal, if it had a henchman to take care of it?*

He slipped behind another pallet and looked at the other two men. They had finished taking the load-puller out from under the new installation, and the one in the jeans and shirt was standing back from it, lighting a cigarette. The other one looked at him with mild reproof and said, "You shouldn't do that in here—You Know Who gets cranky."

"Aah," said the smoker, taking a long drag.

"Besides," said the other man in the overalls, "you said you were giving it up."

"I did give up. Last week."

"You gotta try harder. They say now that if you can go

cold turkey for two weeks, you'll probably give it up clean."

"Huh," said the smoker. He looked up at the installation. "That thing still isn't fitting right around the edges," he said. "Hank, where's that hammer?"

He dropped the cigarette and stepped on it, then went around the corner of the generator to where he had last seen the first man. "Oh, here it is. Where's Hank?"

"Probably went off to take a leak."

"He didn't even say anything."

"He's been that way a lot lately," said the man in the overalls. "Kinda short tempered."

"I don't know," said the man in the jeans, taking a long look at the spot that Hank had been working on. "He's never been too big on social skills, has he?"

"Nah. I think it's 'cause'a not having much family."

Spider-Man spun a length of web between his hands, judged the length and thickness of it, and paused.

"Probably. I think he doesn't have much to take his mind off his work—"

Spider-Man leapt. The ensuing struggle was mercifully brief: in a matter of seconds, the man in the jeans was as thoroughly swathed in webbing as the first, and, also like him, fastened down to the back of another of the pallets. Silently, Spider-Man slipped around to the generator.

"I don't know," said the remaining man, looking absently at the stepped-on cigarette. "I think what he needs is something to do besides work. Maybe a bowling league, or a softball team, or something. If he just— mmmf!"

Spider-Man struck a few seconds later, and the third man joined his cohorts, trussed up like a Thanksgiving turkey and stowed behind yet another pallet full of crates. *Now then*, Spider-Man thought, and he slipped into a new hiding place behind the generator itself.

Hobgoblin's voice could be heard, loud and getting louder, as he came in from the next room. "Look at that," he said testily, "it looks terrible. What am I paying you people for, anyway? Can't you even put simple machinery together straight? Look at that join, it's a mess. And then you stand around gabbing, after what I've paid you. Don't you understand that—Men? Where are you?"

Hobgoblin came through the door. "Where are you?" he demanded. Then he looked around in shock. "I can't believe it," he muttered to himself. "Look at this! This is not a time for a lunch break!" He stalked around—and Spider-Man watched Hobgoblin's face change as he realized it was not a matter of lunch breaks or anything else. He looked up and noticed the window where the grating had been torn out. "They're gone. Where'd they go?" And then his face changed under the mask from confusion to anger.

"Spider-Man!" he hissed. "All right, you two-bit web-slinger, I know you're in here somewhere! Come out!"

Hobgoblin ran for the jetglider. It rose under him, and he began swooping around the room, desperately trying to locate his enemy.

Spider-Man, grinning to himself, cried, "Two can play at this game, Hobby!" He bounded for the ceiling when Hobby was near the floor, for the floor when he was near the ceiling, always using the big installation in the middle as a way to stay out of sight. The effect, Spidey knew, would be utter confusion for Hobgoblin—he wouldn't know which way to turn.

"You've interfered with me for the last time, bug," Hobgoblin shouted, and abruptly, not five feet away from Spider-Man, in transit between a wall and the floor, a flash bomb went off. Warned by his spider-sense, Spidey ducked out of the way easily. It was followed by another, and another a few feet to Spidey's other side. He laughed to himself, though: Hobgoblin was chucking them around randomly, having no clear sense of where Spider-Man was.

"Spiders aren't bugs," Spider-Man called cheerfully as he dodged another flashbomb, "they're arachnids. But then you were never very strong on anything but the applied sciences." A few more flash bombs went off quite close to him. *Trying to draw me out*, Spider-Man thought as he leapt again. He felt exhilarated. After the time spent tonight walking in dark tunnels, the crouching and the claustrophobia, Spider-Man was glad of an excuse to stretch and move. Flash bombs popped and boomed all around him, but Hobby still hadn't seen where he was. Which was just as well; he had no desire to catch one of those up close, even though they were a lot less harmful than the pumpkin bombs were.

That caution, in itself, was diagnostic. *He doesn't want to hurt his generator*, Spider-Man realized. *He doesn't dare. So long as I stay in here, we're okay.*

But—and he grew thoughtful as another flash bomb zipped harmlessly past—*there may be no point in stay-*

ing, since I don't have any proof the bomb is here. And if it's not here, I'm wasting my time.

Hobgoblin was wheeling and screaming around, now, with much more animus than usual. *"I'll get you! I'll get you and squash you like the bug you are, arachnid or no damned arachnid—!"*

"Yeah, yeah," Spider-Man called brightly, continuing with his evasive maneuvers, "the same old song. You couldn't hit your own mother with a flyswatter. Did you *have* a mother? Jeez, she must be embarrassed—!"

Hobgoblin was not amused. "I'll show you—"

There was a sudden crumbling noise from off to one side of the room. Hobby paused in mid-glide, hovering, staring at the wall. Spider-Man, momentarily hiding behind another tall pallet-full of crates, peered around to see what was happening.

The wall was bulging in a very unnerving way. With a sound like a gunshot, a big crack appeared in the concrete, in the place where the bulge was most pronounced. The bulge got bigger, and the crack spread, starfishing out from what seemed like an impact point, a place where the wall was being hit, and hit hard, by something from the outside.

The concrete floor began to vibrate faintly. The other walls thrummed in response, and the thrumming slowly rose to a rumble like distant thunder. The crack stitched wider under the repeated blows from outside, multiplied itself up and down the width of the wall. Then— *smash!*—all at once, the wall fell in.

Hobgoblin threw a couple of flash bombs at something big and black pushing through the rubble, but they had no effect. Another *smash!* and broken concrete and pieces of steel-reinforcing rod came raining down into the room, leaving a great hole into blackness.

Through the hole, striding out of the darkness, came Venom. *Not now!* Spidey thought. *Not again!*

Spider-Man glanced up at Hobgoblin. The jetglider slowly backed away.

"You!" Hobgoblin snarled at Venom. He seemed to be trying hard to sound outraged, but his nervousness showed much too clearly. "Get out of here before I put an end to your nuisance once and for all!" He hefted a pumpkin-bomb, but didn't throw it.

Venom stood there, arms folded, while the symbiote's tendrils writhed about him, and the symbiote's tongue licked the air and reached toward Hobgoblin hungrily. "If you could do anything about us," Venom said calmly, "you would have by now. Which means you can't do anything about us. Or won't." He eyed the big lump of machinery in the middle of the room. "And if this is what we think it is—we believe we know why you won't, and can't, do anything."

Up until now, Spider-Man had been avoiding being seen by Hobby, mostly to see what the crook might do next, where he might lead him. Now, though, it occurred to him that if he didn't do something quickly, Hobgoblin would shortly no longer be a factor in this or any other equation. He leapt out from the wall, where he had briefly been hanging upside down behind yet another stacked-up pallet, and landed between Hobgoblin and Venom. "Listen," he said urgently, "Venom, if I were you—"

The symbiote turned on him with considerable scorn. "You are not us," he said. "Something for which we give thanks, morning and night. You had your chance to be us, and you blew it. Now stand back and let someone deal with this"—Venom glanced at Hobgoblin with the kind of look someone might give a carton of sour yogurt —"this *thing* who can do the job properly."

Hobgoblin's jetglider lifted suddenly, as if he were about to soar away. He never had a chance. The tendrils flung out at him like ropes, caught the jetglider in several different places, anchored to it, and dragged it closer while Hobgoblin fought to get away. Other tendrils sought out and swathed Hobgoblin's hands in steely bands, making the flinging of bombs or the activation of energy gauntlets impossible.

"For you," Venom said, "we have only one desire. Besides ridding the world of you, but we'll get to that shortly. We want to know about this creature which is running about the sewers and tunnels of this city, impersonating us and killing innocent people in our likeness. A simple enough business, it must have seemed to you. Distract attention from yourself by presenting what ill-informed people consider another so-called 'super-villain' so you can continue your schemes uninterrupted. Meantime, blameless men and women are terrorized and killed. It's all just a game to you, of course. But now"— grinning, Venom pulled the jetglider closer, while its engine screamed in protest and useless resistance—"now the reckoning time has come. You've outdone yourself this time, Hobgoblin. You've created a creature sufficiently robust that even *we* have a difficult time subduing it. So you are going to tell us everything we need to know to destroy it. If you're quick, we will be fairly merciful, and we'll be no longer about eating your probably slightly rancid and tasteless brain than necessary. If you waste any more of our time, though, we will start by tearing your arms and legs off."

Spider-Man's first impulse was to let Venom go ahead, but there were more important matters to be dealt with. "Venom," he said, "wait a moment. I take it you've met up with your lookalike down here somewhere—"

"Met it—" A look of annoyance passed over the fanged face. The teeth gnashed as the symbiote expressed its partner's frustration. "We met, yes."

"You came away with your skin intact, but not your ego, I can see that. Listen to me! Good as Hobby here is at stuff like bombs, hasn't it occurred to you that what you ran into is, well, beyond his expertise?"

"This is difficult to say," Venom said, looking at Spider-Man with a slight glimmer of interest, "but we must confess we haven't exactly made a study of this thing's 'expertise.'"

"Then think about it," Spider-Man said. "I don't think what attacked you, what attacked me, has anything to do with him. It's not even from here."

Venom suddenly looked even more interested, a dismaying effect on that sinister face. "We take it you refer to an origin a lot further away than the Five Boroughs."

"It's not from Earth."

"Is this some project of yours that went astray?"

"I can't take credit for this one," Spider-Man said, shaking his head.

"Who then?"

"Look," Spider-Man said, "I can't discuss it now. But it's nothing to do with him. There's more important business of his to deal with at the moment."

"Yes," Venom said cheerfully enough. "Rending him limb from limb sounds like a good place to begin." The tendrils began to pull. Hobgoblin screamed.

"*No!*" Spider-Man launched himself at Venom, trying to web as many of those tentacles as he could, and pull them away from Hobgoblin. The tendrils, though, just kept welling out between the strands of web. "Venom, he's got a bomb down here somewhere, and we have no way to know how it's supposed to be set off! He may have some kind of dead-man switch hooked up to his lifesigns, or God only knows what else he's managed. But if you kill him now, there'll be no way we can be sure of how to deactivate the thing!"

Venom looked at Spider-Man, though the pressure on Hobgoblin did not appear to decrease, and Hobby's screams continued. "Believe me," Spider-Man said, "if we could stick him and his little tinkertoy bomb in the same garbage can, shove them off the planet together, and let them blow, do you think I wouldn't do it? But his finger is on the trigger of an A-bomb, and millions and millions of innocent lives are at stake!" Spider-Man came down hard on the word *innocent*. "This is not the time to go around eating people's brains!"

There came a sudden shriek of the jetglider's engines as they pushed the glider, not back, but forward. All the tension went out of the straining tentacles, and Venom, suddenly pulling against no resistance, fell backwards.

The screaming jetglider engines almost rammed Hobgoblin into the ceiling of the big room. He ducked barely in time, recovered, dove down low, and zoomed off past Venom again—then out through the hole Venom had made in the wall.

Venom staggered to his feet and stared, astonished and enraged. Then he whirled on Spider-Man. The tendrils reached out menacingly toward him, and Spidey got ready to web as many of them as necessary to keep them from closing around his throat, or doing any rending-limb-from-limb on *him*.

"This is the second time you have interfered in our vengeance against this wretched creature," Venom growled. "We should kill you now, but if we waste time with you, we're going to lose him. You may assume, therefore, that our next meeting will be our last."

"I'll save a spot for you on my dance card," Spider-Man said. "And whatever you do, if you want to save this city's life, don't give in to your little urges. You need Hobgoblin, alive and functioning to disarm that bomb."

Venom threw him a furious look and swarmed out after the swiftly retreating whine of the jetglider.

Spider-Man hurried back up the wall and through the opening he had made, recovering his camera and packing it away. *Those flash bombs should have given it good light cues to go by*, he thought. *Hope they didn't fool the strobe into overexposing. We'll see. . . . But if there's any New York City left tomorrow morning, these are going to look brilliant in the afternoon edition.*

Meantime, Spider-Man had an idea. It might take

some doing to set up. If it worked, though, the results could be excellent . . . and the main problem was to get the results *fast*. This was, as he had pointed out to Venom, a gamble, one for millions of lives. In this case, though, it was better to gamble than to do nothing.

Spider-Man plunged back toward the subway tunnels, the way he had come, in pursuit of the last best chance to save New York.

ELEVEN

T he next two hours moved with dreadful slowness and terrible speed.

Spider-Man knew he and his quarry were going to have to find their way back to the underground generator, so he took care to remember his route, marking it with spider-tracers. Several times, where numerous train lines crossed, his spider-sense warned him of an express coming up behind him, unheard because of the omnidirectional clatter and thunder of its brethren. Then he would leap to the ceiling, clinging to it while the metallic juggernaut shrieked and sparked as it passed, inches from his back. There was a certain grim humor in it. New York City might be about to end at five-thirty in the morning, but until then, the subways would keep running.

The whole thing was a longshot, of course, but most of the creature's appearances seemed to be on the west side rather than the east. Perhaps the creature found the middle of the city too populous, too dangerous, too full of machinery and trouble. He was beginning to feel for it, in a way. Here it was, alone in a strange place, confused, frightened, alone. It was more analogous to a lost animal than anything else; it hadn't shown much evidence of high intelligence. Most likely on breaking out of the sub, it had headed straight for open water and had been borne southwards by the prevailing currents where the East River emptied into the harbor. Then eventually it had struck up the far side of the island, westward, coming to a sewage outfall or another entry into the tunnel system. From there it could easily have sought out or stumbled into one, then made its way further underground, where the ambient radiation was less.

As Spider-Man made his way through the tunnels, he again mulled over the creature's bizarre physiology, for exploiting that physiology was now his best chance. The creature was sensitive to very small amounts of radioactive material. Its reaction to the little canister of isotope he was carrying was evidence enough of that. It had sensed that clearly, even through a lead container. *And there*, he thought, *lie the possibilities.*

Spider-Man paused at the junction of two tunnels. Too many of these tunnels looked alike, the only differentiating characteristics being the graffiti on the walls, and sometimes the smell.

He pulled out another spider-tracer. Spider-Man had five or six more tracers left. He leapt up onto the ceiling and slapped this latest tracer there, where it gave off the usual tiny reassuring buzz to his spider-sense.

Spider-Man came down to the floor again, paused. *All right*, he thought. *This should be—what? About Seventh Avenue and Fiftieth. So, about four or five long blocks further west, a few more up. A good way to go yet.*

He started working his way westward again. He was into the utility tunnels again, something for which he was profoundly grateful—the noise of the trains got on his nerves. Still, there would be more interesting things to watch for in the next while. *What time is it?*

He checked his watch. *One forty-eight. Four hours ... less! This is* not *great.* His mission depended on speed, and here he was crawling around in tunnels. Spider-Man desperately wanted to be up in the clear air, swinging on a webline, out where he could see where he was going. But you can't always get what you want. *But hopefully*, he thought with a small grin, *I'll get what I need.*

His mind started drifting as he trudged forward. *I had promised to get something for MJ*, he thought. *What was it?* He laughed ruefully as he ran upside down along the ceiling of a tunnel whose floor was littered with rubble. *Woolite, that was it. I promised I would bring some back.* Even down here, among all the dreadful smells, he was acutely aware that his costume needed washing again.

He stopped at a big intersection, looking around. *Aha*, he thought. Faintly he could hear train rumble again, possibly one of the Broadway lines. *We're in the neighborhood.*

He turned left, slapping another spider-tracer high on the wall, and continued. Another two hundred yards on, an archway opened before him, and he gazed through it into the tunnel where he fell unconscious before. He remembered some broken concrete rubble off to one side.

That's the ticket, he thought. *Now then!*

Spider-Man began retracing his steps with more certainty. These were the tunnels in which he had lost the creature. He followed the path of his escaping bounds and leaps, recognizing a splash of spray paint on a wall here, a dropped cigarette box there. Everything was surprisingly clear in his memory, despite his weary and battered state at that point. But he was feeling a little less battered now. Weary, yes, and he could do serious damage to a steak. Twenty hours of sleep would be nice, too.

Whether he was ever going to get any such things, of

course, was another matter. But it was nice to think about, down here in the dark, amidst the stench, on the trail of something which could probably wad him up like a ball of paper and slamdunk him through the nearest wall.

That's an interesting question, he thought, as he made his way through the ever-more-familiar tunnels. *The creature's strength is all out of proportion to a normal life-form that size.* To determine the cause, of course, the creature itself would have to stand still for analysis, and if there was one thing Spider-Man had noticed, standing still was not high on its list of things to do.

Like a hummingbird, he thought. *It's got to eat all the time to keep going. Its intake of residual and background radiation must be very carefully balanced against its intake of harder, more concentrated sources of radiation. Too much of one or the other might have serious consequences.*

He reached one of the tunnels he had passed through before and stopped. Torn-up metal lay around in strips and shreds. He picked up one piece and fingered it thoughtfully. It reminded him of the metal of those canisters which had been stolen from CCRC. He lifted it to his face and sniffed, but caught nothing more than a vague chemical smell.

Something made a scratching sound not too far away. Spider-Man stopped, listening, and softly put the piece of metal down. *A rat?* he thought. But it was not a rat. It sounded like it might have been underneath. *Below me somewhere?*

Well, he thought. *Let's see. Spend a few minutes here:*

then if that doesn't work, I'll move a little further on, try again. All the same, the thought of having to do this six or eight times frightened him. He had wasted enough precious minutes finding his way back here.

Spider-Man chopped the thought off. Slowly he reached to the canister webbed to his belt. There was no time to rig any protective gear for himself and there was no realistic way to calculate radiation dosage. And there was hardly time to go back to ESU to get a lead apron.

He unscrewed the canister. There inside it lay the little glass capsule, very innocuous-looking. Americium isotope wasn't something you could carry around in lumps; it was enough trouble making it in thousandths of a gram, and half the time you wound up cutting it with talc so you could work with it at all. No matter. No time to worry about it.

Slowly he held up the open canister—and stood there with it open, feeling his skin begin to itch.

Somewhere, below him, came a rustle. Then another.

It can't really make you itch, he reassured himself. Nonetheless, he swore he could feel the stuff burning through his hand. It was ridiculous. His hand was protected by the lead container. Radiation escaping from the end of the canister moved in a straight line. It did not go around corners; otherwise that concrete shield back at ESU would have been useless.

Spider-Man stood there in the darkness, waiting for the creature to hurry up and take the bait. He grew impatient, and muttered, "Oh, come on."

And to his surprise, his spider-sense began to tingle. He turned, looking for the source.

There was a stairway leading downwards, off to one side of the tunnel. Many tunnels had these. Spider-Man had been ignoring them, by and large, trying to stay on one level and not confuse himself too much. Now he saw something come wavering up that stairway. *A snake?* As far as he knew, the New York sewers and tunnels were not famous for snakes.

After that first one came wavering up another of the long, sinuous shapes: not a snake at all, but a long black tentacle. The rustling grew louder as more of those dark tentacles came whispering up out of the stairwell to the lower level. And behind them, the larger shape, dark, humanoid, bigger than a human—

For a moment Spider-Man's heart clenched, as he thought he was looking at Venom. *No, it's bigger than Venom!*

It paused near the top of the stairwell, holding the two sides of the opening with its arms, crouched down, staring at him with those pale patches of eyes. Slowly Spider-Man held up the little canister with the americium inside.

As fast as any number of cobras striking, the creature leaped at him. But Spider-Man was ready for it this time. He leapt faster and away.

On spider-agile feet and single-handedly, he went galloping along the ceiling of the tunnel, retracing his steps, heading for the nearest of his tracers. The creature rushed along after him, bumping, scattering the trash and the rubble, grasping at Spider-Man with its tentacles. Once or twice he felt the wind of one or another of them missing him from behind as it made a hurried grab at him, but fast moves, quick rushes on his part, and the warnings of his spider-sense kept him one jump ahead. Spider-Man began to feel like the snack cart at the college cafeteria, with a whole class of hungry undergrads after him.

He burst into a big chamber, ran right around the walls of it, and was about to turn into the hallway he had marked, when he noticed dark, crouched forms in it, staring at him in astonishment. *Oh, no*, he thought, *people!* Behind him he heard, once again, the bizarre soprano screech of the creature as it came up behind. It was not used to its food running away with such energy. It was taking exception.

I can't bring it there, he thought, and instead led it down a secondary tunnel that led to the train tracks. Here, at least, there wouldn't be too much trouble. It was the middle of the night, the trains were few and far between.

Fat chance, he thought with a gasp of a laugh as he dived out the door, over the third rail, and came down on the tracks running. He sprinted down to the platform, ignoring the almost-empty station, and out again. The creature galloped after him at full speed.

They ran on. Another platform came into view down a long straight run of track, and he could see the glaring lights of a train facing him head-on. No matter for the moment. This tunnel intersected with the one he had marked. He could feel the tracer not too far away.

Behind him there was a bump, followed by a splatter of brightness, a fizz of furious sparks, and a shower of light, as the creature touched the third rail. That soprano shriek went up again, angry this time.

Spider-Man glanced back. The creature was barely thirty yards behind him. *Didn't even slow it down*, he thought in wonder. He kept running. At the end of the tunnel, the glaring lights of the train began to move forward, and he heard the squeak of its wheels as it began to pick up speed.

Where is that opening? he thought. *It was down here, before the station—where* is *the thing?* Behind him he could hear gravel crunching as the creature closed in on him. Its scream rang out again, sounding frustrated and annoyed.

I've done a lot of interesting things in my career, thought Spider-Man, *but I've never yet played chicken with an A train. Where is that opening?* Then he saw it, about fifty yards ahead of him. He sprinted. So did the train. Behind him, the creature was gaining on the straightaway. Not close enough to get him with the tentacles as yet, but they were reaching, and the scream was getting closer. *Okay*, he thought, *just follow me on in here, don't let the nice train hit you, all right?*

Spider-Man dived sideways over the third rail, into the opening of the utility tunnel. His spider-sense told him that his tracer was no more than another thirty yards behind him, and the way to it seemed clear. He paused in the doorway, panting for breath, and turned for a moment—and then heard the scream of brakes as if the train's driver, no doubt used to placid after-midnight runs, suddenly noticed something unusual on the tracks and realized it might be better not to hit it.

The brakes' squeal went up together with the creature's screech—louder and louder as the two closed on one another. Spider-Man peered out from the doorway to see that the creature made no move to get out of the train's way. Perhaps it felt it didn't need to—anything that could knock over a Penn Central diesel had little to worry about from an IRT train. The IRT train, though, and the people on it, had plenty to worry about.

Spider-Man leapt out of the alcove with all the strength he could muster and kicked the creature out of the train's direct path. He used his webbing and the momentum of the kick to bring himself up from there to the ceiling in order to keep himself safe.

The train came to a shuddering halt. There was a long pause, but then the crunch of gravel resumed as the creature made itself thinner and oozed out from between the wall and the train. *Well, it's still alive*, Spider-Man thought. He began to retreat. As the creature pulled itself into the opening of the utility tunnel, neatly missing the third rail this time, Spider-Man turned and ran.

The path was a little more familiar. Spider-Man had the tracer to guide him. Left, then right, right again, left once more—and there was the tracer; he was back on known ground. The creature was right behind him, though. Once or twice he felt the quick swipe of wind on the back of his neck as those tentacles made a grab for him, and a different swipe of cold wind further down as it went for the belt, remembering that the isotopes had been there before. But both times it missed, and both times Spider-Man just raced on, not even pausing to look behind to see if it was catching up. *Satchel Paige would be proud of me.*

The utility tunnels grew quiet as they ran. *As quiet as it ever gets this time of night*, Spider-Man thought, *with the train traffic at its lowest.* The only really noticeable noises were the frustrated screeches of the creature behind. It was a pitiful sound, in its way, and if Spider-Man's breath had not been coming so hard he would have felt actively sorry for it. Not only alone, and the only one of its kind on this planet—if that meant anything to it—but hungry, and afraid it wouldn't get what it needed to survive. *Well, after it finds the bomb for me, it can have this*, Spider-Man thought.

He grinned under his mask as he ran. The shielding on an atomic bomb generally isn't much, so as not to interfere with its being easily transportable. *If my buddy here goes after a little americium like this, it should have no trouble finding Hobby's little Tinkertoy. And once we've found it, it can be disarmed. Even Hobby's scientists won't have bothered working up anything more sophisticated to attach to the stolen trigger device than you'd find in a good James Bond movie. Probably I could defuse it myself . . . though if there's time, I'd sooner call in the folks from the Atomic Energy Commission.*

His spider-sense kicked into overdrive, warning of another tentacle swiping at his ankle; he scooted out of its way. His breath was coming harder. *Can't slow down now.*

He passed another spider-tracer, encouraged. This one he remembered as the third one he had put down. He ran past it, leapt for the ceiling again, kept scurrying on. He threw a quick look over his shoulder, wished he hadn't, turned, and kept on going. *Can't run outta speed now. MJ'll be really upset if the city's blown up at five thirty.*

He was hyperventilating. *It's bigger too*, came a thought. And that was true—the creature was bigger than when he had last seen it. Not incredibly so, but enough to notice. The bit of isotope it had gotten when they met first—*Just that little dose*, Spider-Man thought. *A gram or two, no more. It grew from that. What a physiology!*

He dropped from the ceiling and scurried along the floor again, past the second tracer, the one he had left on the ceiling. *Real close*, Spider-Man thought. *Real close. Pretty soon now, it should stop homing on me, and home on*—

He turned a corner, ran down that last long hall, saw the light of the gratings ahead of him—

—and was knocked flat by the creature, who sprang at him. His spider-sense warned him, but the creature came too fast for him to capitalize on the warning in time. It felt exactly like being run over by a train: legs, arms, tentacles, the creature scrambled at Spider-Man, flung him to the side, and swarmed across him, to his absolute astonishment, completely ignoring both Spider-Man and the canister he carried.

Spider-Man levered himself up on his forearms and stared down the dim-lit tunnel at the creature. It was battering at the wall. It screamed that high unearthly scream one more time, and then arms and tentacles together fastened themselves onto the wall—and the concrete began to crumble. It didn't quite melt, though the stone did run;

it didn't quite crumble, though dust sifted down. The whole big patch of concrete simply slumped in and away from the creature. Spider-Man had a sudden and irrational urge to hide his eyes, as if from an atomic blast. But if that thing were throwing hard radiation at the wall, no amount of eye-hiding would help him—he was toast, every cell of his body sleeted through with gamma rays of such intensity that he would simply come apart in a few days like wet tissue paper. But he felt not the slightest tinge of heat, and people getting lethal doses of gamma typically reported the feeling of a flash of heat.

The creature scrabbled at the wall, and the wall continued to give way in front of it. Spider-Man scrambled to his feet. The effect was occurring only where the creature actually touched the wall. *Not radiation*, he thought, *not as such. It's as if it were disorganizing the shells of the atoms of the wall on a local basis. Collapsing them?* Possibly. Maybe in an earlier time, this creature's kind had normally eaten this way. Fissiles didn't usually occur in pure form, but as very sparse ore. *Maybe this was how they got the good stuff out, and threw away what they didn't need. I guess anyone can get too much bulk in their diet.*

There was no way to tell. Bracing itself with some tentacles, the creature pulled away at the wall, and the concrete and the metal slumped and fell away until they were gone. The creature dived through into Hobgoblin's generator room.

Spider-Man went after it, impressed, but all the same careful not to touch the edges of the hole. The creature tore its way toward the middle of the big room, ignoring both the generator and the piled up crates and pallets, which was fortunate, considering that the goons Spider-Man had webbed up earlier were still stuck down there.

The creature screamed, louder than before. Up came the tentacles again, questing, wreathing around it. "Aha," Spider-Man said softly. "You know it's down here somewhere, don't you?"

The creature began scrabbling at the floor. The floor began to give. *Uh-oh*, Spider-Man thought, hurriedly shooting a webline at the ceiling, and got himself up off the floor before it did something sudden.

The floor beneath the creature crumbled. It looked like a bowl of damp brown sugar being stirred, everything settling inward and downward. A hole appeared, then a space ten feet or so wide fell away from beneath the creature. It dove through roaring, but this time the roar had an odd note in it, one which Spider-Man hadn't heard before. In a human being, it might have been triumph.

Well, let's not miss the fun, Spider-Man said to himself. He swung down on his webline to drop through that hole after the creature—but at a slight angle, so as not to come down right on top of it; he did not want to distract it at this of all moments.

He only had a second or two to take everything in, but there was quite a bit to take in. There was another chamber down here, about the same size as the one above. There had been a lot of equipment in it, big machines like the generator upstairs, a little mainframe computer, some smaller stand-alone PCs. But the phrase "had been" was germane in this case, because a great deal of the machinery lay in broken, shattered piles around the floor: busted circuit boards, smashed monitors, all kinds of plastic and metallic rubble.

Then Spider-Man saw the cause of the destruction: Venom and Hobgoblin. Off to one side, the symbiote had cornered Hobgoblin, who stood on a battered but still hovering jetglider, with one hand clenching a pumpkin bomb and the other something that looked like a cellphone but which Spider-Man suspected was the trigger for the bomb.

I've missed all the excitement, he thought ruefully. *There's been one heck of a fight here. But even Venom wasn't willing to take any more chances with blowing up the city. We're right into the Mexican standoff stage now.*

But now the equation had another element. The creature took only enough time to hit the ground and recover itself. Then all its tentacles and its head whipped around to face a metal box four feet tall and two feet wide that sat by itself in a corner.

The creature flew at it with another of those cries of both hunger and delight, a sound that Spider-Man thought he had only ever heard before from MJ when you took her into that really good Szechuan restaurant at Second and Sixty-Third. It also occurred to Spider-Man at this point—as the creature flung itself at the container of the bomb and began ripping it to shreds—that there was no way for anyone, least of all Hobgoblin, to stop the Interplanetary Gourmet from having what, under present circumstances, was probably the meal of a lifetime.

Hobgoblin stared at it. Venom stared at it too, but

Hobby's look was one of much greater horror. At first, Spider-Man thought the bomb's case might have been booby-trapped, and this was about to be the last second of life for all of them. But then he realized Hobby's horror wasn't at the thought of being blown up, but that his bomb was being ignominiously noshed down like a corned beef sandwich at the Stage Deli.

"No!" Hobgoblin shrieked, "no, no, *no!*" and flew at the creature on his jetglider, pressing the button on his little box. Spider-Man stared in horror.

The creature, busy with the bomb, threw a great wad of wiring and circuitry at Hobby as he came. There was a small explosion which scattered almond-scented shrapnel all around. Warned by his spider-sense, Spider-Man threw himself to the ground—then slowly stood up again, to the sound of more ripping metal. Off to one side, Hobgoblin and his jetglider were on the ground, twisted metal and twisted man trying to disentangled themselves from each other. Spider-Man recognized the almond smell: *semtex*, he thought.

Meanwhile, the creature was still tearing at the bomb, and after a moment it came up with the only thing that mattered to it: a shape very like a giant cold capsule made of lead-coated steel, slit all open down one side.

Spider-Man blinked. One of the most annoying things about an A-bomb is the basic design, which even the most ill-educated terrorists and impecunious foreign governments have managed to duplicate. Any mass of plutonium over a certain size will blow up; it can't help it. The only way to delay this process is to divide the critical mass into two parts and only slam them together when you want the explosion to happen. The slamming is done by a shaped charge of high explosive, this being what had gone off—but, thanks to the creature's hurry to get at its meal, the explosion hadn't been properly confined, and had done nothing but blow out one end of the bomb's containment vessel. Out of this, the creature hooked out the hemisphere of plutonium that had been closest to the charge, and started eating—crooning with joy as it stuffed bite after bite of metallic plutonium-uranium alloy into its face.

Spider-Man was of two opinions whether or not to breathe, since plutonium is about the most toxic thing on the planet. But by this time the creature had put that whole first lump of fissile into its gut, and was hooking the other piece out of the lead and steel capsule. And he didn't feel any warning from his spider-sense.

"No!" Hobby screamed, staggering across the room toward the creature, "don't, you dumb—"

Spider-Man never found out how Hobby intended to describe the creature, for several tentacles promptly came out and backhanded Hobby halfway across the room again. The creature was oblivious: it took bite after bite out of the second dark, shining hemisphere. In a matter of seconds that too was gone.

"No!" Hobby moaned, struggling to his feet again, fumbling for something, anything, another pumpkin bomb perhaps. "You lousy little—you ruined my—I'll—"

"No, I don't think so," Spider-Man said calmly, and going over to Hobgoblin, he reared back and awarded him a roundhouse punch in the jaw that sent him flying as far as the creature's tentacle-whack had.

Hobby didn't move again. Spider-Man strolled over to him, took a good look to make sure he was breathing, saw that he was, then webbed him up and hung him from what remained of the ceiling. With that out of the way, he turned to see that the creature, finished eating, was now holding still. It had slumped into a tired-look-ing puddle of tentacles on the floor, bowed over, like someone overstuffed after a very good meal.

Spider-Man looked past it at Venom. The symbiote looked furious and a little ragged around the edges. The big eyes glared, though.

"How long did it take you to catch him?" Spider-Man said.

"We would estimate," said Venom, looking at the creature sprawled on the floor, "probably about the same time it took you to catch that. He led us a merry chase. He is rather too maneuverable when airborne."

"But he came back here at last," said Spider-Man.

"Oh yes. Home is where the heart is, they say." And Venom looked at the wrecked bomb. "His plan, we're sure, was to lead us as far from here as possible, then to return and wait for his ransom—or do something worse. Who knows what spite lurks in that black heart? We have no desire to."

The creature stirred a little at their feet, and moaned. "So," Venom said softly. "Now it only remains what to do with you."

"I think so, yeah," Spider-Man said, thinking, *I'm in no shape for this. But Venom is still a fugitive and a killer, and I've let this go too long as it is.* He began to edge sideways.

"This is the time, we think," Venom said, "for the settling of old debts. Once and for all, the scores tallied, the books closed, with one gross inequity resolved."

Venom's tendrils lanced out at Spider-Man. He webbed a couple of them as quickly as he could, struck a few aside with fists and feet, and leapt sideways as Venom leapt after.

From behind them both, the moaning sounded again. There was something more urgent about it this time, though, and even Venom stopped to look. "What?" he breathed.

Spider-Man followed Venom's gaze to the creature. Still slumped among its tentacles, which were now stirring and twitching feebly around it, the creature lay—but there was considerably more of it than there had been.

"It's bigger—" Venom said.

"It was bigger before," Spider-Man said. His spider-sense began to tingle. "It's worse now. I think we need to be a little worried about this—"

"Agreed," Venom said, and Spider-Man heard the alarm in his voice too.

The whole creature twitched, and, there was simply no other word for it, *surged*. It was as if its physical structure had suddenly become debatable. *Shell changes*, Spider-Man thought. *The atoms of its own structure suddenly in flux. Energy levels renegotiating themselves— shifting into new patterns—shorter-lived—less stable—*

It surged again. Suddenly it was twice as big as it had been. And another surge, like another breath, and it tripled in size. Venom stared.

And Spider-Man cried out, "Get down! *Get down!*"

He flung himself at Venom. The impetus of his tackle hurled them both to the floor just behind one of the big half-smashed pieces of machinery. *Hobby!* Spider-Man thought, but there was no time. The creature surged one last time—

—and *blew*.

ow long the rumbling and roaring went on, he wasn't sure. Spider-Man had heard a fair number of explosions in his career, some of them at a safe distance, some from entirely too close up. This one unquestionably fell into the latter category. He wasn't entirely sure that he hadn't been unconscious for some seconds in the wake of the initial blast, and the ensuing commotion was so unbelievable that Spider-Man wasn't sure that his protesting brain hadn't simply gone on strike until the noise dropped to a level he could handle.

The problem, of course, was that above ground, an explosion had freedom to move through the air and dispel its force upward. Down here, confined on all sides, the experience was much like being inside a bomb's casing when the explosive detonated. Anything weak enough to be demolished *was* demolished. Anything with any ability to resist the explosion nonetheless had to do something with the huge energy imparted to it, and most of the surfaces in here gave it up as sound, resonating to destruction—ringing like terrible crumbling bells, the walls falling down as they shook themselves to pieces in the aftermath, their reinforcing metal rods letting off prolonged howls like giant guitar strings suffering from terminal feedback. It was a long while before the noise faded to the point where one was conscious of anything but wanting it to stop.

It was almost totally dark, then. Paradoxically, the only light came from a small source which had been attached to the bomb—probably a battery backup of some kind, Spider-Man thought. By the glow of a few red and white status lights, burning stubbornly over switches which no longer worked, Spider-Man levered himself up on his elbows and looked around. Not too far away, a dark form moved feebly again: Venom. Many of the symbiote's tendrils were caught in mid-extension by the blast, but most particularly by the noise. Sound was one of the symbiote's weak points, and now all those usually fearfully active tentacles lay pitifully flat and still on the floor, as if they had been through a wringer. Still, Venom's breathing seemed steady enough. He would recover.

Spidey looked behind him, then, and saw that Hobgoblin lay on the floor, moaning. *I'm glad I webbed his mouth up*, Spider-Man thought, sitting up with a groan and dusting himself off. *The last thing I could cope with now would be him going on about his stupid bomb.*

In the rubble, something else stirred: a quick rustle, quickly gone, and a squeaking noise. *Rats*, Spidey thought, and actually laughed. After what he had been dealing with until now, a rat or two was no big deal. *But I bet they're wondering what the heck happened to their quiet home.*

More subdued squeaking followed, and more sounds of movement, but closer. Spider-Man turned. "Venom," he said. "You okay?" *Though why I'm asking, I don't know. He'll be a lot easier to deal with in this state, anyhow.*

"Nnnnngh." The dark shape stirred, hunched itself slowly up into a sitting position. "We . . . are still in one piece. Figuratively speaking, that is . . ."

"Uh, good." The squeaking was getting louder. "Listen," Spider-Man said, "I think it might be a good idea if we took Hobgoblin and got out of here. I don't know what the structural damage is, but I'd hate to have a building fall down into this hole, now that this *is* a hole. That is, mo— Yikes!"

His spider-sense buzzed just as something was about to run across his leg. He jumped and slapped at it.

"Heel, boy!" he said, and started to scramble to his feet, but before he had a chance, something else ran across his leg, into his lap. He slapped at that too. Then another tried to attack.

He jumped away, guided by his spider-sense to a clear spot in the scattered rubble. The small dark things followed. They were not rats, he knew. No rat alive could jump like that—and even as Spider-Man leapt away, several of them leapt at him. They were small dark creatures—

—with tentacles! Twenty or thirty of them. Bipedal, but not very humanoid-looking as yet, as far as he could see them in the light from the former bomb's telltales. They were little things, maybe about the size of chihuahuas. Shining black, fanged, clawed, squeaking frenziedly—in a tinier, shriller version of their parent's soprano shriek—they went plunging and leaping after Spider-Man, hungry, wanting their first meal.

For a few seconds Spider-Man was lost in a basic and for him slightly ironic response: hatred of swarming things that came at you like bugs, biting, too numerous to stop. They were all over him now, biting, clinging with tentacles, ripping with claws, scrabbling at his midsection. There were only so many he could avoid in his fatigue, even with his spider-sense. The sound of Venom's laughter, still weak but slightly sinister, didn't help at all. Spider-Man jumped and danced and clawed them off, then started webbing them up as fast as he could. But still they kept coming. The floor seethed like an anthill with hungry alien life, newborn, wanting its first meal more than anything.

He jumped to what was left of one wall, but it was no refuge—they fastened themselves to him and clawed and bit all the harder, shrieking with hunger and frustration as he shook some off, webbed others and dropped them in a package, jumped again to another wall, was followed and bitten once more. *Well*, he thought frantically, *MJ did suggest that feeding it might be a dumb idea. After this I'll listen to her.*

Feeding it—oh my gosh!!

He stopped what he was doing and fumbled at his belt. The creatures there bit his hands and arms, protesting; others, encouraged by not being shaken off him, now concentrated there as well. Their little fangs and claws were like razors. He wanted to scream, but Spider-Man concentrated on getting the webbing loose from the canister still at his belt. Revolted at the feeling of them crawling over him, shrieking and biting anything they could reach, Spider-Man flung the canister as far out into the middle of the chamber, or what had been its middle, as he could.

There was a sort of depression in the floor there, a crater blown in the solid concrete by the creature when it detonated. The canister bounced into it. The little creatures stormed into the depression in a black wave, scrabbling, tearing at each other, completely hiding the canister now in a tumble and fury of little black bodies. Hundreds of tiny shrieks filled the air.

Spider-Man brushed off a last couple of confused baby

aliens, possibly clinging to him because of residual radiation from when he had been holding the canister in the open position, and watched them fall toward their ravenous brethren. There was already less noise, and Spider-Man suspected it wasn't because they had gotten the canister open—which they had—but because some of them, desperate, had begun feeding on their brothers and sisters. *Probably some residual fissile material left over in their structure from their parent*, he thought. *It might not have managed to metabolize it all before it went blooey. Or who* knows *what?* He was reminded, slightly sadly, of the sight of some kinds of spider hatching out; an egg-case suddenly releasing hundreds of baby spiders no bigger than a pinhead, only a few of which survive—those fast enough to spin some silk and float away before their brothers and sisters have them for breakfast.

He swung down near the hole in the floor and sprayed a bowl-shape from his webbing, then shot a line of web down into the depression and pulled the halves of the canister up. The young aliens followed—those which hadn't already disappeared into their siblings' gullets. Spider-Man dropped the canister pieces into the middle of his webbed bowl, and the little creatures piled on top of it. When they were all in one place, he used more webbing to cover the bowl, turning it into a tight-woven bag that would hold them all in one place until he could get help.

That left one more problem. Spider-Man turned to face Venom.

Except that the symbiote wasn't there.

Spider-Man blinked. "Venom?"

There was no sign of him. Spider-Man looked around,

but it was not in Venom's style to hide behind something, in circumstances like this, and then jump out without warning. He had a bit too much love of the open challenge, the threat that gave you time to realize what he planned to do with you. He was gone.

Well, he thought, *Brock and I will have our reckoning. Right now, I've got Hobby and a bunch of baby aliens I have to get off my back.*

He picked up the webbed-up Hobgoblin under one arm. Hobby immediately began making strangled noises of rage. "Oh, put a sock in it," Spider-Man said genially. "You're going for a nice trip to the country. People pay to do that in this weather, and you're going to get to do it for free. What're you complaining about? There's just no pleasing some people."

He then picked up the bag of aliens, threw it over his shoulder, and began making his way back up to the surface, feeling like a slightly retro and downmarket Santa Claus, one who comes up from the cellar rather than down through the chimney. Soon enough he found himself in one of the subway tunnels. There were, for once, no trains in sight. Spider-Man walked to the next platform, climbed up its steps, and went out past the token booth, waving at the astonished man who sat there. "Ho ho ho," Spider-Man said cheerfully, heading up the stairs and into the beginnings of dawn.

There was enough light on the streets for things to start being active, and sure enough, with no news to the contrary, New York had started about its business as if there were no bomb theoretically about to go off. Milk and laundry trucks were buzzing around, the traffic was beginning to build up, the morning papers already lay in bundles by the news stands, and were being stacked up on the counters. "THE BIG BANG!" shouted the *Bugle*'s front page, with one of Peter's pictures of Hobgoblin, looking suitably insane and menacing, prominently displayed.

Spider-Man was pleased, and even more pleased by the present contents of his camera, which he had picked up on his way out—assuming the flash and the motion-control system had once more worked properly. *Can't assume, though*, he thought. *The circumstances were different, and with all those flash bombs going off. . . . Oh well.*

He dropped Hobby to the sidewalk and stopped by a pay phone. Hobby made angry but muffled complaints. "Well," Spider-Man said equably as he dialed 911, "if you wouldn't threaten to blow the city up, you wouldn't *get* dropped on your head. Now shut up. Hello? Oh."

Spider-Man found himself listening to the recording that you get when the 911 system is overloaded. *Probably half the city is calling the cops demanding to know what they're doing about the bomb. Or alternately*, he thought, and grinned, looking at a bank's digital clock down the street, *why the bomb hasn't gone off when it was supposed to.* It was quarter of six. He chuckled. Some people would complain about a hoax, and the distress it had caused them, how shameful it was, the city ought to *do* something . . . and on and on. It was true enough: there *was* no pleasing everybody.

"Nine one one, can I help you?" said a weary, inexpressibly bored voice.

"Yeah, this is Spider-Man—"

"Oh?" The cop on the other end sounded skeptical, but said nothing to refute him.

"Listen, I'm at the corner of"—he craned his neck to look at the street sign—"Eighth Avenue and Thirty-Third. I've got Hobgoblin here, all wrapped ready for pickup, and also a bunch of little alien critters that we're gonna have to do something with pretty quick—"

"Wait a minute, Spider-Man," said the cop, suddenly sounding a lot less skeptical. Then again, "I've got Hobgoblin" were probably the words they most wanted to hear right now. "Bernie? Hand me that sheet there, will you? Thanks. Right. Spider-Man, there's a mobile patrol from SHIELD out looking for you at the moment. I'll call their beeper and give them your location. They should be there pretty fast. They've been working the west side for the past couple of hours."

"Hey, that's great."

"Meanwhile, Eighth and Thirty-third? We'll send a wagon for Hobgoblin. What happened to his bomb?"

"It was delicious," Spider-Man said.

The cop sounded slightly dubious. "Does that mean it's defused?"

"Defused, destroyed, the fissile material inactivated. If you'll give me the number of the AEC people out on the street, I'll call them and give them the details."

"Right." More paper rustling. "Ready?" The cop rattled the number off.

"Got it," Spider-Man said. "Thanks. Hey, here comes the cavalry already." For down the street he could hear, faintly, the scream of sirens as the first of several police cars turned into Eighth and roared toward him.

"We aim to please," said the cop on the other end. "Have a nice day." He hung up.

The police cars came howling to a stop all around Spider-Man, and cops piled out, looking delighted to see Spider-Man and to have their hands on the man who had held their city for ransom for the last twelve hours. The police officers who took custody of Hobby had numerous unkind names for him, but one big handsome dark lady simply shook her head and said, "Unrealistic."

"What do you mean?" Spidey asked, surprised.

"This boy," she said, looking at Hobgoblin as they manhandled him away and put him into the newly arrived high security van, "he has no grasp of the economic realities. With the city budget in the state it's in, where did he think we were going to get a billion dollars?"

"You mean," Spider-Man said, "the city wasn't going to pay?"

The police woman looked at him mildly. "What were they going to pay *with*? Now, I hear there were some pretty noisy phone calls from Gracie Mansion to Washington, at about three this morning. Oh, I guess they would have sorted something out in a while. But this boy"—she looked at the van's doors as they clanged shut—"he was just too greedy. A million, the city *would* have given him to get off their case, I bet. Even a hundred million if the feds or Trump or Stark or someone got involved. But a billion? No way." She sighed. "But I guess times change. Maybe a million dollars doesn't go as far as it used to."

Another van pulled up, this one more sleek and streamlined-looking than the police van, with the logo of the Strategic Hazard Intervention, Espionage, and Logistics Directorate, one of the country's premiere military intelligence organizations, painted on the side. Uniformed men stepped out, holding futuristic-looking scientific instruments and futuristic-looking guns, which they pointed at the web-bag lying on the sidewalk. The bag heaved and squirmed, and loud squeaks rose from it.

"We've been looking for you for most of the evening," said the SHIELD team leader—a tall, dark, crewcut man who looked at the bag with polite interest—to Spider-Man. "Sorry we couldn't find you sooner."

"Who sent you?" Spider-Man said curiously.

"Navy Department," said the team leader. "They said they had lost an item and that you were looking for it on their behalf. This it?"

"More or less," Spider-Man said, and he took the team leader off to one side, explaining as much as he could about the creature without letting on that some of the information had come to him from the captain of the *Minneapolis*—no sense getting Captain LoBuono in any trouble. He put special emphasis on keeping the little critters away from any source of radiation. The team leader nodded when Spider-Man was done. "Fine."

"Okay," Spider-Man said. He watched the SHIELD team seal the bag into a small containment vessel in their van and shut the van doors. "Give my best to Nick."

The team leader nodded, then went back to the van. It headed away more silently than the police van had. After a minute or two Spider-Man stood alone on the corner, being passed by incurious traffic, looking up at the sky. It was brightening to full blue now. Eastward, on the other side of this wall of skyscrapers, the sun was peering past Roosevelt Island and up over Brooklyn. Morning, when there had been a strong possibility of there not being a morning, all very pleasant. Even the air smelled less smoggy than usual.

Spider-Man smiled to himself, raised an arm, and shot a line of webbing into the air. It fastened to the top corner of a handy building. He hauled himself up and swung around the corner, heading inward and uptown. He had to make one more stop—then he could go back home and hug MJ.

It was actually more than one stop, and something like three-quarters of an hour later, when he came in through the bedroom window and found MJ lounging in front of the TV, watching news coverage of the police van unloading Hobgoblin, to the delight of the assembled reporters, and Hobby's evident frustration (his webbing-gag was still in place). MJ jumped up and ran to him.

He hugged her hard, pulled off his mask, kissed her, kissed her some more, and then held her away a little. "Did you stay up all night?" he asked.

MJ looked at him as if he was out of his mind. "Could you have slept under these circumstances?"

Peter had to admit she had a point. "Any calls for me?"

"One," she said, with an odd look on her face, and went over to the VCR.

Peter looked at her with amazement, pulling off the top of his costume. "Since when do I get calls on the television?"

"Since this," MJ said, and hit the play button.

It seemed that MJ had been taping the news overnight, including the coverage of Hobgoblin's arrest. The first news that anyone had had of this appeared to have come with a phone call to 911.

"This is Venom," said a voice which Peter recognized all too well, while the news show displayed a file picture of him, with a banner over it saying "POLICE RECORDING—5:30 AM." "We have just been involved with the capture of the criminal called Hobgoblin, who will shortly be delivered to the authorities, and the dismantling of the nuclear device with which he threatened the people of New York City. We have also participated in the destruction of the creature which has for a short time caused the people of this city to believe that we, Venom, were murdering its innocents." There was a pause, and then the voice became, to Peter's informed ear, tinged with just a bit of grim amusement. "Spider-Man, an equal participant in these matters, will be able to confirm to the authorities that it was this creature, and not ourself, Venom, who was responsible for the murders in question. In return for this service, and other favors recently rendered, we find it appropriate for the moment to leave New York to pursue other matters which require our immediate attention—of which, for the moment, Spider-Man is not one."

Peter sat there, looking slightly stunned. Then he yelled at the television, "*Well, don't say 'thank you' or anything!*"

MJ looked at him, and very, very softly, began to laugh. After a few seconds, Peter joined her.

"So," he said, "how *did* that audition go, anyhow?"

"Actually, they offered me the role—"

"That's great!"

"—but I turned it down."

Peter blinked. "What? Why?"

"Because, thanks to Hobgoblin, they were urgent to fly out to LA—immediately. I couldn't just leave when I wasn't even sure if you were okay or not."

Peter stared at her. She had been going on for ages about how she wanted nothing more than to work. Obviously, there was at least one thing she wanted more. He pulled her into a hug. "What did I do to deserve you?"

"You were just yourself," she whispered. She kissed him on the cheek, then broke the embrace. "Now tell me what's in the bag."

"Bag? Oh." He opened it, handed her the bottle. "Is the city having a run on Woolite, or something? I had to try three places."

She grinned. "You remembered! And you need it, tiger, you and that costume both. Get it off."

Peter unpacked the camera and the last few spider-tracers, and the change from the Woolite, all of which he left on the table. "Which of us you going to scrub first?" he said, heading down the hall after MJ.

Her nightgown hit him in the face as he came up even with the bathroom door. "Come find out," MJ said, playfully splashing hot water at him as she climbed into the tub.

Peter smiled and went after her.

DIANE DUANE is the author of a score of novels of science fiction and fantasy, among them the *New York Times* hardcover bestsellers *Spock's World* and *Dark Mirror*, as well as the very popular Wizard fantasy series, and a second Spider-Man hardcover novel entitled *The Lizard Sanction*. She is hard at work on a third Spidey novel, *The Octopus Agenda*. The *Philadelphia Enquirer* has called Duane "a skilled master of the genre," and *Publishers Weekly* has raved, "Duane is tops in the high adventure business." Duane lives with her husband, Peter Morwood—with whom she has written five novels, including the *New York Times* bestseller *The Romulan Way*—in a beautiful valley in rural Ireland.

RON LIM got his start on the alternative press comic *Ex-Mutants*, then moved on to prominence as the artist on Marvel's New Universe book *Psi-Force*. He has since lent his artistic talent to a variety of comics for Marvel, including *Spider-Man Unlimited*, *The Silver Surfer*, *Nightwatch*, *X-Men 2099*, and several *Venom* titles, including *Lethal Protector*, *Death Trap: The Vault*, and *Nights of Vengeance*.

KEITH AIKEN has provided inks for a variety of pencillers, including Ron Lim, George Pérez, Tim Hamilton, and many more, on such diverse books as *The Silver Surfer*, *Dragonlines*, *UltraForce*, *Godzilla*, *Lethal Foes of Spider-Man*, and others. He also provided the inks over pencil illustrations by James W. Fry for the Spider-Man novel *Carnage in New York*.

SPIDER-MAN®